A Queen's

First published in eBook and paperback 2018

This edition 2018

•

© Sam Burnell 2018

The right of Sam Burnell to be identified as the author of this work has been asserted by her in accordance with the Copyright, Designs and Patents Act 1988.

All rights reserved. No part of this publication may be reproduced, stored in or introduced into a retrieval system, or transmitted, in any form, or by any means (electronic, mechanical, photocopying, recording or otherwise) without the prior written permission of the writer. Any person who does any unauthorised act in relation to this publication may be liable to criminal prosecution and civil claims for damages.

Thank you for respecting the hard work of this author.

Please note, this book is written in British English, so some spellings will vary from US English.

Dedicated to

Mooster

CHARACTER LIST

Fitzwarren Household
William Fitzwarren – father of Richard and Robert
Eleanor Fitzwarren – his wife
Robert Fitzwarren – Richard's brother
Jack Fitzwarren – William's son, Richard's brother
Richard Fitzwarren – William's son
Harry Fitzwarren – Richard and Jack's cousin
Edward Fitzwarren – Richard and Jack's Cousin
Edwin – William's Servant
Ronan – William's Steward
Edward Fitzwarren – Richard and Jack's Cousin

The English Court
William Cecil – Secretary of State
Christopher Morley – Cecil's man
Kate Ashley – Elizabeth's governess

Lawyers
 Clement – Robert Fitzwarren's Lawyer
 Luterell – William Fitzwarren's Lawyer
 Marcus Drover – Clement's assistant

Richard's Mercenary Band
Dan – Also a family servant
Marc
Froggy Tate
Pierre
Marc
Thomas Gent
Andrew Kineer
Master Scranton

Knights Of St John
 Claude de la Sengle – Grand Master
 Emilio – A Knight of the Order
 Brother Caron – De la Sengle's aide
 Brother Rodrigo – Head of Ordnance

Other Characters
Lizbet – A Servant
Catherine de Bernay – Servant at Durham Place

Introduction

It had been a long night.

Jack's head was pounding. He'd slept little and when he awoke in the morning the enormity of the previous night's horror returned with sickening suddenness. Sitting up quickly he looked over to the bed where his brother lay. Whether he was asleep or unconscious, Jack did not know.

Lizbet was kneeling near Richard, a hand in his. Hearing Jack, she turned and smiling reassuringly. "He's asleep."

Jack exhaled loudly and lay back down but the refuge of sleep was at an end. Outside a cock was crowing and from the inn yard came the dull thunder of empty barrels rolling across the flagged yard. The cockerel crowed again. Jack winced as the harsh noise seared through his head.

"Here, have this." Lizbet held out a cup of ale.

Jack, sitting up with his back against the wall, took the offered cup and looked across the wreckage of the cold room. The smell of blood was still tangible, the ripped shirt still lay on the floor and the blanket crusted now with dried brown stains lay in a heap next to it. Richard, when he had fallen, had pulled over the table and it was still there on its side, the clothes that had been neatly folded now scattered and creased.

Jack rested his head back against the wall and closed his eyes. He might not be in Marshalsea but he had never felt more alone. This time his brother had left him simply because he did not want to live, and he had brutally forced him to stay. Life was different today, he was alone, and the connection he had always felt was gone. Dropping his head into his hands he couldn't contain the anguished sob that escaped his throat.

"Mary and all the Saints! Not you as well!" Lizbet's voice cut across the room, devoid of sympathy.

Jack looked up. "Shut up, woman!"

"I'll not," Lizbet said standing up. "You made him swear, I heard you. Well, he's here and he needs you." Then she said, her own voice nearly breaking, "We both need you."

Jack looked up, his eyes unusually bright meeting hers.

Before he could reply, Lizbet was righting the chair and table, turning her back on him so he couldn't see the tears on her face. "I can smell fresh bread. I'll be back with some soon."

Closing the room door behind her, Lizbet took two faltering steps before she could contain the tears no more and leaning against the wooden wall, buried her face in her apron.

The door opened behind her and a strong arm guided her back into the room. "You sit down. I'll get the bread."

†

Later on that morning, Lizbet carefully steered the conversation round to the subject of Andrew, giving Jack a constructive focus for his anger.

"We've waited too long already." Jack's temper flared. "That cur has everything, the money, the bloody flintlocks, the men, everything. We have what we are standing up in."

"Not quite." Lizbet slipped her hand in her pocket. "I've still got some of this left." She pulled the leather bag from her pocket that held what was left of the jewels from Elizabeth's shoes.

"God love you, lass. You should have kept your money and left the pair of us to rot." Jack's anger faded seeing the eager look on her face and the offering in her hand.

"I tried to tell you," Lizbet reminded him.

"I know, and blind fool that I am I didn't listen to you," Jack replied resignedly.

Lizbet looked shocked.

"What's that look on your face for?" Jack said.

"I think that's the first time I've ever heard you say were wrong!" Lizbet's eyes were still wide. "That's an admission I never thought I'd hear."

"Well you've heard it now. I thought he was something he wasn't." Jack ignored her attempt at humour.

"If he's shown you that you can be wrong then all was not wasted," Lizbet said a little bitingly.

"He had us all fooled," Jack said sadly, then looking closely at Lizbet, added, "Why not you?"

Lizbet shrugged. "He never liked me. Mind you I think I know why now." Then quickly before Jack could say anything she added, "Do you think Dan and Froggy will come back?"

"I don't know, it depends on what Andrew tells them," Jack replied, adding thoughtfully, "He'll want to keep them with him if he can."

"Especially Froggy, he's the one with the skills to make the flintlock balls, and if he intends to take the Master's place and still put this deal before the Knights then he needs Froggy," Lizbet agreed.

Jack nodded. "Andrew has everything; the only thing he doesn't know is where the rest of the flintlocks are hidden. Richard wouldn't even tell me that."

"I caught Andrew in the Master's room weeks ago going through his papers. Could he have found out then?" Lizbet sounded worried.

"Oh God! When did that happen? Not that it would matter much anyway, he's got the coffer that Richard kept all the papers in so… Oh for God's sake… " Jack stood suddenly as he realised that Andrew had the papers signed by his father proclaiming him as heir. He groaned loudly, pushing his hands through his hair.

"What? Tell me?" Lizbet said, rising to take hold of his arm.

"He's got everything, literally everything."

"What do you mean?"

"Oh God!" The enormity of the situation began to dawn on Jack and he sat down heavily, a tight knot in his stomach. The face that looked up at Lizbet was white. "He knows who I am, he knows probably where the guns are hidden, he's got all the papers Richard took from his father, he's got the communications from the lawyer in England, and Richard's letters from the Order as well. Chances are there would be something in there that will lead him to where the guns are hidden in London."

"What do you mean? He knows who you are?" Lizbet was utterly confused. When he didn't answer she placed one of her small hands on his shoulder and shook him. "What are you talking about?"

"That's not important now. What's important is that Andrew has enough at hand to be able to pass himself off as Richard. I have to assume that he thinks he knows where the guns are otherwise he'd not have tried to kill Richard. So there must have been something in the coffer that told him where they were."

Lizbet was just looking at him blankly.

"What are you staring at woman?"

"Who are you? What did you mean?" Lizbet sounded confused.

"It's a long, long story I would be glad to tell you, lass, but not today. Right now we need to find a way to stop him. So let's think about this. He's going to want to keep Froggy, and he'll not want Dan coming back here to help us, so what's he going to do?"

Lizbet thought about it for a moment. "Dan's loyal to the Master. He'd not leave him, and he'd not watch Andrew press on without him."

A grim expression settled on Jack's face. "That's what I thought as well. He'll need to rid himself of Dan and persuade Froggy to stay with him."

Jack stood suddenly.

"What are you going to do?"

"I need to ride south, catch them up. Warn Dan at the very least, and if I can I will stop Andrew."

"What with, for God's sake? Jack, you've got nothing! Not a sword or a knife, you've not even got a jacket."

Jack was smiling now, and reaching out a hand he ran it down her cheek. "Life has been a lot worse. I've got a lucky lass with a purse filled with pearls."

"There's not much left after we used them to bribe our way into the castle, but you're welcome to them." Lizbet fished back into her pocket and handed Jack the leather pouch.

Jack shook out what there was left into his palm; she was right, there wasn't much left.

"We were in a hurry. I didn't get anything near what they were worth for them," Lizbet said sorrowfully.

"I will fill that purse for you again, trust me." Jack put an arm round her shoulders, pulled her close and planted a kiss on her forehead. "I'll be back soon. Don't leave him alone while I'm gone, and make sure he stays here."

Lizbet, turning to observe the man on the bed, said, "Jack, I don't think you need to worry on that score."

†

Lizbet was however wrong. Richard had dressed with shaking hands and was standing in the room arguing with Lizbet when Jack returned. She looked to Jack for help. "I told him to stay where he was but he wouldn't listen to me."

"Be fair to the lass, she's only trying to do what I told her to," Jack said, then seeing the look on his brother's face he added firmly, "You are not coming with me."

Richard's eyes were unusually dark, the skin on his face pale and tightly drawn, and when he spoke it was with apparent effort. "I am coming with you."

Jack threw his arms wide. "We have between us one horse, one sword that's blunter than Thor's hammer." He tapped the blade he had just acquired, buckled to his waist. "We have with us, do not forget, our gracious sister." He gestured at Lizbet. "Who has neither horse nor money. I cannot take care of both of you! Stop here with Lizbet. I can leave you enough money for that and I will stop Andrew."

"I said, I am coming with you," Richard repeated, staring at his brother from hollow darkened eyes.

Lizbet looked Jack squarely in the face. "Looks like we're both coming with you then."

Richard and Lizbet walked past him, leaving him staring at the wall. "Nobody ever listens to me – it must be a skill," Jack grumbled to the empty room before turning to follow them.

Chapter 1

A Hand Revealed

Andrew shook his head in disbelief. There was so much of interest in the wooden coffer Richard had kept locked that had contained the marked guns. When he had taken the flintlocks from their secure resting place, he had noted the bundle of tied papers, but there had not been the time then for a lengthy investigation into the extent of the Master's secrets. They were resting now, just north of Venice and this was the first time he had been afforded the opportunity to work through them methodically.

The pace of the journey so far had been a brutal one, so determined was Andrew to make it to the Venetian capital and strike a deal for the cargo he was confident he now had to offer. He hoped the negotiations would be swift and that he would be on his way back north to England quickly. Once there he could collect the flintlocks and bring them back to the Knights for a payment that would make up for everything he had lost. He had Scranton and Froggy with him and he was willing to trade their expertise as well, happy to deliver both of them to the Order along with the flintlocks.

Sitting alone, he sorted though the papers. There were Richard's own notes from his conversations with Scranton, clear that he had been intent on recording as much as he could of what the powder expert had said. There were the neatly inscribed results from the tests carried out on the bombarde. Distances, powder weights, shot sizes, all written and recorded in Richard's accurate hand. Andrew smiled. It did not make Master Scranton surplus yet, he still kept close the details of the pellet manufacture, but it seemed he had given away to Richard more of his trade secrets than he realised.

Andrew, putting the notes to one side, pulled towards him another bundle, older looking and neatly tied. A brief review showed them to all be correspondence belonging to Richard's father. There was much, including details of land bequests made after the dissolution. Andrew studied them for a while, but the cracked sheets written in legal Latin did not want to reveal their worth that easily, so he re-tied them and set about looking for easier prey.

The papers Clement had drafted for Richard he found next, tied together with the declaration made by William Fitzwarren stating that Jack was his true son and heir. Andrew had laughed then, but not for long. The enormity of the missed opportunity soon dawned upon him. Jack had been eating out of his hand, he had ensured that the bond between the brothers had been severed. Andrew knew he should have kept Jack closer. If he had known this, he would have. Andrew scowled at the papers. Whatever these flintlocks might be worth, he recognised this could well have been worth more. Jack was malleable; Andrew could have had a Lord in his pocket, a perfect replacement for Seymour. His fist battered the table.

"Damn you to Hell, Richard!" Andrew declared to the silence in the room, before continuing his investigation of the papers.

There was only one letter that was out of kilter with all the rest. General, devoid of information and fact, just a single sheet, seemingly from a friend. Andrew had read it three times. The sentences seemed a little stilted, the letter rambled. He was sure that whatever it was that the writer, Christian Carter, was trying to tell the reader, was entirely different from what the simple words on the page seemed to say.

That a man like Richard Fitzwarren would have kept this banal piece of correspondence seemed wrong, that it had been carefully parcelled along with those damning documents relating to Jack's birth pointed the finger at a connection. The name Christian Carter had also headed the inventory that had set Andrew on the course of action he had taken when he had first discovered it in Richard's room. The letter was just further confirmation that he had the right name. When he'd tried to press the air from Richard's lungs, his reaction to that name had been enough for Andrew to know that Carter was the key. He just needed to find him and he doubted that would be very hard.

†

They were about to arrive in Venice, the trading gateway to the East. The weather was unpleasantly warm, even late into the evening. The men had made a rapid camp centred around the cart containing Fitzwarren's cargo. They were now sat arrayed on the ground, enjoying ale Andrew had supplied from the local tavern. The journey had been a harsh one, travelling even in the heat of the day to cover as much ground as they could.

Andrew strolled among them, coming to stop stand behind Marc where he was sat next to Thomas Gent. "I think that's a drink well earned. It has been quite a task to get here so quickly."

Marc looked up and raised his cup. "It's going down very well, I can tell you."

"Another couple and I might have the dust from the road finally out of my throat," Thomas said, grinning.

"We made it, lads," Andrew said, smiling and looking around the assembled group in the dim evening light. "The Master will be proud of you. He'll be here in a day or so I have no doubt."

Dan's eyes narrowed. "They don't have the cart we have to slow them down. They should have caught us up by now."

"I know, I thought they would have. When I saw the Master, he said he had some quick business to attend to and he would catch us up. He ordered me to bring the men here, and I have, but without the Master I'm not sure what the next step will be." Andrew sounded concerned.

"Something could have happened to them," Thomas Gent said. "You're right, without the cart they should have caught us up easily."

"Do you think it worth heading back to see if there's any news of them?" Pierre asked, coming to sit next to Marc and Gent.

"That's too long a ride for any man here to make, especially after we have just pressed ourselves so hard to get here," Andrew replied. "We have our orders to wait here, and wait we shall."

"I think something's wrong." Dan looked around the group.

"There could be a hundred reasons why they're delayed. It's not our business to second guess the Master," Pierre said.

"I admit I am worried, but I don't see what we can do," Andrew said to Dan. "I can't turn around and take the men and the cargo back the way we came. The Master would be furious if he met us on the road."

Dan, looking at Andrew, made a sudden decision. "I'll go back, see if I can find them on the road. It would ease my mind."

"And mine as well," Andrew said, clapping Dan on the shoulder. "Leave it until tomorrow." Andrew's boot kicked the keg of ale he had bought. "There's quite a lot left in there."

Dan rode away from the camp the following morning before the sun made it over the horizon, determined to make quick progress in the cooler part of the day. What he didn't know was that ahead of him was Thomas Gent. Gent's loyalties lay with Andrew, not with the Master. A man whose life revolved around the execution of orders and who believed completely in Andrew Kineer, he had been sent from the camp with express orders to stop Dan from returning to the Master. The journey had been long and hard and the band's focus had been on the ale provided by Andrew so not one of them noticed that Thomas Gent had drunk little that evening, or disappeared shortly after midnight. Had they been asked, they would have supposed he was sleeping somewhere in the dark with the rest of them.

Thomas Gent took himself along the road carefully in the moonlight. It took him two hours before he found the place he was looking for. They had ridden through it the day before and the location suited his needs perfectly. The road along the track passed through a wide, dried up riverbed. During the cooler months, the wide shallow river would flow slowly towards the sea, but in the hot months it was empty of water, a dried and cracked expanse of mud. The riverbed was uneven, peppered with smooth river boulders caught tight in the dried silt, and it would slow a man as he sought to guide his horse over it.

Gent didn't cross it. Instead he dropped from his saddle and walked his horse further up the bank and secured her in the folds of the olive trees out of sight. Returning, he took up position and waited.

Dan had left the camp early, the sun not yet over the horizon but the light from the early dawn was enough. He was riding hard and Thomas Gent, dozing lightly where he lay, his head pillowed on his arms, amongst the caper bushes, started when he heard the noise of Dan's horse's shod hooves ring out on the riverbed.

At Gent's side, ready, lay the short bow and four arrows. Fletched with white goose feathers, their broad shafts ended with the weighty steel of a point designed to pierce metal plate.

Dan was looking down, his eyes intent on guiding his mare through the uneven dusty riverbed. With a tight hold on his reins, he moved her carefully through the easiest path. Dan was in a hurry, but not enough of one to risk his horse. Gent's impassive face observed the broad back from along the length of the arrow shaft. Satisfied with his aim, he held his breath and released the arrow. The first arrow missed, skimming Dan's shoulder, landing amongst the rocks on the dried riverbed, the metal point squealing across the sandstone boulders.

Gent automatically knocked a second and fired again before lowering the bow to observe his target. Dan's horse had shied as the first shaft had passed it. Had it not, the second arrow would have smashed its way through his heart. As it was, it pierced only the muscle and cartilage in his shoulder. The reins dropping from his slackened hands, Dan rolled forward over the mare's neck, landing with a dull thump that Gent could hear clearly across the distance. His head impacted against one of the exposed rocks and his mind was delivered to instant blackness.

Dan's horse shied for a second time, dancing backward to avoid stepping on her rider. Gent continued to watch. When he was satisfied that there was no movement from the fallen man, he set off quickly to cross the distance between them.

When he arrived, Gent gave the inert form a kick, grunting in satisfaction. Dan lay on his side, propped against a river boulder. Blood welled from a cut on his head and poured from around the arrow shaft protruding from his back. Already some interested insects had begun to alight on his face, dipping their proboscises into the globular blood.

Gent had a short rope over his shoulder. Without hesitation he looped it over one of Dan's feet, tugging it hard to make sure the knot was not just going to pull a boot away. Satisfied, he tied the other end to the saddle and mounted. The horse, wide-eyed and nervous now, neighed and pranced in agitation. Gent, shortening the reins, turned her upstream and slowly guided her through the rocks, pulling behind her the body of her rider.

When he considered they were far enough from the track, he turned her towards the shallow bank and the horse, with her extra burden, dragged the body with her into the cover of the trees on the riverbank. The body was concealed by the shrub. Gent doubted he would be found by anything other than carrion. There was a knife in a scabbard attached to the leather of the saddle, finer than his own, and Gent took it. As he admired the blade, he smoothed a hand down the horse's neck to calm her. Dropping from the saddle, he turned the knife over in his hand, feeling the weight of it. The blade, broad and strong, was well balanced. Gent continued to pat the horse even when he forced the blade into the life-giving vein at the bottom of her neck, stepping back smartly to avoid the spray of blood. Gent didn't want anyone finding Dan's horse.

Chapter 2

A Family Trial

Jack acquired a second horse for Richard, but they simply could not afford a third for Lizbet. Organising their departure and journey south, he adopted both a confident and efficient manner. Jack was neither belligerent nor angry, but took on a role of quiet competence. He was there to help his brother onto his horse and offer a supporting arm when he dismounted. When they reached a fording point he quickly clipped a lead rein to the other horse's bridle, ensuring both horses crossed safely. Jack was quite aware that his brother was not engaged in the detail of the journey; Richard rode the horse blindly without seeing the path that lay ahead.

Jack was surprised, however, that his help was accepted wordlessly and without rebuke. Richard also didn't complain at Lizbet riding behind him, even though Jack knew she was making his journey less than comfortable. They needed to make as much speed as possible in an attempt to overtake Andrew and the rest of the men.

†

Lizbet and Richard, sharing one of the horses, had watched as Jack rode back to join them from an inn, where he had been making enquiry to find out how far ahead their quarry was. The look on his face as he neared them was answer enough, and, sensibly, neither of them pressed him for news. Jack's fears had been confirmed, they were five days behind Andrew, and he rode on at a slower pace. There was little point in continuing with the jolting speed they had been riding at.

Andrew was certainly now at the Italian coast where he could take a boat to Venice. They couldn't catch him, not now, not before they made it to the citadel. Jack rode along in silence, resigned, and sharing with his brother a flask he had purchased from the inn.

†

Lizbet, on the ground already, watched as Jack extended a supporting hand up for Richard to take as he dropped from his horse. One of Richard's feet landed awkwardly and his balance was hopelessly lost.

Holding tight on Jack's arm, he didn't let go, and as he fell back pulled them both to the ground. Lizbet took a step back from them, braced for an explosion of temper from Jack, and was shocked when instead he erupted in laughter.

As they rode along side by side, Jack had been plying his brother with aqua vitae from the flask he had looped over the pommel of his saddle. Between them they had emptied it. Jack had thought maybe the rough spirit would help, and Richard had taken the flask and drunk heavily from it.

Lizbet's disapproving face stared down at Jack when she saw that they had been drinking. "What were you thinking? He's drunk as a monk!"

Richard was indeed laid flat on his back, observing her through partly closed eyes.

"God, stop scolding me, woman. Help me up?" Jack, laughing and on his back on the ground, held up his hand for her to take.

"It's not funny!" Lizbet blazed at the pair of them. "Get up!"

Jack continued to laugh, and a furious Lizbet kicked hard at his feet with her wooden shoes. "Get up, you bloody idiot."

Without warning, Jack hooked her feet out from under her and she fell forward, landing on top of him, yelping. Levering herself up on her hands, she scowled at Jack below her. "You're bloody drunk as well!"

"Only a little!" Jack replied, sounding hurt at the accusation.

"Oh my Lord! What were you thinking?" Lizbet tried to pull herself away.

"I think that was the point, he'd rather not." It was the first time Richard had spoken that morning and his voice sounded hoarse.

Jack pulled her arms from under her so she landed face down on his chest. "Hush your tongue. I'm not that drunk, woman."

"I'll not." Lizbet, intent on righting herself, jabbed her hands painfully into Jack's chest as she pushed herself back up.

"A moment, give me that." Jack pulled an arm from under her again and she landed between them. Lizbet conceded and stop struggling.

"What are you laughing about?" Lizbet demanded.

"It looks like I'm right back at bottom again," Jack replied, still laughing. "Why I ever thought it could be anything else I don't know."

"You'll never be at the bottom," Richard said quietly, his eyes closed and his words slurred.

"What did you let him drink so much for?" Lizbet thumped one of her fists into Jack's chest. "You know what he's like when he drinks."

"He was sober when he did that to himself. I thought it might help," Jack said defensively, then turning to his brother, said, "Did it?"

"Cicero's fool, and one Bacchus would approve of," Richard observed quietly.

"At least you're speaking to me again," Jack said. There was a trace of genuine relief in his voice. "He took both of us for fools. It was only this harridan he didn't convince."

"Not my fault you're bloody fools, is it?" Lizbet turned her head to better observe Jack.

"I am glad we have something at last that we can genuinely share, even if it is defeat," Richard said, closing his eyes.

"We are not defeated," Jack said quickly, turning to regard his brother.

"What are we then?"

"Delayed! There's a difference," Jack stated.

Lizbet swivelled her head to better observe Jack. "Delayed! You actually believe you're going to still carry this out?"

"Of course," Jack replied, then when Richard did not answer, he added, "Why shouldn't we?" Jack pushed himself up on one elbow, blue eyes tinged with the colour of tempered steel holding his brother's, his gaze unmoving. "We can do this. Together."

"I hear you." Richard's hollow eyes returned his brother's serious stare.

Jack nodded, satisfied that his brother had understood him. "I am glad we're in accord."

"You'll be more than delayed if you don't get your backsides back up and on those horses!" Lizbet scolded.

"Whose side is she on?" Jack looked between Lizbet and Richard.

"The answer to that question is a painfully easy one. Ours, and that's a devotion I believe we should both have to earn." Richard, sounding a little more serious, regarded her through partly opened eyes.

Lizbet pushed herself back to her knees. "Aye, well, you're drunk. I'm only here because you both owe me. Don't you go forgetting that."

Jack, squinting a little at the sun behind Lizbet, said, "She does actually bear a passing resemblance to you, it has to be said."

"You think?" Richard replied, turning his head to better observe Lizbet.

"Oh yes, tongue sharper than any knife, definitely your sister."

"Our sister," corrected Richard.

"Now don't start all that again!" Lizbet's cheeks were flushed.

Jack rolled onto his side and grabbed Richard's arm, a look of pure delight on his face. "Just imagine the look on Robert's face when we introduce him to his sister. Can you imagine it? He knows he's a bastard, and after Lizbet opens her mouth he'll be left in no doubt as to where his mother came from!"

Jack fell back, arms wrapped around himself, howling with drunken laughter.

"As funny as that might be, Jack, it isn't fair." Lizbet scowled at him, her voice upset.

Jack had tears on his face. "I know, but I can't help it!"

Lizbet had tears in her eyes, but not ones of mirth. Pulling off one of her shoes, she hit him hard on the shin with it.

"Ouch… Woman, what was that for?" Jack exclaimed, reaching down to nurse the bruised bone.

"For making fun of me." Lizbet's tears ran in two tracks down her cheeks.

Both men looked at each other.

"Lizbet, sorry." In a moment Jack raised himself up and wrapped his arms around her.

"Get off me." Lizbet tried to push him away, still sobbing.

"Come here, Lizbet, and I'll tell you why that was so funny. It wasn't a joke aimed at you," Jack said, and despite her struggles he easily pulled her down next to him on the grass again. "Tell her then, of the family you joined her to," Jack said to his brother.

Richard, leaning over, caught one of her hands and turning it over held it flat in his own. "I told you a long while ago your life was joined to mine and that looks like it has turned out to be true. I am Richard Fitzwarren, and the gentleman pinning you to the grass is my elder brother and heir to the title, John Fitzwarren."

Lizbet swivelled her head to observe Jack. "Title?"

"Don't get too excited, love," Jack said, grinning.

Lizbet listened, opened mouthed, as Jack took up the story and gave her a history of their family past.

"I've heard of your father," Lizbet said in awe at the end.

"Most people have. It's an ability he has," Richard remarked. "Although few, if any, have fond memories of the encounter."

Lizbet lay back, staring up at the sky beyond the tree branches, thinking on what she had been told.

Jack propped himself up on one elbow and leant over her, blocking out the sky. "So, as you see, my brother's declaration, despite what you might have thought, was a good one."

Lizbet blinked away a few tears. "It shamed me, every one of them stared at me as if I'd just crawled from Hell. And the look on Master Scranton's face!"

"And since when did you care about what Master Scranton thought of you?" Jack pointed out accurately. "Master bloody Scranton. He's a man who has society well planned out. You might be from a bawdy house in Southwark, but he'll have no choice now but to call you Mistress Fitzwarren if you meet again."

Lizbet's eyes widened at the thought. "Nooo!"

"I would take a guess that your name is Elizabeth?" Jack asked, after a moment.

Lizbet looked at him blankly.

"Lizbet is a child's name for Elizabeth," he continued by way of explanation.

"Is it? I'd never thought." Lizbet looked confused.

"Mistress Elizabeth Fitzwarren." Jack spoke her name for the first time carefully.

"Stop it, you're not being serious." Lizbet sniffed, and cuffed Jack round the ear.

"Oh, we are. Lass, you've just saved us from the rope, and you've more sense in your young head than Scranton will ever have in a lifetime," Jack replied. "So, sister, welcome to the family." Smiling, he pulled her down and kissed her on the forehead.

Jack's eyes were closed, looking for a moment as if he had fallen asleep, then he added, "We should swear our loyalty to you on our knees, but I hope you'll accept it from me while I'm drunk and flat on my back. Let the manner of the delivery not lessen the meaning. Serva me, servabo te. Semper fidelis."

Lizbet looked between them, but it was Jack she elbowed.

"You saved us, we shall save you. And to you, we will always remain faithful," Jack translated, in a level and serious voice.

After a few minutes Lizbet spoke quietly in Jack's ear. "Do you not think we should set off again?"

"Lie still, lass, there's no rush anymore." Jack's eyes were closed. "It's hot, the horses need a rest." He paused and looked sideways to where Richard slept next to him. "And so does he."

"Let go! You're squashing me!" Lizbet complained, wriggling against his tight encircling arm.

"I want to know where you are." Adjusting his hold on Lizbet, Jack settled himself back intent also on sleep.

Lizbet, though, lay awake, caught in Jack's arm, her head pressed against his shoulder.

†

Jack woke before his brother, an hour later. "How are you feeling?"

There was a pause. "If anyone else asked, I'd lie." Richard's grey eyes met Jack's blue ones and his gaze was frank and honest.

"That's a good start," Jack accepted.

"I trusted where I should not have." Richard spoke with his head tipped back and eyes closed, the words not coming easy.

"We both did," Jack said. "I've sworn an oath once already today. This one should not need to be spoken." Reaching over, he took his brother's wrist in a tight grasp. "Terrible apart and even worse together. Let no-one come between us again."

Richard released his wrist and sat up, his arms shaking with the effort.

Jack sat next to Richard, hesitated for a moment only, then, placing an arm around Richard's shoulders, he pulled him close. "You idiot." Jack had expected Richard to pull away, and was surprised when he didn't, his head resting on Jack's shoulder.

"God forgive me," was all Richard said.

"I can't speak for the almighty, but I do," Jack replied, realising that his brother needed him. He felt strangely content.

"Just get us there, Jack. I need a little time."

Jack tightened the hold around Richard's shoulders. "I will get us there."

†

Jack hated being hungry. It had been the curse of his childhood, where discipline revolved around food and the denial of it. He could never, however, recall an incident when good behaviour had been rewarded with a surfeit of it. Jack looked sideways at his brother, wondering for the second time that afternoon if he had ever suffered hunger. He doubted it. Richard might have missed a few meals here and there, but he doubted very much he had ever had to fight just to stay alive.

They'd travelled now for seven days and progress was painfully slow. It was too hot to travel during the heat of the day. They were forced instead to move south early in the morning and then again when the sun lowered in the sky. But each night had come too early and a waning moon provided little light to show the way. Once, Richard had fallen from his horse after accidentally forcing it to step from the path, the beast losing its footing and bringing them both down.

That Andrew was ahead of them was a thought that Jack dwelt on less and less. Instead his attention was now focused on something far more basic, far more immediate, but which might prove an equally hard battle to win. Food.

Lizbet was feeling it, he could tell from her expression. If his brother was, he kept the thought from his face. The situation was serious. If they did not stop and find themselves more than just the few berries they were taking from passing trees, then within a few days none of them would be in a fit state to continue the journey.

Jack moved closer to his brother and squeezed his arm. "We need to find some food. Soon."

Richard appeared to hear him and nodded, but Jack was not so sure he understood. "Richard, we can't keep going for more than a day or so unless we find something to eat."

Richard met his eyes then. "The next village, we can buy something there."

"With what?" exclaimed Jack.

Richard didn't answer him. He just turned his head forwards and continued to walk doggedly forward, leading the horse behind him. It was then that Jack realised that Richard was still not engaged with what was happening around him. When he'd plied him with aqua vitae they had shared some words, but as soon as the effects of the cheap spirit had worn off he became withdrawn once more, more so than he had been before.

"We need to stop. Why are you not listening?" Jack took hold of Richard's arm and forced him to a halt.

Richard turned dark eyes on Jack, but Jack, swearing, realised he still didn't have his brother's attention. Wherever his thoughts were, they were not dwelling on their current plight.

An hour later they finally stopped, although Jack was not too sure that it was an improvement in their circumstances. A thin covering of wood provided some shelter from the sun for the horses, and Jack was sure they were far enough away from the main track to not attract any attention.

Richard was still not overly communicative and Jack was unsure how long it would take to get to

Venice. They were already way behind Andrew. There was no chance now that they would be able to catch him before he arrived at the Venetian capital. All they could hope was that he would still be there when they finally arrived. Three of them and two mounts was not ideal, the horses moving at little more than a walk. Jack recognised the signs of hunger and fatigue on all their faces.

What little they had left between them they could not trade. Jack recognised he'd be a fool if he swapped the ring on his hand for bread and meat in one of the small farms they passed. He knew he needed to keep as much as possible for when they arrived in Venice, where sleeping on the streets would not be an option. They would need to hire a room.

Lizbet, calling to him from the tree line, told him she had found a stream concealed by a belt of trees and was going to fill the water bottle. Jack, acknowledging her shout, continued to carefully split the thin strips of bark he'd pulled from a tree, making them into narrow enough lengths to begin crafting snares. Although looking around him, at the sun bleached arid Italian landscape, he was not sure that he was going to be able to catch anything. Jack, engrossed in his task, had prepared enough cord to make three snares, when he realised that Lizbet had not come back.

Grumbling under his breath, Jack pushed the cord into his belt, told Richard to watch the horses and set off in the direction she had gone.

†

Richard's reverie where he sat near the horses was broken by the sound of Lizbet's shrill laughter and Jack's annoyed voice in counterpart. Rising, he set off to find them. There was a steep bank in the forest floor and clambering up it, Richard found as he crested it that it dropped away vertically on the other side and beneath him there was a stream and Lizbet and Jack.

Jack was knee deep in the water; Lizbet on her hands and knees on the bank was pointing and directing him. The drop was too steep to go down and Richard was forced to take a longer route to join them. When he arrived, his brother was still in the stream. He'd obviously fallen into the water and was soaked from head to foot. As Richard watched, Jack reached into the water, lifted out a large rock, and then turning, dropped it with a sploosh into the water.

"What are you doing?" The look on Richard's face was one of pure incredulity.

"What does it look like?" came the acid reply from Jack.

"I'm not sure. Tell me?" Richard said, moving closer to the bank.

"Look, there's fish, down there. Can you see them?" Lizbet's raised voice was excited as she pointed over the edge of the bank into the pool.

Richard's eyes followed her finger. In the pool were a number of sizeable fish, coiling and twisting in the water. As Richard watched, Jack hoisted another sizeable rock, lugged it behind him, and dropped it back into the water. Richard realised what he was doing. Jack was building a dam to contain the fish. The pond was small and the water was coursing over the top of the wall of stones. The gaps between them were too small for the fish to make an escape.

"Get in here and help me," Jack called.

Richard obediently stripped to his shirt and hose and was knee deep in the pond a moment later.

Lizbet, a rock ready in her hand, on her knees shouted down at them. "There, that big one. Get it."

The pond was small, and they could even feel the fish brush past their legs, but their repeated efforts to plunge grasping hands into the water were failing to bring a fish to the surface. It was Jack who eventually dropped to his knees in the water and waited patiently until the fish swam too close to his submerged hands. He hooked a fish out of the water but with Richard's clumsy help, he lost hold of it, cursing. They watched it twist free of their grasp and plunge back into the pond.

Lizbet berated them from the bank. "You useless pair of bastards."

"Get your backside down here, woman, and you try, if you think you can do better," Jack shot back at her.

"Shut up moaning and get on with it." Lizbet continued to offer helpful instructions "There! Behind you!"

Jack ignored her and kneeling in the small pond, side by side with his brother, waited until the fish brought themselves close enough. It was Richard this time who hooked one from the water, and between them they managed to throw it to the bank. Lizbet delivered the rock to the fish's head, ending its squirming quest for escape.

Lizbet, her hands still holding the dead fish on the grass, called down to them, "Come on lads, two more like this and we'll have a meal."

They had two more landed onto the grass soon after. Jack hefted a rock from the pond to the bank and on it he quickly gutted the fish. Lizbet had taken herself back over the ridge and into the trees to collect firewood. Jack still had the blood-covered knife in his hands when he heard Lizbet screaming. He was on his feet in a moment, his brother at his shoulder.

Lizbet, still shrieking, an arm whirling round her head, the other clutching the wood, crested the bank.

"Get away from me!" Lizbet screeched.

Jack had taken two quick steps towards her before he realised what was happening, the tension suddenly leaving his body. "Christ, woman! It's only a wasp."

Lizbet leapt past him, letting out another shriek. "Have you seen the size of it? Get it away from me."

"Just leave it be and it'll leave you alone." Jack pulled the wood from her arms.

"I hate them." Lizbet was looking around nervously. The wasp, it seemed, had for the moment disappeared.

"It probably doesn't like you much either," Jack muttered, turning his attention to lighting a fire.

The summer sun had dried the wood to a crisp. One of their remaining possessions was a small tinderbox and he had the fire started quickly, the spark catching easily and the glowing ember soon turned from smoke to a hot flame as he added kindling.

Lizbet soon had the fish roasting over the flames, skewered on some of the longer sticks she had brought.. They ate in silence. Jack savoured every mouthful. Picking the last of the fish from the bones, he was wondering whether they could quickly catch more. Richard had already lain back on the grass next to the dying flames, one arm over his eyes to keep the light from them. Jack settled back, his head in a patch of shade from one of the trees on the bank. Closing his eyes, he realised he was more tired than he had thought.

He would catch some more fish in a while. It was just good not to feel hungry.

"While you laze there, I'll get the water skin and fill it, I suppose," Lizbet grumbled.

Jack heard Lizbet stand up, but kept his eyes shut. "Aye, you do that." He suppressed a grin as he heard Lizbet cursing and making her way back up the bank to where the horses were to get the water skin.

Jack was never sure how long he had been asleep. He supposed it couldn't have been long when Lizbet's piercing scream ended his slumber.

Sitting up, suddenly awakened, Richard said, "Another wasp?"

Jack smiled, and was about to agree when he heard her scream again. "That's not a wasp."

They both heard her next cry for help. As both men scrambled to their feet, Lizbet crested the bank and ran screaming towards them. In close pursuit were three men.

Jack ripped the wooden scabbard from the blade as Lizbet made it down the bank, only an arm's distance from her pursuers. The men dug their heels in, coming to a crashing halt at the sight of the blade in Jack's hand. There might have been three of them, but none were armed with anything but a knife, and the sword was a formidable threat.

The man in the middle, his arms wide, prevented his companions from moving forward. Grinning broadly, his eyes never leaving Jack's face, he took a precautionary step backwards. "We just thought the woman was lost," he offered in heavily accented Italian.

It was Jack who spoke, the sword in one hand and his other hand wrapped tightly round Lizbet's wrist as he pulled her quickly behind him. "Thank you for your concern, our sister is a constant worry to us."

The man's face creased into sun-burnt wrinkles. His eyes switched for a moment from the steel in Jack's hand to his face. His own hand was open now in a gesture of supplication as he stepped back two more paces, the men on either side matching him.

Smiling the Italian said, "We are pleased she is safe."

The three of them took more slow cautious steps backward before they turned to walk up the bank to the crest. Jack and Richard stood immobile and watched them as they disappeared over the rise. Only then did Jack release his tight hold on Lizbet's wrist.

"I'm sorry," Lizbet wailed, rubbing the skin where Jack's fingers had left an imprint.

Jack sheathed the aged sword in the wooden scabbard, and put his arm around her shoulders. "It could have been worse, it could have been a wasp."

"Don't, Jack." Lizbet hit him on the chest with her small balled fist. "I was just unhooking the water skin when they saw me."

"Christ!" Jack exclaimed.

The brothers looked at each other at the same moment.

"The horses!" screamed Lizbet. She set off to keep up with Jack as he launched himself at the bank in pointless pursuit. By the time they crested the rise they could see that the two tethered horses were gone. Lizbet made to run down the bank and Jack's hand stopped her.

"We'll never catch them, lass," Jack said, his voice bitter.

"It seems our fall from grace is complete," Richard said, meeting Jack's eyes.

Jack swallowed hard, rubbing a rough callused hand over his face. They'd lost not just the horses, there had been two cloaks rolled behind the saddles and the water skin was gone from the branches. He wanted to scream.

Lizbet wrapped her arm around his. "Jack, I'm so sorry, if they hadn't seen me."

"It's my fault, it's my fault. I should never have let you out of my sight," Jack replied, anguish in his voice. Then, "Where's Richard?"

His brother had gone back up the bank and back down to the stream. When they got back, they found him standing looking down into the pond.

"I was wrong, it seems," Richard said wearily. "There was a little further yet to fall."

The pressure from the water had forced away the central stone from the dam and the fish, no longer trapped in the pond, had made an escape.

Chapter 3

A Poor Acquisition

If progress had been slow before, now it was bitterly painful. Without the horses, poor beasts that they had been, they were reduced to covering at most ten miles a day. If their situation had looked dire, now it was verging on the desperate. Avoiding towns was something they could no longer do, they needed to trade what little they had left, and the small villages were no place to do that.

"We find the next town, and we sell the rings," Jack had declared, and before Richard could say a word he'd added, "We have no choice."

After that they had walked on in silence. On the third day, when the heat of the sun was starting to lessen, they found a destination. In the distance they could see a walled town, although it seemed to get little closer as the afternoon wore on. It was early evening before they finally arrived, dusty, foot sore and hungry.

As they neared the town, the smell of cooking and the noise of cheering and music drifted across the dry plain towards them.

"This is good, it looks like the town is having a fiesta. They'll not notice a few more people on a night like tonight," Jack said quickly as they approached.

The smells from the cooking fires and the aroma of roasted meat were causing loud complaints from all of their stomachs. The town's population had moved outside of the walls for the evening's entertainment. Two large fires were set up and above them were roasting pigs. Near the flames was a vendor selling hot bowls of pottage and nearby, for a coin, you could purchase bread from a basket. Ale sellers, with stoppered casks and earthenware cups, had ranged themselves near the food, and there were two women selling small, round, sweet-smelling buns peppered with fruit.

"I think I'm going to be sick," Lizbet complained, as they neared the food stalls.

Jack leant his head close to hers. "Soon you'll have your fill, girl. I promise."

Jack had seen something else beyond the food sellers that had claimed his attention. Raucous shouts rang out from a crowd of men gathered in a group and he pressed forward to find out what it was they were betting on.

The crowd were ranged in a rough circle around two combatants who were trading blows with their fists. The pair looked badly matched. One was huge bear of a man with the build of a wrestler, his arms thick with corded muscle, and his sweating grim-set face was balanced upon a broad wide neck. His opponent, half his size, was lithe and fast, making his blows repeatedly and with a speed the big man could not match. As soon as the smaller man had delivered a punch to his opponent's flesh, he darted quickly back out of the way of the retaliatory swings. If the big man could make just one of his meaty fists connect, no-one expected the smaller man to continue to fight.

Suddenly, Jack felt nails bite into the skin of his arm. Lizbet's voice close to his ear hissed, "No, Jack. You'll not win."

"I'd rather be knocked out flat on my back, than continue to feel like this." Jack pulled his arm roughly away from her and turned back to watch the fight.

The smaller faster man continued to taunt the bigger. From the comments that met Jack's ears, it was obvious that they knew each other well. This fight was not only providing entertainment for those gathered to watch, it was also settling a score between them.

Lizbet, freeing her long hair from the plait it had been kept in, was quickly pulling a bone comb through the long brown tresses, tugging at the knots and tangles that had lodged there from rough sleeping and neglect.

The hand that grasped her wrist nearly made her drop the comb. "You I can stop," Jack growled in her ear as he pulled her towards him. He knew exactly what she was proposing to do. Lizbet, twisting, tried to wrench her arm free, but the grip was like iron, and she yelped as his fingers pressed her flesh to the bone.

"Stop trying to pull away and I'll stop hurting you." Jack dragged her close to him for a moment.

Lizbet stopped struggling and the tight, painful grip relaxed, but he did not let her go. Jack was still watching the bout before him closely. The smaller man had landed a blow that had brought blood to the other man's nose along with a delighted shout from the crowd. It also delivered him the opening he needed. Joining his hands together, he brought them up hard under the other's jaw, rocking his head back. The blow broke three of the other man's teeth as the balled fists cracked him under the jaw. Blood spilled from between his lips, pouring from the gash his shattered teeth had cut in his tongue. A kick to his exposed groin took the remaining strength from his knees and he crumpled to the ground in the middle of the circle of cheering onlookers.

Richard tried to place a restraining hand on Jack's arm, but Jack, intent on presenting himself in the ring, pulled from his grasp. Before he left, he pushed Lizbet towards Richard. "Keep hold of her."

"Stop him!" Lizbet hissed Richard's his ear. "He's not eaten for days, he's going to get the Hell beaten out of him now. He should have let me go." Lizbet yelped in pain as Richard shifted his grip to her upper arm and brought her face close to his.

"Would you have been able to stop him?" Richard demanded.

Jack's earlier assertion that the town's folk would not notice them had been quite wrong. As he entered the ring to declare himself a contender, his appearance caused a wave of comment throughout the crowd. Summer sun had stripped the colour from his hair and it shone now like white gold, in stark contrast to their dark Mediterranean hair. Taller by a foot than most of the men gathered there, he was of immediate interest. The lithe and agile man who had won the last fight was not stopping in for another round; his score had been settled, and collecting his winnings he joined the other spectators.

A match was soon found. Jack looked at his opponent with bitter resignation, wondering just how long he was going to last. It was immediately apparent that it was not a fight he could win. Jack, his skill blunted by lack of food and sleep, took two blows to the head before he managed defend himself. Blood welled from his lip and the crowd cheered as he staggered backward. Looking round quickly, his eyes found Lizbet's. He made a quick signal with his hands that anyone from London would recognise and hoped she'd seen it. It was the hand signal used to warn of pickpockets. Jack hoped Lizbet understood he was suggesting that he would keep their attention while she dipped their pockets.

"Let me go." Lizbet twisted her arm against Richard's hold and tried to pull herself free on the hold.

Richard had seen the gesture as well. Realising that Jack was going to take a beating as a diversion, he had no choice but to let Lizbet go, muttering as he did, "Now I am a poor man stealing."

Lizbet was gone in a moment, pushing her way through the crowd, jostling the spectators and looking very much like she was just trying to get herself to the front for a good view. The crowd roared with laugher at Jack's poor performance in the ring. He made a comic figure, and they watched as he hid behind his hands, tried to deflect the blows with opened palms and even tried to reason with his attacker in broken Italian. Jack fervently hoped that this painful method of keeping their attention well focused, and away from the woman pressing between them, was going to work.

Lizbet was back at Richard's side very soon, saying urgently, "What's Italian for 'my stupid husband'?"

When Richard did not answer, Lizbet shook his arm, repeating the question. "Hurry up, what is it?"

"Moi stupido marito," Richard supplied a moment later, looking at her in confusion.

"Moi stupido marito," Lizbet repeated.

Richard nodded.

Turning, Lizbet dived back into the crowd clearly intent on making it to the contestants in the ring, shouting as she went, "Moi stupido marito." Arriving at the ring side, she yelled once more, "Moi stupido marito."

Jack's attacker, too stunned by the appearance of Lizbet forcing her way between them, dropped his fists. Jack threw his hands in the air, then Lizbet, reverting to English, began to scold and swear in equal measure. If the crowd had been amused before by Jack's antics, now they were howling with laughter, as he was pulled from the ring by his wife. Lizbet continued the tirade, dragging her reluctant husband away from the fight, some of the spectators clapping him on the back as he passed them, offering their condolences. Lizbet ignoring them, continued to berate him, blindly pushing through the crowd and pulling him with her.

"You foolish man." Lizbet's shrill scolding voice had gone and there was real concern in it now. "Look at you."

Jack had a split lip and a swollen eye for his pains. His opponent had landed a good few telling blows on Jack in the short time he had been in the ring. Lizbet ripped his shirt up and saw the plume of purple settling on his ribs where they too had taking a beating.

"Maybe," Jack agreed, pulling the shirt back down and wiping the blood from his mouth with the back of his hand. "At least I've got something in my mouth with some taste."

"We can do better than that in a minute." Lizbet was leading them back towards the cooking fires. The freshly acquired coins in her hand were enough for pottage and bread for each of them with some left over. The remaining stolen money she gave into Jack's keeping. The plan was simple, they'd remain outside the walls tonight, then tomorrow they would go into the town and trade what little they had left.

†

The town of Marostica was an affluent enough place for them to trade. A quick tally in the morning showed that they had three rings, one of Jack's and two others belonging to Richard, plus four pearls that had come from the shoes, which Lizbet still had in her pocket.

"In the right place, when we don't look as if we stole this lot, we would get a good price," Lizbet said, bitterly, "but here, looking like this, I doubt if we will get enough money for more than a meal each and a place to sleep."

"Well, we can keep them and starve," Jack said, cheerily, "or trade them, and live a little longer." He dropped the three rings back into Lizbet's bag along with the pearls. "We trade the pearls first – if we say we are fishermen then these are something we might have come across."

"No-one in Christendom would believe you two are fishermen," Lizbet scoffed, looking at Jack's grazed face.

"I know. But the rings will brand us as thieves for sure. And although being hanged for theft would be a fitting end, it would spoil the day a little," Jack said, darkly, instantly regretting his words.

"There would be some justice in it," Richard replied, dropping his eyes from Jack's.

Together they set off to see if they could find anywhere in Marostica to sell the pearls. They eventually found what they were looking for – attached to an apothecary's was a usurer's shop, indicated by the symbols on the faded wooden sign.

"You'll have to go," Jack said, pointing at his face. "I look too much like I just relieved the owner of them."

Richard reached for the bag, and as he did, Jack saw his hand shake and abruptly changed his mind. They could not risk this going wrong.

Jack took the bag with the pearls and opened the door to the apothecary's shop. The usurer had a small corner of the shop that was given over to his wares, all neatly stored on cramped shelves. In front of the shelves was a worn desk, one leg blocked up with a stone. Behind the desk, watching his approach with assessing eyes, was the thin and spare frame of the usurer. Jack knew that he had already been well appraised by the little man.

There was a set of small scales on the desk. Jack lifted the top brass dish from it, set it down in front of the man and into it he placed three perfect pearls from Elizabeth's shoes. If the usurer was surprised he didn't show it. Without meeting Jack's eyes, he picked up each one in turn, and examined it closely before replacing it in the dish with the others.

"Quanto?" Jack asked quietly.

His accent raised the man's eyes to his face. Jack knew the man was thinking about how low an offer he could make.

Still the man did not speak. Instead he opened a box near the scales, took from it a coin and lay it down next to the dish. It was a silver piastra. It would feed them for all for a week, but nothing else.

Jack's eyes never left those of the usurer. "Di Più."

The usurer's mouth twisted into a hard thin line and there was an almost imperceptible shake of his head. Jack nodded, slowly picked up the three pearls and turned to leave. His back was to the usurer before the man spoke.

"Quanto?" the man put the question.

"Doppio," Jack replied, without even turning back. He was still walking towards the door. He reached it before the man spoke again, hastily this time to stop him from leaving.

"Si, si."

Jack, hiding a smile, turned back. In a few moments he had the two silver piastras in his hand. Leaving the apothecary's shop he crossed the street back to Richard and Lizbet.

☥

An hour later, fed and preparing to leave the town, they were back outside the apothecary's again.

"Let me try?" Lizbet pleaded, for the second time, and then added persuasively, "What harm can it do?"

"It's money we don't have," Jack replied, bluntly.

"You need to do something to help him. If you don't, he's not going to be of use to anyone soon." Lizbet had her back to Richard, who was sitting with his back against the wall, staring at the ground between his feet.

Jack, casting his eyes over the forlorn figure of his brother, had to agree. There was a meeting coming soon and there was little chance of anyone taking his brother seriously in his current state. Richard was withdrawn, disinterested and seemed permanently pre-occupied.

"When you were ill, remember, Lucy gave me some medicine for you. Let me see if they have it," Lizbet pressed Jack.

"Dwale? You're not giving him that? Christ, he's hardly moving as it is. If you give him dwale it'll stop him in his tracks," Jack said, his expression horrified.

"Not dwale. Lucy had some other medicines I gave you. It used to bring you back from wherever you were. He needs something like that now," Lizbet continued.

Jack looked over the top of Lizbet's head at Richard; he could remember only too well the torment and the demons of Marshalsea. Maybe, if there was something that would help, they should try it. Then his mind ran back to the practicalities of their current situation. They had so little. To risk what little they did have on an apothecary's remedy seemed rash.

"Here, I was keeping this for myself." Lizbet produced one last pearl that she had palmed from the small bag. "Let me use this, please."

Jack relented. "How are you going to know what to ask for? I doubt the apothecary can understand you."

Lizbet tapped her nose and grinned. "I know what it smells like."

Jack returned with her and negotiated silver for the final pearl. Standing back, arms folded, he kept half an eye on his brother where he still sat, back against the way, staring in front of him while Lizbet approached the apothecary's counter.

Behind the counter, a neatly attired short man, wearing a linen apron and a close fitting cap of the same material, watched her closely. His eyes raked over her body, earning him a scowl from Jack, where he stood near the door.

Lizbet put both her hands to her belly and twisted her face in an imitation of pain.

The little man's face became a depiction of immediate sympathy. Rounding his counter, he reached out a hand laying it gently on her stomach.

"Does it hurt here, Senora? Or here," he asked, in quiet Italian, as he moved his hand further up her abdomen.

Lizbet heard the tread of Jack's boots on the boards behind her, but she did not see the look he bestowed on the apothecary that discouraged him from any further exploration.

"Just here." Lizbet tapped her stomach again.

The little man smiling returned behind the counter and lifted down a large earthenware pot, placing it on the counter he removed the lid. "A spoonful in wine, three times a day, for the stomach pains."

Lizbet didn't fully understand his quick Italian, but she knew what she was looking for. Pulling the pot quickly towards her, she sniffed the contents and shook her head. The brown acrid dust inside was not what she wanted. Wrinkling her nose and replacing the stopper for him, she turned to Jack. "Tell him what I want smells like ladies' perfume."

Jack rolled his eyes, then addressing the apothecary, said, "She says it smells like ladies perfume."

The apothecary's face brightened. "Ah, ask your Senora if it is like the scent of flowers."

"He says," translated Jack, "does it smell like flowers?"

Lizbet turned back to the Apothecary and in her broken Italian addressed him. "Yes, like summer flowers."

The apothecary turned, his fingers running along the packed shelves, until they arrived at the jar he was looking for. It was smaller than the first he had shown her. He lifted it down, prised the stopper from the top and tipped it so she could smell the contents.

Lizbet sniffed experimentally, and shook her head, saying, "More."

The apothecary looked confused. "More?"

Lizbet turned to Jack. "Tell him, what I want is like this, but it smells stronger."

Jack, his face turned away to make sure Richard had not moved, spoke to the apothecary over his shoulder, telling him what Lizbet wanted. Another jar appeared and Lizbet sniffed a second time. "This is better, but the stuff Lucy had made your eyes water when you took the top off. Don't you remember?"

"No, I don't," said Jack, not at all liking to be reminded of his own incapacity.

"Ask him if he has anything that smells stronger than this," Lizbet said over her shoulder.

The apothecary repeated Jack's words looking slightly askance at Lizbet. Lizbet nodded enthusiastically. The apothecary returned the jar to the shelf, and this time retrieved one from under the counter and opened it for her. As soon as the lid was removed, the cloying sickly aroma met Lizbet's nose and she smiled and nodded.

The apothecary, shaking his head, addressed Jack. "This is expensive. Ask the lady how many measures she would like?"

Jack translated.

Lizbet, placing her hand over the pot, said quickly, "All of it."

Jack tried to object. The price was high. When he tried to argue though, she told him in no uncertain terms that it was her pearl that was buying it. The deal was finally sealed, when she pointed across the street to Richard, sat against the wall hugging his knees to his chest, and asked him, "Do you want him to stop like that?"

Jack conceded that he didn't, and paid the apothecary. From the market they then bought bread and pale yellow cheese, Lizbet adding the sickly substance to the ale that she passed to Richard.

Chapter 4

A Change Of Fortune

It was several days after they had left the Italian town, still heading south to the coast, when Jack finally felt their luck was changing. He had woken in the morning, and was delighted to find that his snares had finally worked. Two rabbits had been caught and were still fighting to free themselves from the snares. Jack quickly dispatched them, then quickening his pace, he took them triumphantly back to Lizbet.

Holding them high and grinning, Jack said, "Get a fire lit, lass. At least we won't start today with empty bellies."

Lizbet, on her feet in a moment, her eyes wide, skipped towards him. "They're a good size. Well done. Get them skinned while I get a fire going."

Soon, Lizbet had a small smoking fire set between three stones. The two rabbits, skewered on long sticks, were set to cook in the gentle heat at the edge of the fire, Lizbet on her knees making sure neither of them burnt.

Fat dripped, sizzling into the fire, and the aroma of roasting meat was a delight they had not smelt for some time.

"A feast fit for a king," Lizbet declared, handing the larger of the two rabbits to Jack. "It's hot. You've been warned."

Jack pulled at the roasted meat tentatively, determined not to wait.

Lizbet had rinsed down the largest of the three stones and set to cutting the other rabbit up. There was little point giving Richard anything but one small amount at a time, and she didn't want to waste Jack's catch. The best meat was on the breast. Cutting it away, she held it out on the edge of the blade for Richard.

"Here, take it. It will make a welcome change from bread," she encouraged, proffering the meat a little closer. "You need to have something…"

Lizbet never finished the sentence. Richard lashed out, sending the offered meat into the flames. Lizbet, startled, knocked the rest of the cooked rabbit from the stone into the fire. The blow had been hard enough to make Lizbet yelp, and she sat holding her arm where he had struck her.

A moment later, seeing the flames consuming the rabbit that had fallen into the fire, Lizbet screamed and sent her fists to land ineffectual blows on Richard's head. Jack was too intent on the task of saving their meal from the flames to intervene.

"Get up. Damn you to hell," Lizbet screamed, continuing to hit him. Richard, kneeling with his head in his hands, ignored her. "Get up! Damn you."

She hit out one more time before standing. Taking in two whooping gulps of air, heels of her hands pressed hard into her eyes, she sobbed in despair. Her whole body shook.

The rabbit safe, Jack planted a hand on his brother's shoulder, sending him sprawling over backwards on the ground.

"If I hit you, you won't get up again." Jack's eyes were dark with fury. Rising, he said not a word to Lizbet, simply wrapping his arms around her and fixing a hard stare on his brother over her head. Richard was kneeling again, his head bowed, face covered with his hands.

Lizbet recovered herself quickly and pushed away from Jack, wiping the back of her hand across her wet face. "I'm sorry, that was my fault."

Jack gave her a final reassuring squeeze before loosening his arms. "He's not getting any better. Give him some more," he instructed.

Lizbet sniffed and nodded.

"I'll sort him out; we've not the time to treat him like a child." Jack said, looking down at his brother he rubbed his hands over his face. "Get up, face me and face the world."

He received no response.

Next he delivered a kick to Richard's boot. It was a warning, and not heeded. He kicked him again. Still there was no reaction.

"I warned you." Jack leaned down, took a fierce hold of Richard and hauled him to his feet. "Face the bloody world. Do you hear me? The lass deserves better from us. Do you hear me?" Jack held him up, his face close to Richard's.

Something flickered across Richard's face, his eyes focusing on Jack. It was as if he'd just become aware of him and he stared at his brother in confusion.

"Do you hear me?" Jack said again, adding a violent shake to reinforce his words.

"Jack, don't!" shouted Lizbet behind him.

Richard looked between them, then peering at Jack's face, he asked quietly, "What did I do?"

Jack still had a tight hold of his brother, but he could feel Richard supporting his own weight now and he lessened his grip. "You don't know?" Jack sounded incredulous.

Richard's face was answer enough and Jack let him go.

†

The journey that morning was both sombre and long. They stopped eventually at a small town, Jack telling Lizbet and Richard to wait whilst he made enquiries.

"Wait here with him. I'll go and see if I can find news of Andrew passing through here," Jack said, looking around the marketplace.

"Don't leave me with him," Lizbet said, quietly so Richard didn't hear.

He'd already lowered himself to the ground and sat with his back to the wall and his knees drawn up.

"He's alright now. He'll be no trouble." Jack squeezed her arm. "I just need to clear my head, and some time out of his company would help."

"Alright," Lizbet accepted, adding, "but don't be long."

Jack smiled. "I won't."

Lizbet sat next to Richard in the shade on the edge of the market and watched Jack disappear from view. From a broken loaf in her lap she passed a hunk to Richard. Absently he shook his head and Lizbet sighed. "You need to eat more. You'll be nothing more than skin and bone soon."

His unshaven face disguised how much weight he had lost, the angular cheek bones seeming to provide a fragile framework for the tanned skin.

When she didn't get a reply, she continued, "He needs you." Lizbet swallowed her mouthful of bread. "We both need you."

Those final words did get a reaction and Richard turned to regard her closely for a moment before lowering his face into his hands. "I don't know if I can believe again," was all he said.

"It wasn't your fault," Lizbet said quickly.

Richard laughed harshly. "The price of the lesson was too high."

"It wasn't a lesson…"

Richard cut her off. "Don't pick over my soul like a raven on a carcass."

They sat in silence after that.

Richard raised his head from his hands and stared across the marketplace. It seemed a long while before he had a sense of what he was staring at. Opposite them, on the other side of the marketplace was a church. White limestone walls shone in the sunlight, its two high arched towers dominating the centre of the small town. Whether it was to avoid any further comment from Lizbet or whether he genuinely wanted to cross to the church, he didn't really know. Richard pushed himself up from the floor, and strode away from Lizbet into the crowd in the marketplace. He didn't want her company. He didn't want any company.

The steps up to the church were busy. The market stalls butted up to them on either side, breaking for a short distance only to allow access to the church. On the bottom step was a row of town beggars who had taken up a strategic position. The only way up the steps was over them, and they could ply their trade on the faithful who had to press closely to pass them.

Pronouncing the words of a psalm in Latin, and using a stick with alarming accuracy, a priest rattled shins, bestowing bruises on arms and heads as he cleared the beleaguered beggars from the steps. Richard was pushed to one side as two of the men, who had looked close to death's door, leapt up and scampered neatly away before the priest could deliver a second chastening attack upon them.

As if sensing Richard's eyes upon him, he turned and met the grey assessing gaze. He said in Italian, "Beggars on the steps are bad for the business of the Lord, get you gone, wasters and thieves the lot of you." Advancing towards Richard, he waved his stick threateningly in his face.

"Does that not deny the proverb that says, whoever is generous to the poor, lends to the Lord?" Richard said, holding his ground.

Lowering the stick the priest looked him for a moment, then suddenly his face broke into a huge smile. When he spoke again, it was in English. "Come in. The Lord's house is blessedly cool."

Richard answered in the same language. "I was undecided. But it seems that now you have cleared a path for me it would a shame not to use it."

The main door stood solid, dusty and closed. Following the priest up the steps it became obvious that the entrance to the left of the main door stood open. As soon as Richard entered the shade afforded by the huge doorway, he could feel the cool air rolling from the church's interior in tempting invitation.

How long had it been? Six months? No, more like nine months, since he had walked up the aisle, and nearly collapsed in St Ethelrede's in London. Richard had to admit he did not feel much steadier on his feet this time either, and his steps down the side of the church were equally as heavy.

Reaching out a hand for the carved wooden end of the pew, he leant heavily on it, his heart hammering in his chest and his throat dry and tight. Stepping sideways, Richard lowered himself onto the wooden seat, raising his eyes to the image of Christ on the cross hanging above the altar. Sunlight, piercing the windows high up in the walls, struck the gold leaf on the suspended carving, the bright light stabbing painfully at the back of his eyes. He changed his focus instead, watching the dust motes dance in the shafts of sunlight that poured from the windows down to the tiled floors.

"A long way from home?" The voice, that of the priest he had spoken to outside, came from behind him. "How long has it been?"

Richard was about to deliver a curt reply, but the question was softly put, and he even thought he detected a note of sympathy behind the words. The priest continued, "I recognised your accent. I'm from a village a little way north of Hexham if you would believe it, and I've not spoken English in so long… it would please an old man to talk to you."

Richard turned in his seat. The priest was indeed, on close inspection, older than he would have first guessed. The face beneath the brown tan was creased with age, the skin wrinkled around the smiling eyes.

"North of Hexham," Richard echoed, "that's a rough part of England to come from."

"I left when I was boy, went down to Durham, from there to Canterbury and then here. My ageing bones are not regretting swapping English winters for Italian ones," he said smiling. Then suddenly he laid a light hand upon Richard's shoulder and said, "Do not think there is a sin on earth I have not heard, in English, or Italian." He rose without waiting for Richard to answer. "Come, let me ease your soul. That is why you came in here?"

"Some souls are beyond redemption," was all Richard said in reply.

"That I cannot believe. The dust will fall on the earth and the spirit will always return to God who gave it," the priest stated quietly.

"Ecclesiastes," Richard replied, distractedly.

"Whatever your sin, it cannot place you beyond salvation."

Richard reached out for the back of the pew in front with both hands as his head swam. Maybe it was the thick incense. The priest was still talking to him, but the words were just noise, order-less noise, soothing but without any sense or meaning.

Richard was never sure exactly how he made the journey across the church. The next time he was aware of his surroundings, they had changed to the inside of the small dusty confessional, which seemed to harbour an even stronger scent of incense. Eyes closed, he saw again the bodies laid in the street, smelt the rank burnt flesh, heard the wails and pitiful choking screams of those caught within the buildings, looked again for the last time into Mat's clouding eyes. A tight breath caught in his throat. A half gasp, half sob escaped as he screwed his eyes tight shut against the image in his mind, his nails biting into the palms of his hands. There was silence only from the other side of the screen as the priest waited patiently for him to begin.

"God forgive me for I have sinned," he managed on a hoarse breath.

The words of the priest issuing his penance were still filling Richard's head when he left the cramped confines and made his way back to the pews in the middle of the church. "For such a sin as the one you carry on your soul, the penance must be a weighty one. Look for the innocents you can save. Return them to the Lord, and he will grant you salvation from your sin."

†

Jack couldn't find him. He had only left them for a few minutes, and he could not believe Lizbet had let him walk alone into the crowd. Swearing loudly at her, he cast his eyes over the crowd for sight of Richard, before sending Lizbet to search in one direction while he took the other.

It was a flower seller who remembered seeing him talking to the priest on the steps of St Maria's. She had no idea where he had gone after that. Jack looked wildly up and down the street and then at St Maria's. Could he be in there?

He took a path straight up the steps. Heedless of the beggars who had to scramble out of his way, he strode through them and finding a side door open, ducked into the dark interior.

It took a few moments for his eyes to adjust to the dim light inside. There were people scattered around the interior. Jack moved to walk down the aisle, not caring about the noise his boots made on the flagged floor, or the incongruous metallic clank that came from the sword tethered to the belt at his waist, the sound rattling around the vaulted ceiling. In a moment he had made it to the pew where Richard sat, Jack dropped heavily next to his brother on the narrow bench.

Richard, head still bowed, eyes closed, said, "You couldn't sneak up on a deaf man."

"I wasn't intending to. When I make an entrance I expect people to notice," Jack said none too quietly.

"Oh, they notice," was all Richard said wearily.

"What are you doing in here?"

"It's a church," Richard supplied, as if that was answer enough.

Jack looked around him. "Yes, I can see that, so why are you here?"

"I know you don't believe you have an immortal soul, but some of us are not blessed with your self assurance, I am afraid," Richard said, icily.

"Ah," was all the reply Jack made, then leaning over, he placed a hand heavily on Richard's shoulder and asked, "Did it help?"

Richard stood suddenly. "Has anyone ever told you how insensitive you can be?" He spoke loudly. It earned him several stern glances from those in the church, along with a loud shush from a nun trimming flowers near the Lady Chapel.

Jack frowned. "Not recently." Then smiling, he put a guiding hand on Richard's arm and began to lead him down the aisle towards the door. "But someone did tell me I was in charge. And I don't remember telling you that you could absent yourself without notice on the grounds of your eternal salvation. Next time, tell me where you're going."

Richard pulled his arm from his brother's grasp, and, squinting against the noon light, stepped outside the Church. Jack ducked to avoid the low lintel and followed him.

†

Meanwhile, in London, another difficult conversation was taking place. One in which the name of Fitzwarren featured, heavily. The lawyer Clement's filed petition had come to the attention to William Cecil.

"Take a look at this?" Cecil threw the folded velum, with the heavy lawyer's seal, across the desk towards Morley.

Morley didn't take it. "It will take me a more than a few moments to decipher this legal Latin. What is it for?"

Pulling his spectacles down his nose, Cecil observed Morley over the frames. "It's Fitzwarren again," he supplied.

"Which one?" Morley was forced to ask.

"Robert has applied for a writ of guardianship over Catherine de Bernay. Which strikes me as strange as she is no longer resident in his household."

"I agree. Unless he knows where she is and believes he can extract her if he needs to present her to the Chancery Court," Morley pointed out.

"Find out if he knows where she is. The fact that more than one person might be using her does remain a possibility," Cecil said, removing his spectacles and rubbing at the glass with a cloth.

"I'll go and see Robert again and see what I can find out," Morley accepted, nodding.

"No need." Cecil returned his glasses to his nose and looked quickly on his desk for the folded document he needed. "Robert Fitzwarren's application has been dealt with a little more speedily than his lawyer would normally expect. He has been summoned to appear at the Court in a week with the de Bernay girl. So tighten your watch on her and attend this hearing."

Morley scanned the document, making a note of the time and date for the hearing, before absenting himself to undertake his master's bidding.

✝

Clement's face split into a wide, and unusually genuine, smile when he received back, sooner than he would have ever anticipated, a reply to his petition for a writ of guardianship for Catherine de Bernay. It would be the turn of at least one of the Fitzwarren's to suffer, and that, as far as Clement was concerned, was a good start.

Penning a letter himself, Clement enjoyed the process of letting his esteemed client, Robert Fitzwarren, know that he had pressed his case in Chancery as swiftly as he could, and the de Bernay case was set for a preliminary hearing the following week. This would, he advised his client, be all very routine, however Robert Fitzwarren and the subject of the writ, Catherine de Bernay, would be requested to attend the proceedings. Clement assured his client he would meet them at the Court to assist him through all stages of the proceedings. Clement finished by signing his own name with a little more flourish than was usual. He would not be suffering next week, oh no, now it would be Fitzwarren's turn.

His thin reedy voice called in his secretary, Marcus Drover.

Marcus, bent over a desk copying out Clement's fearful scrawl, swore silently as he heard his master's summons from the adjacent room. "Coming, master," he called back obediently as he pushed himself from the chair and made his way to the dusty confines of Clement's office.

Clement was already proffering the sealed note across the desk to Marcus. "See this gets to Robert Fitzwarren, don't trust it to a servant. I want you to go yourself and make sure he gets it. Do you hear?" Clement ordered.

Marcus nodded in ascent, groaning inwardly. The Fitzwarren house was on the other side of London. This errand would take him the best part of half a day just to get there and back. It was hot and the city was at its most putrid. Everything smelt rank. The population sweated inside clothing that was more suited to the cooler months, the river festered between cracked dried banks and the fumes rising from the gutters and slop heaps were eye watering. Marcus Drover had no desire at all to spend a day amongst the heat and smell of London in August.

The journey was worse than he expected. He hired a horse from the Swan's Neck Inn, a dozen doors away, and with the thinnest cloak over his shirt he could find, Marcus set out for the Fitzwarren's London house, Clement's note in a bag slung over his shoulder.

Marcus cursed his master vocally after half an hour. He had managed to pick the one day of the month when the pig market was held at Smithfield. His journey necessitated him crossing Chardwell Street, which was now packed with swine being driven down the sweltering street to the pens. As far as Marcus could see up Chardwell Street were pigs being herded by their shouting jostling owners.

A fight, someway further down the street, had broken out between two of them. Several lots of pigs had become mingled together, and an argument broke out as to who actually had the rights to the largest sow in the group. A good-natured crowd had gathered to listen to the men first trade insults and then blows.

All this led to Marcus being forced to sit on top of an agitated horse that was up to its hocks in a tight press of hairy pig flesh. Just when Marcus was convinced his stomach was going to rebel against the smell from the snorting squealing mass, the argument resolved itself, and the pigs pressed on slowly down the street. It was another half an hour though, before Marcus could navigate away from those bound for Smithfield, and turn his horse into the relatively clear Sandpike Lane.

Arriving at the house, Marcus knew his place. Dismounting, he went towards the back where the gates stood open.

The stable yard was swept clean, the cobbled yard showing barely a wisp of stray straw. It was empty, apart from a young lad. He was bent over a horse's hoof clamped between his knees, with a bone pick in one hand.

"Hold still, old lad, will you?" the boy was saying to the horse as he sought to retain the hoof and lever from it one last pebble that was wedged between the hoof and the shoe. The pebble, once pried loose, rattled off one of the cobbles and the boy released the horse's hoof. Rising, he patted the animal affectionately on the neck before noticing Marcus standing by his own mount, watching him.

"I've a note for Master Fitzwarren," Marcus stated, then said to add weight to his words, "It comes from his lawyer."

The lad bobbed his head. "I'll fetch master Ronan, sir." In a moment, the lad was gone and Marcus was left alone with the two horses in the empty yard.

The boy reappeared a few moments later, beckoning him to follow him. Marcus looked about him helplessly and then quickly hooked his horse's reins through a tethering ring and followed in the boy's footsteps. He met the steward coming down the corridor towards him.

"Ronan Hitchson, Lord Fitzwarren's steward," he supplied, then reaching out a hand he cuffed the boy round the back of the head . "Did I tell you to fetch him in here?"

"No master, sorry master," the boy blurted, a hand going to his head to protect himself from another blow. Marcus winced as he noticed the boy's right eye was a milky white. Blind.

"Get off with you, before you earn another beating!"

The boy didn't need telling twice. Without a backward glance, he disappeared into the gap between Ronan and Marcus, then dived through the open door and back into the yard.

"Lad's simple," Ronan said, then turning his attention to Marcus, he asked, "How can I help?"

Marcus sounded relieved. At least his errand was finished and he could begin to pick his way back home through London before the day was finished. "I have a note for Master Fitzwarren from his lawyer. I've been instructed to deliver it in person." He had the square of parchment in his hand.

Ronan reached out to take it. "Master Fitzwarren is not here at the moment, but I will make sure he receives it."

Marcus hesitated. "It's urgent, please impress this upon him, sir. Can you let me know when he returns so my master, Lawyer Clement, will know when he has read it please."

"He will be back tonight. He's sent ahead to have a meal prepared so I'll make sure he has this as soon as he returns," Ronan supplied.

Marcus had little choice but to hand over the parchment and leave. He knew Clement would not be satisfied with his answer that he had left his message with a steward and had not made sure it was directly in

Fitzwarren's hands, but there was not a lot else he could do.

Ronan watched Marcus leave and tucked the note inside his leather jerkin. As soon as he turned, he heard the voice of William Fitzwarren through the panelled corridor behind him. Since the Lord had moved from the top floor, there was little that got past him and he had his nose stuck firmly into everyone's business. Ronan opened the door to William Fitzwarren's room and stood on the threshold, hoping for a quick dismissal.

"Who was that?" demanded William Fitzwarren, turning in his chair and glowering at Ronan who stood in the doorway.

"Just a messenger for Master Fitzwarren," Ronan provided accurately.

"Come in here, man. Don't make me twist round in the chair. Stand where I can see you properly, and don't address me from the threshold of my own room – damn you."

Ronan kept his expression blank, eyes downcast, and moved into the room to stand in front of William.

"A message from who?" William demanded when Ronan was finally stood where he wanted him, and William was sat back in his chair.

"From his lawyer, my lord," Ronan provided.

William's eyebrows shot up. From his lawyer? What was his scheming son up to now? "Give it here."

William held out his hand for the message and Ronan hesitated for a moment too long. "I said give it here, you churl, now!"

There was little Ronan could do but produce the square and hand it to William who immediately waved him from his presence. Reaching for his glasses, William pushed them onto his gnarled nose and looked at the letter. It was one sheet, folded and sealed with the lawyer's crest on the reverse. William tapped his fingers on the arm of his chair thoughtfully. He badly wanted to read it but at the same time, breaking the seal was likely to rouse Robert's violent temper and he could do little to resist it these days. A moment later and he had made his decision. He pulled repeatedly on the chain attached to the table next to him and was rewarded moments later when Edwin presented himself in the room.

"Close the door," William demanded.

Edwin complied immediately.

"You are going to do something for me, and not a word to my son – do you hear?" William said slowly.

Edwin's eyes widened in fear. "Of course, My Lord."

"Swear it."

"My Lord, I swear I will say not a word." Edwin's voice shook as he wondered exactly what he was about to be involved in.

"Good. Get me those two candles from over there." William nodded and watched Edwin as he collected the two silver candle holders and brought them to the table and laid them where he was bid. "Now light them and fetch me that silver plate from over there, not the large one, you idiot, yes, the small one."

Edwin, with trembling hands, lit both candles.

"Hold that plate over them, hold it with your sleeves, man, it's going to get hot," William commanded. With his nail he rasped away a tiny curl of wax from the side of the seal on the Clement's letter and waited.

"Hold it closer."

Edwin holding the hot silver plate presented it before William who tipped the curled wax shard on to the plate and watched with satisfaction as it melted. "Now hold it still." William pressed the letter flat onto the silver plate. His fingertips, holding the paper down, could feel the heat through the sheet, and in a few moments he smiled as his nose registered the smell of the melting wax on the underside of the seal.

Taking the letter from the plate, he lifted the seal and the top portion of the seal peeled away intact from the page. William smiled, even more so when he saw the horrified look on Edwin's face. "Not a word, remember." William reissued his warning as he quickly read the short half page of script from Robert's lawyer. Now William Fitzwarren also knew of Robert's folly in trying to press a case in Chancery. He knew the girl had disappeared, lost to the stews of London. Everyone had supposed that she had run away, but William knew better. –It seemed now from this letter that she had some worth attached to her as well. It looked as if Richard had not just robbed him that night, but that he had robbed Robert as well.

It could only mean that Richard was looking to profit from her himself. Why else take her? He had to admit he was developing a grudging admiration for the cur. Robert would amount to nothing – William realised that – but Richard on the other hand had easily outsmarted him and, for some reason William did not understand, he had the Privy Council after him as well. At least he was involved in the country's affairs. Shame he was on the wrong side, William lamented.

William, with Edwin's assistance, reversed the process so that Clement's seal was once again firmly in place on the front of the letter and William placed it on his table awaiting his son's return.

✝

Morley had eyes at Durham Place and he was not surprised at all when they informed him that no one had made an attempt to make contact with Eugenie, or, as he knew her, Catherine de Bernay. And so, knowing that the girl who was the actual subject of the writ was elsewhere, it was with mild interest that Morley found himself in the outer chambers of the Chancery Court the following week. He didn't particularly want to encounter Robert Fitzwarren, but Morley knew that he looked a man of no particular note and doubted that Robert would notice him stood in the shadows cast by the columns around the court entrance.

He heard William's heir before he saw him. Loud, ill-mannered and foul tempered, Robert was bellowing orders at his steward Ronan to clear the press of Chancery petitioners away from him and leave him with ample space. As Morley watched, the steward shoved, shouted and pushed to make a space around Robert, and it was then his eyes alighted on the woman standing eyes downcast at his side. This could be none other than the subject of Robert's Chancery application of guardianship, and it was certainly not the de Bernay girl. Pushing himself away from the wall, his job done, knowing now that Robert had not a clue where Catherine was, he made his way politely through the pack of early morning petitioners and made his way out through the open Chancery gates.

Chapter 5

A Matter Of Education

Jack looked down at himself and sighed. How exactly they were going to convince anyone to give them a hearing he didn't know. The shirt he wore was filthy, the usable, but old, leather jerkin he had bought was coming apart and the knees were ripped from his hose. The leather of the sword belt had broken and showed two rough repairs and a third break had been repaired with twine from one of the snares. The scabbard made of pressed wood and cloth was frayed and splintered, the blade showing through in several places. Thankfully, Jack had retained his boots. They were the only part of his sorry ensemble that showed any worth.

Richard, lacking even a sword belt, looked in an even sorrier state. He wore a similarly filthy linen shirt and a loose, waist length, brown hessian over-jacket. His belt contained a knife, but one that was little better than an eating knife. A tumble from his horse before it was stolen had torn holes in his hose, and his boots, once fine, and made of soft kid skin, had fared worse than Jack's and were worn through.

They had stopped for food. Jack was deep in thought, wondering what they were going to do when they arrived in Venice.

"Will you eat something, please?" Lizbet said to Richard. "Otherwise this scavenging dog'll have it." Lizbet elbowed Jack who sat next to her.

"If all you feed me is scraps, what do you expect?" Jack said, reaching across and helping himself to more bread. Lizbet made to slap away his hand but he was already grinning at her over the lump he had stolen from her lap.

Richard raised his head, eyes searching around him, as if he had just suddenly become aware of his surroundings. He was sitting with his back against a tree. In his lap lay two hunks of bread along with the two roughly carved pieces of cheese Lizbet had given him. He'd said little all morning, so when he spoke directly to Jack, his grey steel eyes for once were focused. Jack stared at him, his face immediately serious.

"Chester Neephouse," Richard said, when his eyes had found Jack and he had his attention.

Jack repeated the name slowly, he was confused, unsure whether or not the name should mean something to him.

"Remember, I told you about him when we were in London?" Richard continued.

Lizbet sat and watched the exchange between the two of them in silence.

Jack was desperately searching his memory, but he found nothing. Richard had spoken to Jack only when it was necessary for the last two days, Jack was determined to keep him talking and draw him out. "I honestly can't remember a lot about what happened in London. Tell me again."

Richard continued. "I was at University with Chester."

Suddenly a light blazed in Jack's memory. "I remember, he was from the North. That's where you got that terrible accent from."

Richard nodded slowly. "More than that. Chester was about the same height as me, and the same build. He always wore his father's money. He spent more on clothes and finery than anyone else; it marked him out."

Lizbet and Jack stared at him when he stopped his narrative, but it was Jack who prompted him to continue. "So how can Chester help us now?"

Richard took up the story again as if he had not heard Jack's words. "I had Chester's accent off perfectly. He'd spent no time on study and when it come to his exams I took his place. Dressed in his gaudy clothes and with his voice nobody gave me a second look. It wasn't difficult, he hardly even attended college, so none of the tutors truly knew what he looked like."

For once Jack could almost read his brother's mind. "And where is Chester now?"

"Last I heard, managing his father's import business and spending the profits in Venice," Richard supplied quietly.

Jack pushed himself up from where he was sitting, crumbs spilling from his lap to the floor, and lowered himself down next to Richard dropping an arm around his brother's shoulders. "Tell me more about Chester."

"There's not much to tell." Richard's voice was still quiet, barely above a whisper. His eyes closed and his head fell sideways resting on Jack's shoulder.

"Come on, tell me a little more. Please," coaxed Jack. He caught Lizbet's eye, and she smiled at him. It did look as if she had been right to buy the remedy from the apothecary. Maybe Richard had a plan in mind after all.

"Chester will help us, I'm sure," was all Richard said in reply.

Jack wanted to know more about Chester, but realised he wasn't going to find it out now. Richard was soundly asleep.

✝

When the day was done, and they had walked as far as they could, they slept not far from the roadside. Lizbet and Jack had spent plenty of nights in worse places. The nights were warm enough, and the weather dry, the downpours of the earlier summer now all well past. Lizbet doubted if Richard had ever had as little as he had now. It did not, however, seem to bother him; indeed nothing did. A fact that worried her more and more as the days wore on.

Jack, as she well knew, had only to close his eyes, and within moments his breathing would become the level, even breaths of a sleeping man. Richard, on that journey, slept as badly as Lizbet did. Lying awake, listening to the sounds of the night, she'd hear him moving restlessly near her. Lizbet slept close to Jack. Jack slept close to his sword. It lay beside him, unsheathed, and next to the hilt was his knife.

Jack might have the ability to fall asleep in a moment, but from a lifetime dedicated to self-preservation, he woke at the slightest sound. Lizbet needed to get up. Squeezing Jack's arm, she whispered in his ear and received a grunted reply. Rising stiffly from the ground, Lizbet made her way towards where a water skin hung from a tree. Jack had grudgingly bought a new after their first was stolen along with the horses.

A new day had not yet broken ; the darkness was still almost complete, the only light coming from a the moon. Lizbet leaned heavily against a tree, her eyes closed, waiting for the nausea to pass. With a trembling hand she tried to unhook the water skin. Her stomach convulsed one more time, cold sweat beading on her forehead. Cursing, she groped for the tree for support.

"What's the matter?" The quiet voice was Richard's.

Lizbet shook her head, waiting for the sickness to subside. Richard reached past her, unhooked the water skin and held it out for her.

Lizbet took it in shaking hands and drank before uttering a word of thanks. Squeezing her eyes tight, the dizziness seemed to leave her and the nausea in the pit of her stomach quietened as the water reached it. Richard took the flask back and Lizbet wiped the back of her hand across her mouth, her expression one of thanks. She saw the question in the expression Richard's face and the enquiry in his eyes but Lizbet looked quickly away.

"Well, as we're all up, and you've decided I no longer need to sleep, we might as well get going," Jack said, grumpily from behind them.

Lizbet took the opportunity and ducked past him before Richard could vocalise his thoughts.

✝

Five days later they were on the Italian coast, looking at the stretch of water across which lay the trading centre that was Venice.

Jack, catching Lizbet's look, threw his arm around her shoulders. "Are we shaming you, lass?"

Lizbet reddened, and said quietly, "I've seen better dressed beggars than you."

Jack was thankful that Richard could not hear her words.

"He doesn't care, Jack," Lizbet continued. "About anything. He doesn't care about anything."

"I know," Jack said quietly, giving her shoulders a squeeze. He knew he needed to find out a little more about Chester Neephouse before they arrived in Venice. He'd tried a couple of times already, but his brother had been unresponsive.

Richard was sitting quietly but he had eaten some of the food Lizbet had put before him. Jack had watched. They knew now that if she gave him too much he'd not touch it, but if the amounts were smaller he would eat.

Jack settled himself down next to Richard. His tone conversational, he asked, "Tell me more about Chester Neephouse. How was it that you ended up sitting his exams for him?"

Jack thought he wasn't going to get an answer. Then Richard's grey eyes flickered and he said, "Chester never attended lectures, hated work. However his father was not going to let him take over the business unless he passed at University. Chester had something, however, that we all wanted."

"Would that have been money?" Jack said, having a good grasp of the situation. His brother's voice was very quiet and he moved closer so he could hear.

Richard nodded. "Our father was not overly generous on that score. Chester never went to lectures, not one of the tutors knew him well, all they recognised were his appalling clothes and his northern accent which marked him out. It wasn't difficult to become Chester for a few hours."

"He's good," said Lizbet, through a mouthful of food. "You should have seen him in London. Came into the drapers and everyone thought he was a bloody sodomite."

"One tale at a time," Jack said planting a hand on Lizbet's knee. "Chester first, then be sure I want an account of why my brother parades like Patroclus." Returning his attention back to Richard, he asked, "So why will Chester help us?"

"I passed his exams for him. If he had failed, his father would have denied him his inheritance," Richard supplied. "He'd not wish to be reminded of it."

Jack grinned. "Let's hope he is still as affluent as you remember, and has a conscience."

"He might have," Richard said, absently picking up the food Lizbet had given him.

Jack drove on. For a few minutes he'd held his brother's attention, he didn't want him to sink back inside himself again. "What exams did you take for Neephouse then? Philosophy at a guess?"

Richard didn't look up, his eyes already unfocused and his attention on the ground between his feet.

Jack tried again. "So you did actually complete a course at University then, even if it wasn't in your name."

"Mathematics. Neephouse was studying Mathematics," Richard supplied, and then he added, "I was studying Philosophy."

"And you passed Mathematics?" Jack did sound impressed.

"Philosophy and mathematics have a lot in common," was the last Richard said before his attention was gone, and nothing Jack tried could draw him back into the conversation.

†

Sleeping on the streets in the Doge's narrow city was not permissible. Being found on the streets after the curfew bell rang for the night would likely lead to relocation to one of the city's many prisons, which supplied a labour force for maintenance work. Jack was thankful he had kept coins in reserve and knew they had enough to pay for a room, even if it would be a poor one. He was relying heavily on Richard's plan to find Chester Neephouse.

They paid for the passage into the citadel on one of the flat bottomed, pontoon-like boats that moved people, animals and commodities between the mainland and the city. Richard found a seat in the middle of the pontoon next to piles of stinking baled furs. Lizbet objecting to the stench, stood next to Jack as far from the smell as possible watching Venice rise before them as they crossed the lagoon towards the vibrant city.

Little did they know they were watched by Thomas Gent. Diligently following orders, he was watching, as he had done for weeks, those entering the city. His attention was drawn by the sound of Lizbet's voice, incongruous and clashing with the local Italian lilt, and his narrow brown eyes had found her standing on an approaching boat. As Gent had watched, Lizbet raised an arm and pointed towards something on the shore. The man stood to her left inclined his head towards her and seemed to supply the answer to a question. Gent's eyes widened.

The man Lizbet was talking to wore clothes more suited to a peasant. But when Gent looked a little closer, the messy hair, unshaven face and the blue unforgiving eyes were those of Jack Fitzwarren. Gent quickly scanned the rest of the boat but Richard, sat on the other side of the fur bales, was out of sight. As the boat neared the quay, Richard stood. Gent saw the man with the dark hair, and knew then that the brothers were still together.

    Gent, moving as quickly as he could, headed down the steep steps from his vantage point. But the exit onto the narrow street was blocked by two carts bearing fresh bread. By the time he was close enough to observe the quay and the boat they had arrived on, it was empty. He methodically checked the surrounding streets but could find no trace of any of them.

Chapter 6

A Legality

The preliminary hearing had passed quickly, and as far as Robert was concerned with a most unsatisfactory outcome. He had presented Ronan's eldest daughter as the de Bernay girl and had expected to leave the Court with a writ of guardianship. Robert had supposed that the hearing would produce what he wanted: control over the woodlands appended to the manor at Assingham. So sure had Robert been, he had already dispatched men to gauge the full size of the holding, and draw up a detailed document outlining the extent and quality of the tract of land. There were several interested parties already and Robert wanted a quick sale. He was, if nothing else, an opportunistic man, recognising that any delay could jeopardise the sale – especially as he had lost the actual heir.

The preliminary hearing took place in the presence of a minor court official seated at a desk in a crowded hall. He had been interested only in checking the identities of the parties involved. When it was over, it was Clement who found himself once again on the receiving end of the Fitzwarren temper.

Robert, the colour rising to his face, contained his temper only so far as the Chancery gates. Turning on the stooped form of Clement who stepped quickly and nervously behind him, the lawyer was well aware that the day's proceedings were not going at all the way his client had planned.

"You told me there was to be a Chancery hearing?" Robert almost screamed at Clement.

Clement took a quick pace back, standing on the feet of Marcus Drover who was directly behind him, clasping the case file to his chest. "There was, this was a preliminary hearing. This will be the first one and then a date will be set for the full proceedings," Clement said defensively. He had no intention of leaving the relatively safe precincts of the Court. There were armed men here employed to keep the peace within the Court and he could rely on them to intervene if Fitzwarren's threats became physical. If he took too many more steps down the street then he was not so sure his safety would be assured.

Robert had a firm hold on the girl's upper arm, gripping so tightly she let out an involuntary yelp as he propelled her into the arms of her father. "Get her away from me." Then, turning back to Clement, his face inches from the small lawyers, he added, "Do not fetch me for your errands again, master lawyer. Next time I hear from you, it had better be to tell me I have the writ and control of the lands."

Clement's mouth was opening and closing but nothing coherent emerged. His hands held the summary signed by the Chancery clerk. As Robert shouted at him, his trembling fingers released their hold on the folded sheet and it was only Marcus Drover's intervention that saved it from ending in the street.

Robert, followed by his steward, his steward's weeping daughter, and three of his men, left the Court confines. Clement was rooted to the spot. It took a tug from Marcus on his elbow to revive his attention.

"Sir, please, we cannot stop here. We are drawing the attention of the crowd," Marcus said, his head close to Clement's.

Clement, looking about him, saw that Marcus spoke the truth. The harsh loud words from Robert along with his aggressive departure, pushing through the assembled crowd, had brought the stares of those waiting onto Clement and Marcus.

Clement cursed under his breath and shuffled from the yard. Marcus, laden with his files, followed closely behind. Why, Clement grumbled, had the Lord saddled him with such an insufferable client?

†

Catherine had not been aware that there were eyes following her around Durham Place and even if she had, she could never have guessed the reason why. It would never have crossed her mind that Robert would drag the most presentable looking of his steward's daughters to Chancery to impersonate her. Clement had been stunned by Robert's audacity as well.

After the arrest and internment of Kate Ashley in the Fleet gaol, Durham Place itself became a prison. Guards from the Queen's own household appeared, the rooms allotted for daily use by Elizabeth were reduced to just three on the second floor, and the large arched entrance now housed a constant guard day and night. The gates, which had previously stood open, were now closed. Morley was satisfied with the new security arrangements. He was sure that there could be little contact between those inside Durham Place and London beyond her walls.

Elizabeth was less than pleased with the new security, but at present, there was no one to complain to. After her beloved Kate had been removed, no provision had been made to replace her. The princess was left with only a minimal serving staff and two waiting ladies, both of whom she despised. Elizabeth had been completely isolated from the politics of Court. She had no idea what was happening, and it gnawed at her. Finally, she resolved that she would rather be at Court, despite the dangers of the place, than a prisoner in her own home.

An ivory comb, inlaid with mother of pearl and bearing a gold handle, was still just a comb, and it snagged in the princess's hair just as easily as a bone one. Fiery auburn hair came with a price. The hair at her temples was fine, short and delicate, and presented daily a tangle of threads for the comb to snare in.

"Will you be careful!" Elizabeth blazed and turned on the girl still holding the comb. The sudden movement dragged the hair tight in the teeth, jarring the comb from the girl's hands. Elizabeth lashed out, the back of her hand impacting with a resonating neat slap on the side of the girl's face. Yelping, the servant backed away, a hand to her face.

"Get out!" Elizabeth shouted. She tried to prevent the comb from tangling further in her hair, but when the maid had let it fall, it had wrapped itself firmly in her unruly auburn locks.

By the time Elizabeth had extracted the comb there were more than a few strands of hair that had been pulled painfully from her temple. The final hairs were wrapped so tightly around the teeth that she had to use both hands to tear them from the comb.

Elizabeth was not in a good mood. Denied any outside contact, and with no idea of what was happening at Court, she was pining for news as if she had lost a lover. Weeks ago she had thought of an idea, but it had been so abhorrent that she had pushed it to the back of her mind. However, during her lonely isolation, she had begun to dwell upon it more and more. Now it was becoming not just an idea, but a course of action, that Elizabeth, characteristically, was putting rapidly into place. There were few servants who entered her apartments, but there was one she wanted very much in her company.

After a raging argument, of which her father would have been proud, Elizabeth was left alone with another furious woman. Catherine de Bernay had now been selected to wait upon the petulant princess. Catherine took up both the comb and the task reluctantly. Elizabeth's hair was brushed, pinned and shining like a wet autumn chestnut leaf. Her task complete, Catherine quietly placed the comb back in the box containing the matching brush and mirror. Treading quietly, she turned her foot towards the door, murmuring under her breath, "Will that be all, my Lady?"

"No, it isn't. Bring me pen and paper. Tell Travers I wish to write a letter to our sister, her most Gracious Majesty."

Had Travers seen the look on Elizabeth's face he would have denied her access to anything to write with.

Catherine returned soon after with all that Elizabeth needed, and under her direction, laid it out for her on the writing desk.

"Now wait," commanded Elizabeth, "you can take this to Travers when I am finished. I am sure he will want to read it before sending it to my dear sister."

Elizabeth had been right. Travers did want to review it and he was shocked by the contents. Sealing the letter inside another of his own, he dispatched it under guard, wondering what reaction it was going to produce.

✝

"Marry! She says here…" Mary paused while finding the line in the letter she wanted to quote from, "she writes - That after careful consideration, I feel I am of such an age that marriage must be my utmost consideration. A husband would be a great aid to steer and direct me." Mary's narrowed eyes met those of Cecil. "And she says here, that Philip's offer to aid her with the issue of her marriage is a cause she would wish to consider again. Apparently, she has had many months to ponder the issue, since she spoke of it with my gracious husband, and is now well disposed to becoming a wedded woman."

"Marriage is every woman's final condition. Should it not be the lady's wish to be so?" Cecil replied carefully.

Mary's cold assessing gaze met Cecil's. "I am not sure I can believe it."

Elizabeth married was a very pleasing idea. There were many, she knew, that thought of her sister still as a prospect for the throne. However, suitably wedded and filed away, that threat could be reduced. Philip had counselled Mary to consider a Spanish match for her sister, one that would tie the princess firmly to both Catholicism and Spain, two alliances that her supporters would baulk at! That thought twitched a smile to the corner of Mary's mouth. A Catholic match would be another slap in the face for Protestants; they could hardly still cleave to her as a figurehead then. If the match was made to one of Philip's courtiers, as he had urged, then her new husband might very well take the irksome woman to Spain, away from Mary and the political stage. That thought appealed so much that the reply summoning her sister to Court to discuss the matter quickly made its way back to Durham Place.

Philip had left his wife, and England, in August. Mary was distraught. Her Prince, her consort, some eleven years younger than her, had persuaded her he would return. Mary was left only with promises. As time dragged on, the daily letters she sent to him were returned in an increasingly smaller ratio. Her ladies assured her endlessly that Philip was occupied with the war with France, with securing her Kingdom and above all else with retaining Calais. Publicly Mary took heart from their words, but in private, she grieved for her love with an intensity that she found sometimes shameful. Was it wrong to want her husband this badly? Why did her love for Philip fill her with more meaning that her love for the Lord and the lady for whom she was named?

That was when her ladies began to worry. Mary would leave them frequently to turn back to her faith, the faith that had been her rock for her whole life. Between appearances in her presence chamber and meetings with her councillors and advisors, Mary had little enough time for herself, let alone for sleep, yet still she still spent hours on her knees in devotion to the Lord, her ladies joining her in uncomfortable obedience.

Mary became convinced that the cause of her own problems was her leniency towards the Protestants. They were set to undermine the Catholic faith, worming their way through every level of London society like maggots. This rotten and rank infection had incurred the Lord's displeasure, and it was only she, as Mary I, her most gracious majesty, who had the power to exorcise this Protestant heresy from England. Because she had not, Mary became convinced, the Lord had punished her, first by taking her child and then her husband.

Her actions became those of a deranged and lonely women, seeking the approval of two masters, and gaining neither.

In London there were several burnings, well publicised and well attended events. Her Councillors, leading nobles and key figures from her religious institutions, were forced to attend to watch their Queen's physical assault on the Protestant blight.

†

Robert Cecil, flanked by Morley, waited at Smithfield. Both had worked to bring about the morning's executions, and neither could be absent. Cecil was a man who preferred to tread a middle path, and he was well aware that the recent orders were not popular. At first the prisons had supplied sufficient victims for the piles of blazing faggots, but Mary's redemption needed more. The low-ranking, illiterate peasants that were sent to the hereafter in smoke did little to ease Mary's troubled soul. These offerings did not strike at the root of the Protestant threat; they did not issue the warning to England that she wanted them to. So today's spectacle sent a worrying tremor through the ranks. Those who were to burn were people of rank, they had powerful friends, they were well liked and their passing would be mourned.

Cecil's schooled face was impassive. His eyes, which were turned on the unfortunate, were unfocused. His mind was dealing with a particularly difficult property dispute between Lord Rochester and the Earl of Essex, both of whom claimed they had rights to the same parcel of monastic land. Henry, it seemed, had sold the same land twice, both had receipts and both had good title, it seemed. The problem was not who the land should vest in but rather ending the matter with both parties, if at least not happy with the situation, accepting of it. Both had seats on the Privy Council and it was in no-one's interest to have two of its members at each other's throats over a petty land dispute. The dispute was providing a welcome distraction and adequately distracting him from what was about to happen at Smithfield.

So Cecil did not really see the men and woman arrive, wearing only linen shifts. They were led from the wagons to the platforms, raised high to give everyone assembled a good view of the wrath of a vengeful God and Mary his loyal and obedient servant. It was Morley's words, pitched so only his master could hear, that caught his attention.

"Could you have not found someone else to attend you today?" Morley's tone was abrupt, and at odds with his usual soft and amenable voice.

Cecil glanced round at him, annoyed, his attention instantly drawn back to the events before him. "Surely this does not irk you?"

Morley's mouth, clamped in thin line, regarded his master levelly. If he had been about to reply he obviously thought better of it and remained silent.

"That's Mistress Harrington." Cecil pointed towards a middle-aged woman making a poor attempt to clamber up a ladder in bare feet to the staging. "Were you not instrumental in her internment in the Tower in the first place?"

Morley looked carefully about him before replying. There were none close enough to hear his words. "You know I was. These exhibitions, they serve no other purpose than to make a man wonder if he will be next."

Cecil's horse moved beneath him, and for a moment he moved closer to Morley. "I hope very much that this will be a finale. Mary needs to ease her conscience, and if this will bring that about then it has served a good purpose. Do you not agree?"

"If it will be an end…" Morley's words trailed off as the first of the screams reached his ears. Seated on horseback, his view was far too good for his liking, and he could see across the heads of the gathered Londoners to where Mistress Harrington's humble prayers had given way to screams of abject terror. The lady, a grandmother, with a ready wit and a quick turn of phrase that Morley had found enjoyable, was now screaming for help and begging for her own mother to save her. If the crowd had been gathered for an entertainment, this was one that they no longer wanted. Morley, casting his eyes over the assembled, saw many of them looking away, faces twisted in disgust. Some wore pitying looks and some even had tears on their cheeks.

Her hair caught fire then and her screams turned to shrieks. Mary had forbidden the mercy of the gunpowder bags around their necks, so there was not going to be a quick end for the poor old lady. As the smoke cleared for a moment, both men were afforded a good view of the blood coursing down what had once been her legs to hiss and spit in the flames.

Cecil must have sensed Morley's discomfort and said quietly through gritted teeth, "In a few more moments, her torment will end. Pray for her."

And Morley did pray. He prayed for her instant and quick death, prayed for an end to her suffering. But it was not a matter of a few moments. Her torment continued. The flames that had lit her hair and scorched all the skin on her face to bubbling blisters receded and now Mistress Harrington was only ablaze from the knees down.

Morley's hands tightened involuntarily on his reigns and the horse beneath him, smelling the smoke, stamped and neighed, tossing its head.

Cecil's surprisingly strong fingers dug into his arm, warning. Morley, shaking, lessened his grip on the startled mount's reins and tried to show an outward degree of composure, knowing that those close to him were now looking in his direction.

Mistress Harrington begged until Morley thought he could take no more. Then suddenly, her face fell forwards, chin on her chest, dead. Morley sent up a silent prayer of thanks. Had he known it though, his troubles were only just beginning. Mistress Harrington's end had not been brought about by the cleaning flames from the faggots stacked against the stake to which she was tied, but from the arrow that had grazed the stake and severed the vertebrae neatly in her neck. It did however bring about a swifter death than that promised by the fire.

There were six others burnt that day, but it was the flames that took them to their judgment. None had the mercy of the arrow that had ended Mistress Harrington's sufferings.

Chapter 7

An Honest Assessment

Soon after their arrival in Venice, Jack resolved that they should press Chester Neephouse and his conscience. It was a matter of necessity. What little they had left had paid for the room. If Richard could obtain money from this man, then the sooner the better. Jack left Lizbet and Richard and set out to find Neephouse. He soon found his offices, and quiet enquiry confirmed that the man Richard had known in England was indeed in control of the business here in Venice. All Jack had to do now, was to guide his brother back through the narrow streets. Returning to the rented room, and casting his eyes over the wreckage that was his brother, he was not sure he would be able to convince anyone to do anything anymore.

"Drink this," Lizbet said, her voice encouraging, as she held out a cup for Richard.

"Is he going to be able to do this?" Jack was looking at Richard critically but spoke to Lizbet.

"I don't know." Lizbet sounded equally worried.

The cup Lizbet had given Richard shook in his hand, the contents beginning to spill to the floor. Reaching out quickly, she wrapped her hand around his to steady it, and shakily he raised it to his lips and emptied it.

Jack, turning towards the window, ran his hands through his hair in a savage gesture. "He's going to be taken for the village idiot."

"Shush, Jack, you're not helping," Lizbet admonished.

Richard pushed the emptied cup back towards her, his eyes meeting Lizbet's. "Another."

Receiving the cup she refilled it quickly, careful this time not to overfill it.

Richard watched her carefully. As she passed it back to him, he said, "With whatever it is you put in it."

Lizbet hesitated for only a moment. She'd not realised he knew she had been putting the herbal mixture into his drinks. Quickly she added some from the stoppered pot in her pocket. When he received the cup this time he needed no help, the shakes had lessened, he emptied it quickly and held it back out for more.

"I've not much left," Lizbet warned.

Richard thrust the cup towards her without a word. Lizbet obeyed the unspoken order and filled it.

Jack had his palms flat on either side of the stone window opening and was staring through the partly opened shutters into the street below. "Richard, I've found Neephouse's offices. Are you ready to go there?"

Lizbet took the cup back from Richard. As she watched, she could see him emerging slowly back from the shell he had existed in. When he spoke it was to Jack, "You found Chester?"

The sound of his brother's voice was like a knife in the back. Jack wheeled around to find Richard, bright eyed, observing him with a serious expression from where he sat on the edge of the table.

"Can you do this?" Jack asked, carefully.

"Shall we find out?" Richard pushed himself up from the bed. "When the Devil is at your heels it's best to run. Come on."

Richard had already set his feet towards the door. Lizbet and Jack exchanged a quick confused look before they set off to follow him.

Jack, catching Richard up, walked close to him. "Are you listening to me?"

"Yes, Jack, I have ears. I hear you," Richard replied.

"Forgive me," Jack said, sarcastically, "but it's been like talking to a wall for the past weeks."

"I asked you to get me here. You did," Richard replied, as if that was sufficient explanation.

Jack was exasperated. "So now we are here you are willing to engage with the world again?"

Richard stopped for a moment, and turning to Jack, he said, "Yes, the journey has ended. And a new one begins. Is it far?"

Jack looked at him in confusion. "Yes," he said, then, "No, a few streets away. He has a warehouse near the fish market."

"Ah, so he's not moved. Good, well come on then." Richard was already striding away from him.

Jack, taking a hold of Lizbet's elbow, pulled her along to keep up with rapid pace Richard was setting.

"Don't complain, Jack," Lizbet warned. "We need this to work."

Chester had a warehouse near the Rialto Fish Market. The smell in the summer heat was enough to turn any stomach not used to it. Lizbet caught hold of Jack's arm and pulled him to a halt.

"Please, stop."

Looking at her pale face, it was obvious why. "For God's sake woman, it's only fish! Come on, or we are going to lose him." Jack linked his arm though hers and propelled her back into the throng in the street.

Richard was already disappearing ahead of him. Jack became acutely aware that his brother seemed to be quite familiar with the narrow twisting maze that was Venice. The narrow packed streets would suddenly open to a canal, the traffic from several of them converging and pressing across the narrow arched bridge, spilling into the shaded, tightly streets, on the other side. If Jack had not kept a tight hold on Lizbet she would have been swept from him and become lost in the crowd.

Chester Neephouse's warehouse, and Venice offices, provided the administrative centre for trade across Europe in rare spices from the East. Most went to France, Spain and Italy but much of his wares made it to England. Chester's father, a shrewd merchant, recognised that the further you took your wares, the higher the price you could demand for them. A lifetime of trade had given him secure trade routes to move his spices easily and quickly north from Venice.

Jack, with Lizbet pale and hanging on his arm, caught Richard up at the entrance to the Neephouse trading centre. Richard, walking backwards in front of them, told them to wait and disappeared through the entrance.

Jack let go of Lizbet. She leant heavily against a wall and he was forced to stand close to her to avoid the continuing stream of traffic that packed every artery in the city.

✝

The arched entranceway opened into a small yard, small storerooms and offices leading off it. The scene inside was no less chaotic than the city beyond the walls. Two liveried men, wearing the same red and green colours that adorned the Neephouse sign that graced the archway, were involved in a heated discussion with the owner of a cart that was taking up most of the space in the small yard. All around the edge of the yard were piled a seemingly chaotic mix of boxes, sacks, and earthenware jars. On one side of the yard, half a dozen women were working with quick hands sewing accurately weighed measures into small sacks. Brass scales and weights were set up on a pile of crates. Two men weighed and checked the black grains before the scoops were dropped into the waiting closely woven Hessian bags.

Picking up a dusty sack from the wall, Richard hefted it to his shoulder. He headed towards an open doorway in one corner, beyond which he knew were the stairs to the offices on the next floor. Dumping the sack at the bottom of the darkened stairway, he made his way quietly up the stone steps. Above him he could clearly hear men arguing. Both voices were heavily accented. If one belonged to Chester, he was unable to tell which it was. Making it to the top of the stairs, he took up a position to the right of the door and listened carefully.

"…Toby knew they were short measures. Why did you buy them?" The voice was angry and accusing.

"I knew they were short. But there's no more to be had in the market. Even short, they are still worth double the purchase price," came the loud, unapologetic reply.

"It sets a precedent. They'll think they can dupe us again with the same trick. Before you know it everything we take in from the De Givan's will be short. Mark my words, we went through all this with the Morrocci Company two years ago, and look where that ended up?" The voice was raised, the speaker exasperated and angry.

"It won't end up the same as the Morrocci's. Toby knows fine well we'll not buy anything else from him in short measures, I've already told him this." The reply was impatient, the words clipped and curt.

"It doesn't matter what you told him. You allowed him to sell you short this time and he'll do it again. You've made a fool of us in the marketplace. You can be sure this will become common knowledge." Disappointment edged the words.

"Father, this will not become common knowledge. I have bought enough to fulfil our commitments. We needed it, to make the Jevani order up, that you have taken part payment on already. I bought no more than that. I didn't really have a choice, did I? Would you have had me refund their money, cancel their orders?" The tone was at odds with the words.

That was enough to quieten the older man for a moment. "No, no, that would make our reputation even worse in the market. Just be aware that Toby is likely to try this again. It's a bad footing to be on when your suppliers know they can cheat you like this." The words were sullenly spoken.

"I will be careful. It's just to fulfil the orders to Jevani. They need to leave this week otherwise they will be late," Chester Neephouse said, his voice quietening now he realised the argument was coming to a close.

"Good. Have we had the final payment through from Jevani yet?" The anger had left the older man's voice.

"His men are here now, in the offices downstairs with Alfredo, checking through the inventory for their order," Chester supplied.

"I'll go and see them. Alfredo might need some help."

Richard heard the footsteps approaching. Flattening himself against the wall as the door opened, the figure of Chester's father emerged and descended down the darkened stairs. He watched as the man stepped through the doorway into the light. Richard quickly flipped the door back open and closed it behind him, leaning against it. Chester Neephouse was standing behind a desk, hands resting palms down on either side of a ledger he was studying. He looked up as soon as the door opened.

"Alfredo doesn't…" The reply he had been about to deliver died, as he realised the man facing him was not his father returning to his office.

"Yes, I am sure Alfredo doesn't need your father's help, but it will keep him occupied for a while, do you not agree?" Richard replied.

Chester's eyes widened. "Jesus Christ! Fitzwarren." And then taking in the man standing in his room, added, "What the Hell has happened to you?"

"It's more a case, I rather think, of what hasn't," Richard replied dryly. Turning, he dropped the latch down, pushing the wooden peg into place to stop the door being opened from the outside.

There were wine glasses, expensive engraved Venetian ones, next to a glass flagon. To cover his initial shock, Chester moved quickly to pour himself a glass.

"Bacchus would disapprove," Richard commented quietly, eyeing the glass in Chester's hand.

Chester looked at him over the rim for a moment, then sighing, poured a second glass, holding it out for Richard to take. Richard stepped away from the door, closed the gap between them and accepted the glass from Chester's hand.

"Christ man! You smell like the gutter." Chester took an involuntary step back. "So what was it? Your father throw you out? Gambling? Women? What happened?"

Richard looked thoughtful for a moment, then his eyes flicked back to meet Chester's, staring into the other's for a moment too long, before he replied, "All of those, plus a few extras I added in myself."

"What else?"

"Murder. Treason. The usual exploits that disinherited second sons involve themselves in," Richard replied tranquilly. He finished the wine and held the empty glass out for a refill.

"Christ, Fitzwarren. You were never anything other than trouble," Chester said, tipping the decanter to swill more wine into the glass.

"I don't remember that bothering you particularly," Richard countered.

"What is it you want?" Chester said, ignoring the comment.

"Surely you can guess?" Richard answered, before he drained the glass.

"I can guess. So what will it cost to get you gone from my doorstep never to return?" Chester said, his tone hard.

Richard put the emptied glass down and folded his arms. "Let's negotiate, shall we? You are a merchant, after all. What would my lack of presence be worth to you?"

"I should imagine a few angels would be wealth indeed to you right now," Chester sneered, his eyes running over the dishevelled form of the man before him. Then they settled on Richard's hollowed eyes, and his sneer deepened. "I think there might have been something you omitted from your list of sins."

Richard did not reply to that, and Chester laughed loudly. Opening his purse he dug his hand in and pulled out a number of coins. He shuffled them in his palm for a moment, sent half back into the purse, and the rest he scattered on the desk. "Take those, that should be enough for you."

Richard didn't even look at the coins. "I need, as you can see, clothes, food and…" Chester waited for his next words expectantly. "…slightly more money than you would throw at a beggar in the street."

"Fitzwarren, you are a beggar in the street. If you don't take that and get yourself gone, I will call my men to drag you from here and dump you back in the gutter you crawled out of," Chester said angrily. "If you think you can blackmail me, think again. Do you think my father is going to be interested in the ravings of an opium addict from the gutter? Do you?"

†

"Something has gone wrong," Jack grumbled, from where he sat against the wall next to Lizbet opposite the entrance to the Neephouse warehouse.

"You've said that a dozen times," Lizbet replied, exasperated. "We've no choice but to wait. Lord, you are not a patient man, are you?"

"Have you only just noticed that?" Jack replied, casting a sideways glance in her direction.

"If something was wrong, we would have known by now," Lizbet assured him. They were sitting some distance away from the entrance to Neephouse's business, in the shade cast by one of the wooden bridges spanning the Rialto canal.

When Richard finally emerged from the archway, both Lizbet and Jack were on their feet instantly. Richard dropped a handful of coins into Jack's hands and immediately set his feet back in the direction of the rooms they had rented.

Jack looked in disbelief at the money in his hand, then stepping quickly after his brother, he said, "Is this it?"

Richard, ahead of him, replied over his shoulder, "There will be more. I'm to call back in three days. That will be enough for now."

Jack, relieved, tucked the coins away, and followed his brother to the rented rooms. On the way they'd pause at an apothecaries. Lizbet, knowing why Richard had stopped there, took coins from Jack and ducked under the low beamed door. After that, they returned to the room. Richard, saying barely a word, lay on the only bed, and shielding his eyes from the light, sank into sleep, or at least what looked like sleep.

It was too much for Jack.

"You said I had to get you here," Jack said, speaking though clenched teeth, his temper barely in check. "I've done that."

"Jack, leave him alone." Lizbet's voice was weary. She'd hoped for more as well. When he'd emerged looking tired and uncommunicative, she'd felt as disappointed as Jack had. "If there is something to know, he will tell you when he wakes up."

"I'm awake." Richard's voice was a hoarse whisper. "Find another room, get me some clothes and for God's sake, feed Jack!"

Lizbet and Jack exchanged a look. Lizbet picked up the purse containing the coins Chester had given Richard and hefted it in her hand. "You heard him, come on then."

They left Richard apparently asleep and set out towards the centre. Street sellers provided Lizbet with skewered meat, and sweet crusty pastries still warm from the oven. Jack's temper dropped from him as soon as he had a full stomach.

Enquiry of the stallholders directed them towards a row of respectable boarding houses clustered above small narrow fronted shops.

Lizbet stopped Jack from setting his feet towards the doors, a restraining hand on his arm. "You'll not get in looking like that."

Jack realised her words were true. He was filthy, his hair crawled with lice, and he had no doubt he smelt worse than the canals.

"The market near the fish sellers, we can get everything we need there." Lizbet said, turning her feet back toward Rialto.

Lizbet was almost right.

She bought hose, shirts and a used, but good, doublet for Richard. Jack, however, was never going fit into any of the selection of clothes available, too tall and too broad for anything the sellers had to offer. He had to make do with hose, shirt and boots. Jack still had the doublet he had taken from Robert, and Lizbet resolved to try her best to clean and repair it.

Returning later they found Richard still asleep. Jack stripped, shaved and sluiced himself with water that Lizbet hauled up from the street. Lizbet, ,satisfied, dispatched him back to hire another room closer to the centre that hopefully would have fewer rodents than this one. She had the unsavoury task of dealing with the less predicable brother. They had brought back food, but Richard was little interested in it and wanted only something to drink. She was thankful though, that after the ale with the herbs she had bought, he was quietly cooperative.

An hour later they were gone, Jack leading them back across Venice towards the room he had rented. Lizbet was delighted with the sudden and dramatic improvement in their circumstances. Richard, though, simply walked across the room and lay himself upon the bed, eyes closed to the world, Jack staring after him.

Chapter 8

A Truth Recognised

Thomas Gent needed to find Richard. This had not taken as long as he thought it would, although it cost more than he had wanted. When Andrew had arrived in Venice, believing that Richard might be close behind them, he had hired men from the Almilio family. Andrew had left Gent, along with these hired mercenaries, to prevent Fitzwarren from following them. After three weeks, when there was no sighting of either of the brothers, Gent dispensed with the services of Almilio's men. It was a burden in terms of cost and Gent disliked their company.

After Gent had sighted the brothers on the boat, and then lost track of them, he had returned to Almilio. This was not his city, Gent was very much on his own, and he knew he needed help if he was to find them again. He had provided Almilio with a description of the one man who would stand out in crowd in Venice – Jack. Blond, a head taller than most men and English, he should not be hard to find. Almilio had thought differently, and had set a high price on the information. Thomas was forced to agree to it, knowing that without

Almilio's help he had little chance of finding Fitzwarren.

A boy, dark skinned and brown eyed, had come to find him. Gent trailed through the blisteringly hot streets after the boy to where he finally found Almilio playing dice. The boy's patron was drinking wine in a canopied courtyard, wafted by the draft from a large fan operated by four boys. Jewelled water sprang from a trickling fountain in the centre of the courtyard, a constant cooling cascade pouring from the open mouth of a lion. Almilio saw Gent and beckoned him over. The boy snatched the coin that was sent spinning towards him, then darting through the doorway, he was gone, leaving Gent alone.

"You've news for me?" Thomas Gent asked, striding forwards.

Almilio nodded but did not look up, intent on rolling the bone dice on the board between himself and the other two players. They stopped their rolling dance and displayed an unwanted two and a one. Almilio groaned, cast the coins from his side of the table into the centre, and excused himself.

Rising, he made his way to Gent. "It looks like you have saved me from ruin." He nodded behind him at the dice table.

Gent doubted very much if a few games of dice would reduce Almilio to a state of penury. He waited until they were out of earshot of the gaming table before he said, "Did you find him?"

Almilio nodded. "My brother rents accommodation near St Catherine's, and the man you are looking for is there."

"Are you sure?" Gent asked.

"He is with a man and woman, the descriptions fit. The boy who brought you here can take you there," Almilio said, and then added, "There are two of them. Surely you will want my men with you again."

Gent considered this for a moment. Almilio was trying to maximise his profit from the deal, but on the other hand he had a valid point. The two brothers were skilled and he had no desire to face them together alone.

An hour later, Thomas Gent flanked by two of Almilio's men, was striding through the narrow streets following the small boy who guided them through the crowds. By the time they arrived the Fitzwarren brothers and the bitch they had with them had left. Gent, furious, left empty handed.

†

Richard told them what he wanted, and more importantly, where to get it. Jack was happy to go have something constructive to do, and taking Lizbet with him set out to get it.

The Piazza De Fino had long been associated with scribes. They sat in the shade of the columns, surrounded by their low wooden writing tables, attended by their apprentices. The Piazza, reached though a narrow passage, was away from the hustle of Venice; a haven of peace and tranquillity, a small quiet isolated place that had been home to scribes for as long as anyone could remember. They spent their days quietly around the piazza where a statue of Venus poured perpetual water from a jug; it was both a calm and quiet place to be.

Venice's very lifeblood might be her canals that veined their way through the city, but they were fed by a heart, and that heart was fuelled by trade. Commerce was life in the Doge's Venetian empire. Most of the larger merchant houses had scribes and clerics on staff completing bills of lading, invoices, letters and notes of credit in stuffy airless small offices. The smaller merchants, though, still used the ad-hoc services of the scribes in the Piazza De Fino, rather than carrying the unnecessary expense of such staff when they were not always needed.

At the end of the day the apprentices stowed away the tools of their trade and folded away their masters' wooden writing tables. Richard had told Lizbet exactly what he wanted and it did not take her long to find it. A balding man was haranguing his apprentice for tipping over a pot of ink on the flags. The boy had already placed a bare foot in the black spreading stain, the imprint of his toes appearing repeatedly over the alabaster white flags, as he hopped from foot to foot in increasing agitation.

The writing tables, when folded flat, were carried by means of a leather strap clipped onto each side of the table. The second clip, having been twisted by Lizbet's quick fingers as she passed, was no longer properly closed. As the boy hoisted it to his shoulder, the strap fell away, the wooden box hitting the stone with a crack. There followed a clatter as the lid slapped open and a rolling rattle as the contents tumbled out.

Lizbet threw her arms wide. With an exclamation on her lips that was certainly not Italian, she claimed the scribes and apprentice's attention as she descended upon them. Her helpful hands were unwanted, but the scribe's polite gestures and accented Italian did not deter her. Eventually all the pens, pots of ink and sheets of velum were stored again inside the writing table, the leather strap was fixed firmly back to the side of the box. The scribe, retreating from Lizbet, his hand firmly on the elbow of the boy, backed from the Piazza, muttering words of thanks. He clearly wanted to absent himself from Lizbet's attentions as quickly as possible.

Soon afterwards, Lizbet put down her stolen offerings one by one in front of the Master. Two sheets of velum, rolled and creased, two short ink-blackened pens, a pot of dark ink with a cracked and blackened cork stopper and a small block of sealing wax.

Richard drained his cup, then slid both pens towards him and observed their sorry state. Meeting Lizbet's eye over the nibs, he said, "This one…" He held out the shorter and fatter of the two. "…is for marking and tallies and not much use for writing." He rolled the goose quill between his fingers before placing it on the table and picking up the narrower longer one. "While this one is split from here…" He tapped his finger on the top. "…to here." The split ran half way down the length of the ink stained pen.

It was Jack who spoke in her defence. "How is Lizbet supposed to know a good pen from a bad one?"

"Maybe you should teach her to write?" Richard said, absently pulling one of the creased sheets towards him.

"Don't you say anything about that. It's not my fault it got creased. This great oaf here squeezed my arm and squashed it where it was rolled up."

"Sorry," interrupted Jack, sounding not at all apologetic. He selected the split pen, inspected it and threw it back on the table in front of Richard, placing his knife next to it. "Trim that down and it will serve you well enough."

"Any complaints about the ink?" Lizbet asked grumpily.

"None, and the sealing wax was a nice addition as well," Richard said.

Lizbet met his eyes. They were bright but lacked humour. She yanked a chair away from the table and dropped down heavily into it, elbows on the wood. It was obvious she had every intention of watching him write the letter.

"Come on then, I've never seen it done before," Lizbet announced.

"Trust me, it's not that exciting to watch," Jack supplied. He was leaning against the window frame, observing the narrow street below, from the crack between the shutters. His next words were directed at Richard. "So you think this letter will get a reply?"

"Certainly," Richard replied. Under Lizbet's scrutiny, he trimmed the quill back and set down the knife on the table. "I expect it will bring about our arrest, which should place us where we want to be. There we go, the shortest pen I've ever used but it should work." Richard held the pen out for Lizbet to see. It was barely long enough to grip. Lizbet's small quick hand took a rapid hold of his wrist and turned it over to view the back of the pen.

"Are you satisfied with my work?" Richard said, sounding annoyed.

Lizbet nodded.

"If I may…" Richard opened the sheet out, rolling it in reverse to flatten it. "Pull the stopper from the ink pot," he instructed.

"Why?" Lizbet exclaimed.

"I don't want ink all over my hands, that's why."

Lizbet twisted the gnarled cork from the small bottle, sniffing at the contents, her nose wrinkling.

Jack rolled his eyes. "It's not meant for drinking."

"Good. It smells as bad as your feet."

Jack shot her a dark look, and Richard ignored them, turning his attention to the sheet of paper.

"Are you watching?" Richard said as he held the pen over the inkpot. Lizbet nodded. Dipping it in he turned it over so she could see the wet mark of the ink on the reverse. "No more than that much at a time." Then smoothing the sheet out with his hand, he began placing the black cursive marks of the letters on the page.

"Each block is a word, is that right?" Lizbet asked.

Richard nodded.

"Well, you have a lot to say then, don't you?" Lizbet remarked.

Richard's eyes met hers as he paused to dip the pen into the ink once more. "Not as much you, woman."

Lizbet heeded his words and watched him compose the rest of the letter in silence.

Richard sat back when he was finished, staring at the completed sheet before him.

Jack turned his gaze from the street. Seeing that the letter was finished, he crossed the room and lifted it from the table. His brow furrowed in consternation as he read.

"Christ, Richard! You've missed out words. It doesn't make any sense." Jack raised his eyes from the letter to meet Richard's. His brother's gaze had returned again to some point between them and he didn't meet Jack's look. "This looks like a child wrote it!"

Richard still didn't reply. Wordlessly he raised himself from the chair and returned to the bed, lying down on his back, his eyes fixed on the ceiling. Jack swore, took the vacated seat and, pulling the unused sheet of vellum towards him, carefully copied out the letter in his own neat hand.

Lizbet watched him. His confident strokes contrasted markedly with the shaky indecisive lines she had watched his brother create on the page. When he had finished he picked up the uneven lump of dark wax. "Can you melt that?" he asked Lizbet.

Lizbet looked between Jack and the lump of wax, and then said, "We've no fire."

"It's hot enough out there to melt hell," Jack replied.

Lizbet watched as he opened the shutters a degree more and placed his knife on the dusty stone sill. He sat the lump of wax on the widest part of the blade and as she watched the wax closest to the hilt began to run.

Jack balanced the molten wax on the blade, carried it back and poured it to the folded sheet. The room was warm and the wax remained soft and pliable long enough for Jack take his ring from the purse and press it carefully into the seal, staring at the Fitzwarren crest he imprinted there.

Soon after Jack left the room. A few coins ensured that the letter would be delivered. He was about to return to the room, but instead took himself further along the narrow street to the end where it met the canal. On the left, facing the water, was a tavern he had seen earlier. It was of the cheaper type, he could tell from those sat drinking and playing cards outside. It catered for the city's workers, the bakers, the dyers, the tanners, the boatswains, the men who toiled to make Venice the city it was.

He wasn't sure if he wanted ale. What he did know was that he didn't want to go back to the room. He certainly didn't want his brother's company. Not at the moment. The meeting with Chester had obviously not gone his brother's way, and the letter he had written had shocked Jack.

A small earthenware jug of ale was delivered to his table. He smiled at the girl as she placed it quietly before him, waiting until she left before he poured the ale into the cup. The jug was small and quickly emptied. Jack was considering another and attempted to summon the girl who had brought him the ale over. She was, he saw, more profitably employed, her hand in that of a man wearing a floury apron and with his dark hair full of wheat dust. She was leading him towards a narrow alley that led down the side of the tavern. Jack cast his eyes around, looking for another serving wench, but apart from another handful of men sitting talking quietly over their drinks he was alone. It looked like he would have to wait.

She was back soon enough and he waved her over. Fetching another glazed brown jug, she made her way between the tables towards him. Did he really want to sit here and get drunk? Jack knew the answer to that question was a resounding yes, but he knew he couldn't. Lizbet and Richard were back in the room and he had no right to leave them while he drowned his sorrows.

The girl put the jug down and leaned across the table to stroke his arm, an invitation playing across her face. Did he want a woman? His body supplied the answer to that question. He was on his feet a moment later, being led to the alley along the side of the tavern. Behind the tavern there was a low crumbling wall that served the girls well. Perched on it already, her legs spread either side of a grunting man, was another girl, who acknowledged with a smile the girl leading Jack.

Letting go of his hand and hopping up onto the wall she hoisted her skirts for him, leaning back and spreading her legs wide. Jack needed no further invitation. The man to his right finished with a loud groan and a moment later the girl pushed him away, her eyes now on Jack. Holding his gaze and reaching down between her legs, she matched his pace.

Jack felt guilty when he paid her from the small supply of coins he had. Then when she nodded at the other girl and said, "You give Nicole money as well," he felt even worse. He had no choice but to pay. Somewhere close would be the girl's owner ready pounce on those who failed to part with coin. That he had been rolled by two prostitutes was something he would be keeping to himself.

Jack sat down at the tavern table and slowly drank the remainder of the jug of ale, his mind wandering back to that appalling letter drafted by his brother. Richard would have berated him for an age if he'd done something like that. When he'd been stupid enough to poach pheasants, he'd not heard the last of it for weeks. So what had changed? He knew Richard didn't care overly about what happened to himself and Jack could recognise a pain felt on the inside, he had suffered it himself, but this was something different. There was something else.

As they had travelled south he'd become less and less talkative. The only times he'd ever really spoken to them were when Lizbet gave him whatever it was she'd bought at the apothecary's.

Jack's hand, reaching for the jug, stopped in mid-air.

What had the apothecary given her?

Jack didn't finish the jug. He was on his feet and strode quickly back to the rented room, finding Lizbet and Richard where he had left them. His brother was sprawled out on the bed, Lizbet was sitting at the table, the ink pen in her hand. She was busy making patterns on the reverse of the abandoned sheet of vellum that had Richard's failed letter on it. Lizbet looked up at his entrance, guilt on her face as she discarded the pen quickly on the table.

"Lizbet, the herbs you've been giving him, where are they?" Jack asked as he closed the door behind him.

Lizbet looked confused. "He doesn't need any now. I gave him some a while ago just before he was writing the letter."

"Let me see them." Jack held his open hand out for them.

Lizbet patted her skirt and found the small jar, extracting it and dropping it into his hand. "There wasn't much left, but I got some more today."

The ale cup Richard had drunk from earlier was on the table. Jack slopped more into the cup and pushed it towards her. "Put in there what you give him."

Lizbet looked confused.

"Please, I need you to," Jack reassured her.

Lizbet took the jar back, pulled away the stopper and tipped in what she normally gave Richard.

Jack took the cup, stirred it with his finger, and tipped the contents into his mouth. A moment later he spat it onto the rushes in the room. "Christ, woman! No wonder he can't write."

"Jack, what's the matter? It's just herbs." There was an edge of panic in Lizbet's voice.

"Yes, it is. The type that robs a man of his senses. The kind that he can't do without once he's started. You've been giving him poppy tears," Jack exclaimed.

Lizbet pulled the stopper out again and looked at the brown ground mixture inside aghast. "Are you sure?"

"I'm sure." Jack sounded grim.

"I didn't mean to," Lizbet sobbed

"It's not your fault. He knew." Then addressing his brother where he lay on the bed, he said, "Didn't you? You knew damned well what she was giving you."

Richard did not reply.

Jack's temper snapped. Reaching down, he grabbed Richard by the shoulders and tore his shirt open. Jack could count his ribs, and the skin was sunk and taught around his shoulders and collarbones. "When was the last time he ate?"

"He's no appetite. He has a little sometimes. You've seen me trying to get him to eat." Lizbet had tears in her eyes.

"Are you listening to me?" Jack shook his brother hard. "You've an appetite for this, haven't you?" Jack held the half empty cup he himself had just drunk from in front of Richard's face. That did get a reaction and Richard reached for it. Before he could take it, Jack hurled it across the room to smash against the wall spreading a dark stain across the stone.

Richard's eyes followed its flight. "Please," was all he said.

"No, damn you."

"Will he be alright?" Lizbet was wiping tears from her eyes.

"Not while he's drinking that he won't be," Jack said, pushing his hands roughly through his already untidy hair. He dropped heavily into the chair. "Tomorrow we set off back north."

"North?" Lizbet said, shocked. "What about Andrew? What about the flintlocks?"

Jack shook his head. "Richard couldn't even convince a merchant to give him more than a few coins." Jack spoke to Richard, fury in his voice. "Those few coins were all you were getting, weren't they? You had to tell us there was more coming so we'd buy you more of this."

Lizbet looked at Richard horrified.

"How well do you think he will fare with the Knights of St John? They'll take one look at him and recognise the opium in his blood, then they'll not deal with him charitably that I can tell you. Look at him, for God's sake!"

Lizbet did, and like Jack, she saw what they both hadn't wanted to see. A wasted body, black sunken hollow eyes and a demeanour that she knew was that of an addict.

Richard was sitting on the edge of the bed with his head in hands. "They'll trace the letter here. I don't care how you sent it, they will trace it." The effort of speaking was evident.

"We will be gone in the morning," Jack said, with finality.

†

Venice had long been home to various Orders of Knights. The Templars, before their fall, had land, property and churches, some of which had been bequeathed to the Knights of St John of Jerusalem. This surviving Order had headquarters in the Venetian state, a church dedicated to St John the Baptist, along with a convent attached to it with a hospital and barracks. The Knights of St John now had a permanent home on Malta, granted to them by The Holy Roman Emperor, Charles V, in 1530. From there, they continued their running battle with Suleiman the Magnificent who had ejected the Knights from their original base on the island of Rhodes in 1522. Suleiman had no intention of letting them remain in the Mediterranean on Malta.

Dragut, Suleiman's corsair prince, attacked Malta in 1551, however the siege lasted only a few short weeks and he had turned his attention to easier pickings – carrying away most of the population of the neighbouring isle of Gozo as slaves and then ousting the Knights from Tripoli on the North African coast. The hatred between the Turks and the Knights ran deep.

Provisioning an Order the size of the Knights of St John was an administrative task, that was coordinated from their headquarters in Venice. This southern European port, a centre for trade between east and west, was the perfect place to stockpile provisions and ship them to the Mediterranean island of Malta.

Brother Franco put his pen down, reaching for the cool cup of lemon water that had just been placed on his desk. It was August and it was hot. Franco was originally from Northern France, where the summers were comfortable pleasant affairs to be enjoyed, where a man could sit in the sun and soak up the warmth. He resented Venice in the summer. It was too hot to go out in the afternoons, the sun burnt his tonsure and to wear a hood was to suffer even more. The city was pleasant only in the very early mornings, before the real heat of the day took hold, then again late at night.

Franco also resented the smell. On his desk, scented oil burnt steadily in a brazier, the aroma just about enough to mask the stench rising from the canal outside his window. Franco regularly lamented that it could not be much worse if he had been forced to conduct the Order's business from the middle of a rotting fish market. The canals through Venice were liquid rubbish dumps, the summer sun fermenting them to eye-watering levels. In the central canals, the sea did not flow as easily as it did nearer the outskirts. The filth of daily living failed to wash away into the open lagoon. Instead it remained, festering and rotting beneath his shuttered windows.

The shutters were a necessity for a second reason as well. The flies. In the hot summer months the air-borne pests multiplied and Brother Franco had found that he was one of life's less fortunate people when it came to insect bites. The small red pinpricks from the fly bites would spread in hours, becoming hot and painful swollen welts that could take weeks to dissipate.

The uniform of the Order, covering his skin from neck to toe, should have afforded his body some protection. However, the flies still managed to penetrate the layers, delivering their painful poison to his arms and legs. On his desk lay a fly swat and his Venetian serving boy, Angelo, was now well acquainted with Franco's hatred of insects. He would diligently, morning and evening, inspect the walls and ceiling in his office, and later his sleeping quarters, flattening any of the biting, flying insects he found. As far as Franco was concerned they were the Devil's own creatures on earth and he hated them.

The Order required all kinds of provisions, and when the requisitions came in from Malta, they were all processed in his office. Goods were ordered before being stored in the Order's warehouses in Venice, until such time as there were enough to fulfil a shipment. Then Franco either sourced a merchant ship, or the Order's own vessels would come and collect the stores. As such, there was constant traffic between Malta and mainland Europe. Although the island did have its own resources, there were a lot of items they lacked, and these came through Venice.

Two letters had been delivered that morning for Franco. One he recognised immediately. Heavy, bearing the seal of the Order, it was a requisition for stores to be procured that could not be found on the Mediterranean isle. Franco broke the seal, his eyes quickly scanning the list. Oak, pig skins, leather hides, brass billets, nails and sail cloth. Nothing difficult.

Most of the items on this latest order could be dispatched immediately from stores, the rest Franco had good supply contacts for. The second letter he did not recognise, the seal being unfamiliar to him. Turning it over in his hand Franco regarded it carefully. The paper was still bright and uncreased, the ink wasn't smudged, and the corners of the letter were still crisp and angular. It had not been penned long ago and it had not travelled far.

Reaching into his top drawer, Franco pulled out a thin flattened blade, the end of which he applied to the candle flame on his desk. The strong, wafer thin steel heated quickly. Judging the moment right, Franco slipped the hot blade under the seal, the wax melting to the touch of the metal and the seal lifting from the page intact. If he wanted to trace the impression on it he still could, having avoided breaking it.

Dropping the blade back into the drawer, Franco read the letter from Richard Fitzwarren.

Franco let the letter drop back to the desk in front of him and stared at the closed shuttered windows. A moment later Franco pulled open a drawer and drew out two other letters carefully tied together. One was from Thomas Tresham, alerting him to the fact that a man would be contacting the Order regarding the missing Italian arms shipment, a Master Garrett, by all accounts. The second had been from Richard Fitzwarren a few weeks ago, announcing his intention to open negotiations with the Order for the same shipment and requesting a meeting.

The meeting had indeed taken place with Brother Franco, and Fitzwarren, his men and the arms he had brought with him, should have arrived in Malta by now.

So Brother Franco had no idea why he had received a second letter from another, purporting to sell the same shipment, and using the same name – Richard Fitzwarren. Franco tapped his fingers on the table, the puzzle for the moment taking his mind off the infernal flies.

Jack had signed the letter in his brother's name, unaware that Richard had used the name Garrett as an alias.

Richard had been right, the missing munitions had caused ripples. Indeed, had he known it, more than he could have guessed. The finger had already been pointed at the Knights for having plundered them for themselves almost two years ago. It was well known that if they had ended up on Malta, then there would be very little anyone could do to prove otherwise. For all intents and purposes they would have permanently disappeared and this was generally what was assumed to have happened to them.

The Knights however, on this occasion, were not guilty. Two years ago when such accusations had been levelled at the Grand Master, by an emissary from the Pope, he had been ejected from Malta with abject fury. Quiet orders had then been sent out. Find out where the arms are. Find out who has them. However, nothing had been found.. The trail was cold. Senor Monsinetto had taken the arms to England and then lost his life on the return journey, along with everyone else on the ship. It had been supposed that he had the shipment with him, although quiet enquiry and a stolen copy of the bill of lading for the vessel suggested that this was not the case.

Franco had received a copy of the dispatch enquiring after them two years ago. He had contacts in Europe for everything, and knew who would deal in such items. Those that were less than honest in their dealings he had pressed, hoping that one of them would have heard of the location of the arms. Nothing.

Now here they were. Thomas Tresham in England had been alerted that they were for sale if the Order was interested. A Master Garrett would be in touch shortly and would have with him examples of the wares he was trafficking. Franco found himself quite annoyed with Tresham who had let this man, Garrett, walk free. Franco had no contact details for Garrett, no idea who his master was. There was just a vague promise that Garrett would be in touch with the Order in Venice. Tresham's communication alerted the Order to the fact that a possible deal was on the way, and nothing more.

Was the Order interested? Franco snorted. Of course the Order was interested!

Franco re-read Tresham's letter.

Tresham obviously had no idea what these munitions were worth. Garrett could be anyone. The only piece of information he could glean from this was that the arms were probably in England. That was where they had been destined for in the first place, but Franco had no idea who would have held them for nearly three years. Greed was, Franco knew, generally not that patient.

Now Franco had two men, it seemed, both trying to sell the same missing shipment to the Order, and both laying claim to the same name. Richard Fitzwarren he had spoken to himself a few weeks ago. Franco had been shown samples of the full cargo and had despatched the men and the samples under heavy guard to Malta. Franco had felt little liking for Fitzwarren, the man was boastful and overly confident. Brother Franco had little doubt that his manner would change once he found himself on the Knights' island fortress.

Little did Andrew know that the name Richard had used in his dealings with the Order had been Garrett when he assumed the guise of Fitzwarren in his meeting with Brother Franco.

Franco was about to reach for a pen to send a note to the Order's barracks. Then, grumbling, he threw the pen down, knowing he was going to have to go himself. The matter was too important to trust to a note.

"Angelo…" Franco called the boy into his rooms and Angelo diligently knelt at his feet helping him on with his sandals.

Brother Franco, as controller in Venice, arrived at the barracks with an escort that befitted his rank. Angelo had run ahead, with a note, letting them know of his master's imminent arrival.

The barracks were positioned next to the Order's hospital, and although number of men stationed here were small by the standards of the Order's Maltese force, they gave the Knights a well-respected presence in Venice. Their principal role now was to ensure the safety of Brother Franco's precious stores in the Order's warehouses adjacent to the barracks, before they were despatched to Malta.

The commander was an Italian Knight, Brother Emilio, and he had no liking for Franco. Emilio was in his prime, and resented his current posting guarding Franco's storehouses. Emilio longed to be on Malta, fighting the Turk, side by side with his brother Knights. Nothing happened in Venice. None of the local criminal class were stupid enough to take on the Knights over their provisions, not when there were easier pickings in the city.

"Brother Emilio, how good of you to see me," Brother Franco acknowledged, as he was shown into Brother Emilio's sparely furnished office. A table, two chairs, and a portable shrine to the Virgin against one wall were all it contained.

Emilio nodded in acceptance of his words and motioned for Franco to take one of the chairs. "How can I help you, Brother Franco? It is not often I receive two personal visits from you in such a short time."

Franco had been forced to visit Emilio and employ his services several weeks ago, to keep Richard

Fitzwarren and his men close until they could be secured on one of the Order's ships.

Franco didn't miss the hint of sarcasm in Emilio's words, but he chose to ignore it. It was true that normally he communicated with the Barracks by note or messenger, rather than take the hours-long journey himself. "I need the services of some of your men at my offices."

Emilio raised his eyebrows when he heard the request. "Don't you have your own security?"

"We do," Brother Franco was forced to admit. "However there is a man about to approach the Order, and when he does, it is very much in our interests not to let him slip through our fingers. My Venetians are not as dedicated as your men are, as I am sure you are aware."

Emilio's attention was riveted on Franco. Very little ever happened in Venice that was not simply the day to day mechanics of trade. The recent brief internment of Fitzwarren and his men had been the closest Emilio had got to using his military skills for nearly a year.

"If this is a matter of security of the Order, I would of course lay at your disposal as many men as you need," Emilio affirmed.

Franco nodded. "Good, I hope to meet with him soon. Release him and find out who he travels with before taking him back into our keeping."

"One man?" Emilio repeated.

Franco confirmed. "There is not time to contact my superiors about this, so I propose a small number of your men billet themselves at my offices, then when he arrives, or we find out where he is, they can follow him. I want anyone he travels with, and everything he travels with, in our custody. He has sent me a letter announcing his intention, and I have men trying to trace whoever it was delivered it. We might be able to find him before he approaches us."

"May I ask why you want this man?" Emilio enquired.

"You may not, just know that it is important to the Order, and have men posted today," Brother Franco snapped. He had no liking for Emilio, who had the blaze of youth that had long since abandoned Franco and an Italian arrogance that he loathed. Franco was sure, though, that Emilio would follow his orders.

Brother Franco made his way back to his offices, a feast for the flies as he went, despite Angelo's best efforts to keep them at bay. On his return he penned a letter to Malta and sent it directly to the Grand Master de la Sengle informing him that there appeared to be a second person in the market to sell the Order the missing munitions. And more, that the seller was in Venice and about to approach the Order to negotiate a sale, and that this second seller also laid claim to the name Richard Fitzwarren.

There was little else Franco could do now but wait, until either he was contacted or his own men traced the origin of the letter. Within the hour Franco's quiet offices had been overrun with Emilio and his men, and he found he had a lot more irritations to deal with than just the flies.

Chapter 9
Forced Duplicity

It had been a sobering evening, the three of them in the room, all alone with their own thoughts. Richard had lain back on the bed again, his face turned towards the wall, his knees drawn up to his chest. Jack was sat at the table, his head in his hands, desperately trying to think of a way forward and Lizbet was left to sit on the floor, back to the wall watching them both.

Eventually it was Jack who broke the silence. "Well, we can't spend the rest of the night like this. I'm hungry and I dare say you are as well, lass."

Lizbet, raising her head, nodded.

Jack shook out the coins he had left onto the table and viewed the sorry selection. It would, he mused, have been more had he not been a fool and let himself be duped by the prostitutes. Casting a sour look towards the figure on the bed, he asked, "Do you want something to eat? Or is it something else you'd like?"

Richard rolled over, regarding him with dull dark rimmed eyes. "Something else," he admitted.

"I should let you have all of it, damn you." Jack's anger with his brother had not dissipated yet. "You swore an oath – remember?"

"I swore to live, I didn't say how I'd do it," Richard replied, wearily.

"This isn't living, you're killing yourself. You'll last another month like this and then you'll be a sack of shaking bones. That's all that will be left of you," Jack shot back.

Richard didn't reply. His gaze had dropped to the earthenware jar that held the opium. It had rolled to the floor when Jack had dragged his brother from the bed earlier and none of them had picked it up.

Jack saw Richard lick his lips and followed his brother's gaze. Rising, he crossed to the wall to where the jar had ended up, scooping it from the floor. "This is all you care about, isn't it?" When Richard didn't reply Jack pulled the stopper from the jar and held it close to his brother's face so he could smell it.

Richard, unable to resist, reached out with a shaking hand to take the jar. Jack, taunting him, moved it quickly out of his reach.

"If you want this, get on your knees. Beg for it. I want you to show me how much you need this rather than me," Jack growled, holding the jar just out of Richard's reach.

"No, Jack, stop it." Lizbet was on her feet, trying to push in front of Jack.

"I won't stop it," Jack snapped in Lizbet's face. Then pushing the jar back towards Richard, he watched with delight, as his brother reaching for it, missed and fell forwards from the bed. "On your knees, damn you."

Lizbet lunged for the jar, wrapping both her hands around it. "Stop it, Jack. This isn't helping."

"I should have let you go. I should have let you bleed out like a pig." Jack ripped his own shirt open so his brother could see the healed scar that lay on his chest. "I would have gone to Hell with you."

Lizbet tightened her hold on the jar, pleading with him, "Please, Jack, let go. He's ill. Please stop it."

Jack suddenly let go of it and clamped his hands to his face. "Why are you doing this to me?"

"Jack, please. It's not you. He's doing this to himself." Lizbet put the jar on the table and wrapped her arms tightly around Jack.

Bending his neck Jack lay his cheek on the top her head and returned her embrace fiercely. "I just want to hurt him as much as he's hurting me."

"I know you do. But please stop, you're both hurting me as well."

Jack squeezed his arms tighter around her. "I'm sorry," he muttered into her hair.

"Christ! Let me go, you oaf! I can hardly breathe," Lizbet said, with mock seriousness after a moment.

Jack loosened his hold, but still kept his arms around her.

"That's better," Lizbet said. "I think you've cracked at least two of my ribs."

If Jack made a reply, Lizbet didn't hear it. A moment later she was spinning backwards, Jack's hand in her chest pushing her hard away from him. Staggering, her feet banged into Richard who was still kneeling on the floor and she cannoned over him, bringing them both down in a heap. From where she lay on her back, her feet above her head resting on Richard, she saw why.

When Jack's head had rested on Lizbet's, he'd heard the unmistakable sound of a blade rattling from a sheath, beyond the door. Jack had needed his arm free. In the same instant he'd pushed Lizbet from him, he'd drawn his sword, which had stood propped against the wall.

The door came in at Jack. Kicked hard from the outside, swinging back and cracking loudly against the stone wall.

"Thomas Gent." Jack regarded the man who stood in the open doorway from along the length of his blade. "You have chosen the right moment to step back into my life."

If Jack's words were disconcerting, or the fact that his prey was not as surprised as he would have liked, it did not show on Gent's face. Steel in his own hand, he advanced into the room and, taking in the scene before him, he grinned. "See you've still got your whore of a sister with you. Share her, do you?"

Jack knew better than to engage in banter. His blade was already coming up under Gent's, sending it back in his face. The move forced Gent to take a step backwards, stopping the two men behind him from entering the room.

Gent's face darkened as he felt the steel in his hand reverberate from the impact. He growled at Jack, "Still full of tricks?"

Jack's eyes narrowed. "Tricks?" he repeated. "I don't think you and I ever sparred together, did we?"

Gent was looking past Jack and Jack snorted. "Now who is trying the tricks?" He lunged as he spoke and the blade point went though Gent's sleeve and cut through his arm. Gent screamed, his own blade point embedding itself in the wood floor as the sword dropped from his grasp.

Jack, his sword withdrawn, quickly leant forward and with his left hand took a hold of Gent's doublet, hauling him into the room. Gent stumbled forward, tripped over his own blade and landed awkwardly on his knees, his left hand pressed hard over the bleeding cut.

The two men behind him faltered on the threshold. There were shouts behind them from the rooms below. Jack couldn't hear them as clearly as they could. Both men exchanged a quick glance and darted away from the open doorway.

Jack dropped to his knees facing Gent. There'd been a knife in Gent's belt and as he'd stumbled forward Jack had neatly extracted it. He held it now, none too gently, against Thomas Gent's stomach.

"Where's Dan?" Jack demanded, increasing the pressure on the point.

Gent grinned through the pain, his face contorted and ugly. "Where do you think he is?"

Jack's fist, tightening around the hilt of Dan's knife, drove it straight into Gent's stomach. Gent fell against him, eyes popping from his head, mouth open in a silent shocked scream. The blade was still tight in Jack's hand, and he twisted it viciously. This time he was rewarded by a piercing shriek of pain from the dying man.

Jack pushed Gent away, and he collapsed on the floor, blood pouring to form a dark pond beneath his body as he writhed on the floor.

Lizbet still on the floor on her back, feet on top of Richard, stared open mouthed as three men, armed and wearing the unmistakable emblem of the Knights of St John strode into the room. Richard pushed himself up onto the edge of the bed. Lizbet shuffled back on the floor until she felt the wall behind her. Only Jack remained on his knees, immobile and staring at Dan's knife still held firmly in his hand.

A third Knight entered the room, taking in the scene before him, his eyes running over both the dying and living occupants.

"Richard Fitzwarren?" the new arrival enquired of the room in general.

"I'm Richard Fitzwarren," a voice replied.

The Knight looked towards the man who had spoken, disgust plain on his face. "Bring them all," were his final words before he strode from the room.

†

Brother Franco's offices were in the Castello district, in the centre of Venice, accessed down one of the narrow streets near St Mark's Square. The door was not a conspicuous one, although a plaque attached to the wall next to it told that these were the offices of the Order of St John of Jerusalem.

As instructed, Emilio and his men returned with the prisoners. Their bang on the outer dusty door was answered quickly. It was opened by an elderly serving brother, who admitted both Emilio and Richard Fitzwarren, leading them quickly up a flight of stairs to Franco's room.

The controller sat. He didn't offer the man before him a chair, but stared at him with hard eyes. Franco was, after all, a Knight of St John. Emilio had been forced to wait outside. The questions Franco wanted to put were not ones he wished to share with the younger Knight.

"So, Richard Fitzwarren, I assume?" Brother Franco said, steepling his fingers.

The man before him nodded in acceptance of the name.

Franco ran an assessing gaze over him. The Knight leant back in his chair, his bright eyes locked with those of the man who stood before him. His stare was returned in equal measure.

"I am surprised to say the least," Franco said, eventually. "You do not appear to be a man who would have anything to trade. We've searched your rooms and found nothing. Nothing at all."

"I did not bring them with me," came the poor reply.

"Why was that then? Perhaps someone else did?" Franco said. The man before him opened his mouth to speak, but Franco held up his hand to still his words. "Satisfy my curiosity, if you will. Why did a man using your name, travelling with both men and these flintlocks you seek to sell, stand before me not that very long ago?"

The man who stood before Franco stiffened. "The explanation is simple."

"Come on then, if it is so, simple supply it," Franco said, his eyes widening, anticipation plain on his face.

Discomfort flitted across the face of the man before he spoke. "It was a thief who laid claim to my name. He stole the arms he has with him from me. However, he only has with him samples. He does not know where the main shipment is stored. Only I have that information."

"How unfortunate for you," Franco said, sarcastically.

"As you say, unfortunate," came the acid reply.

"You had the audacity to trade in stolen goods with my Order? Then you were betrayed by your own men. This is not a good stand point, is it?" Franco's voice sounded slightly incredulous.

"I can assure you, these are not stolen property," Fitzwarren countered, ignoring the point about betrayal.

"Alright, shall we use the term lost property then? Would that offend your sense of right and wrong a little less?" Franco said pointedly.

Fitzwarren inclined his head. "Lost property," he said, in agreement.

"Well, if it is lost, why not take the Godly path, and return it to the owner?" Franco asked.

"If the Order is not interested then I will have to find someone else who might be. It may very well be that they could find their way back home again," Fitzwarren supplied smoothly.

Franco laughed loudly. "You are currently my prisoner. A man is dying at the moment. You indeed still have his blood on your shirt. Shortly your crime will be one of murder. Your fate should, by rights, lead you into the Piombi." Franco leant forward, his elbows planted on the desk, watching the man in front of him closely. "You are not in a position to negotiate."

There was a slight nod of acceptance from Fitzwarren.

Franco, satisfied, continued. "One of these you sent, and it bears the Fitzwarren seal. The other doesn't. So which of these is the true bearer of the name?" He reached into a drawer and dropped two letters onto the desk.

"I have the seal, here." The man held his hand so Franco could see the signet ring.

"Possession of a seal is little proof, is it? You could very easily have butchered the owner, just like the man we found bleeding to death at your feet earlier today," Franco pointed out accurately. "Which does bring me round to asking the question of why you tried to kill the man?"

There was a pause. "He had remained in Venice with the sole purpose of preventing me from contacting the Order."

"And why was that?" Franco put the question quickly.

"Kineer, Andrew Kineer, is the name of the man who has taken my name and who purports to trade with your Order."

"Perhaps he has good reason?" Franco said, thoughtfully. "Perhaps you were a poor leader. It does seem that he also has all of your men with him. Did none at all think to remain with you? Did all of them desert you?"

Franco did not receive an immediate answer, so he added, "Your brother and sister appear to be the only unfortunates travelling with you. Was that their choice, I wonder?"

The reply was quick and automatic. "Can I trust the Order with their safety?"

"And the dying man you were found with – are we charged with his safety as well?" Brother Franco said, smoothly.

"I have access to a something of significant value. It is of interest to many parties. I am sure you can understand how it is when you are dealing with something so valuable."

Franco raised his eyebrows again. "I can see how it might be problematic. Your brother, and your sister, will be safe. You have the word of the Order, and my word."

Relief showed plainly on the man's face as he stood before the Monk.

Franco said accurately, "So they are of importance to you? From the look on your face you hold them in higher regard than the flintlocks you are in the marketplace to sell?"

"I hold my family in higher regard than money," Fitzwarren replied, carefully.

"It is a shame this interview will be so brief. I must say I prefer you to your namesake who stood where you do now some weeks ago."

"Can you tell me what happened? Where he is now?" Fitzwarren asked.

"No, that is not something I can discuss. Sit down," Franco gestured to the seat opposite him. "You are to be our guest, just for a few days. Then you can go and plead your case before the Grand Master. He is more than a little intrigued by the cargo you allegedly have for sale. I can imagine that soon you may well be wishing yourself in the Piombi in Venice rather than in Malta. The Order does not like to be treated like fools."

"And my brother and sister?" Fitzwarren asked, still standing.

"Will go with you. Brother Emilio will escort you. A task I am sure he is suitably looking forward to. He has a great desire to serve the Order and finds his posting in Venice a tedious one."

"You assured me…"

"I assured you they would be safe, sir. And they are safe. They are not, however, free. I think you are about to find out the price of impudence," Franco replied, curtly.

"Where is the impudence in trade?" Fitzwarren asked, from where he still stood before Franco, having ignored the invitation to take the seat.

"And you are a merchant, are you?"

"I have goods to sell, and trade is…"

Franco cut him off. "Trade, sir, demands that you have a right to the title of the goods. You have no right to the title of these goods. We both know that. I do not know how, or where you think you have got them from, but I can assure you, very soon you are going to regret that you ever had the slightest idea of trying to sell them to the Order. What kind of fools do you think we are?"

"No fools at all." Fitzwarren held Franco's eyes with this own. "But this cargo needs to be in safe hands, and if I can assist with its delivery then I would hope to be recompensed."

"Where is it?" Franco knew he would not get an answer, but it was a question he badly wanted to put.

The man before him smiled.

"Very well, smile now. However I fear that you'll not be keeping that information to yourself for overly long," Franco finished wearily, then rising he opened the door and called loudly, "Brother Alfonso."

One of the armed men who had escorted Fitzwarren appeared.

"Make sure a close guard is kept on him until Brother Emilio collects him."

The room they took him to was cool and quiet, both of which he was thankful for. Apart from the door that had closed behind him, there was just one small grilled window, high in the wall, letting in a narrow streak of sunlight. The floor was damp. Up to waist height the plaster had fallen away, exposing brickwork bristling with salt petre. The wall beneath the window on the far side of the room was running with water and he guessed this one faced the canal. On the drier side of the room was a low lying bed frame, topped with a packed straw mattress. There was little else in the room.

He had known that this was coming from the moment he had found out about the flintlocks. That seemed a very long time ago. The interview thankfully was over, and his breath came easier now. The moment they had closed the door behind him, a pressure that had felt like a leaden weight on his chest had lifted. That he had got through it, without betraying himself, seemed a miracle. How long he could keep up the ruse was another matter entirely.

Pulling the bed away from the damp wall, he lay down on his back. Pushing blond hair from his eyes, he cast an arm across his face to block the light from the grilled window. Soon his breathing became even and shallow as sleep claimed him.

✝

Claude de la Sengle was the Order's forty-eighth Grand Master, and he was nobody's fool. Under his hand, the Order's military strength on Malta had increased, as had her defences. Completing Fort St Elmo and expanding Fort St Michael, de la Sengle had created powerful bastions at the mouth of Grand Harbour, as he tightened his hold on the Mediterranean. A lifetime of sea and land battles against the Turk had taught him to never underestimate his enemy. As a leader of one of the foremost fighting forces in Christendom, de la Sengle was a man who knew his trade, and his trade was war.

De la Sengle had received Franco's report and there was a fury burning within his chest. It was already assumed that the Knights' armoury was stocked with the missing Italian munitions. The Grand Master had little intention of paying in coin for what the Order had already paid for in diplomatic humiliation. That they had the flintlocks had, of course, been denied. There were no powers on earth that were going to open the Order's armoury doors for anyone to check. And even if they had and the missing Italian weapons were not on show, then it would have been assumed that, for the time of the visit, they had been stored elsewhere.

De la Sengle had not been able to win. Having drawn their conclusions, and the weapons never having surfaced anywhere else, the powers that be in Europe had satisfied themselves that their suspicions had been correct. The military Order of St John of Jerusalem, along with some of its more questionable procurement methods, was to blame.

Monsinetto had died when his return ship had sunk off the coast of Spain, which was no longer viewed as a freak accident of weather and poor seamanship. It was indeed the perfect cover for the removal from the ship of its lucrative cargo, and then, God rest their souls, the consignment to the deep of the crew and Monsinetto. Piracy was not a crime beyond the Order, they had an unfortunate record that bore that out.

In 1553 Emperor Charles V had offered the Order the city of Mahdia on the Tunisian coast. In 1551 the Knights had lost their hold on Tripoli to the Ottoman Turk. The cost had been extreme. Mahdia had looked very much like another Tripoli, difficult to defend, at the end of very long supply route and splitting the Knight's resources from Malta. They declined the offer. Charles knew Mahdia would fall to the Turks and the Spanish garrisoned there sacked and burned their own citadel before leaving it to its Ottoman fate.

Relations were stretched. The refusal to offer their protection to Mahdia two years previously had caused a deep diplomatic rift between the Charles V and the Order. The disappearance of the ship, supposedly returning the missing Italian arms, in Spanish waters had Charles V's diplomats beating on the Order's door, demanding return of the weapons they had seized at sea en route to Italy.

So De la Sengle, and the Order, had already borne the cost of them in loss of diplomatic faith and honour. As a rich organisation with full pockets, payment for the consignment was a secondary consideration. As far as de la Sengle was concerned, he had already paid for them even if the currency had not been coin. Now he just needed to secure them. The fact that it now seemed he had two impudent men brave enough to try and sell these arms to the Order, left the Grand Master incredulous.

☨

They woke him from his slumber in the dim storeroom after a few hours and escorted him to the Order's barracks in Venice. Once there, he was shown into an empty barrack block, the door closed and locked. An hour later the door opened and a serving brother, backed by three capable men, armed and blocking the door, entered carrying a jug of tepid ale and food.

He aimed his words at those behind the servant, who was standing in the doorway. "How long do you intend to keep me in here? I was travelling with two others. Where are they?"

None of them replied, but they grinned, and he saw the nudge one of the men gave the other, a moment before the serving brother backed out and the door closed once more.

"Well, that went well!" he said, under his breath.

An hour later, the door opened again. This time there was no nervous servant, just the three armed men who he had seen before. "Brother Emilio would like you to come with us."

"At last!" He was stripped to a linen shirt in the stifling heat of the barracks. Grabbing his doublet, he shrugged his shoulders into it as he followed them.

Brother Emilio was seated outside, under the shade of several clustered olive trees. There was a table, cups and an empty chair. He had obviously been waiting for his prisoner's arrival, smiling broadly when the men opened the door to the small enclosed terrace, before closing it securely behind him.

"Do you keep every door locked?" Fitzwarren asked, remaining standing.

"Only when we don't want to lose anything, and it would be a shame to lose you," Emilio said. He extended a foot and pushed the chair out from under the table.

Fitzwarren read the look on Emilio's face, one he'd recognised before in others. Holding Emilio's eyes with his own, he slowly, and with care fastened up all the loose buttons on his doublet. When he'd finished, his face expressionless, arms folded, he said, "Unless you have word of my release, or, of my brother or sister, I would prefer to return to my room."

Emilio sighed, then waved him towards the door. Applying his hand to it he found it swung open, and on the other side one of the guards waited to return him to the barracks.

He recognised his mistake soon after he returned to the room. When the evening came and the serving brother arrived carrying food and drink for a second time, he informed the armed men behind him, that, if Brother Emilio wished it, he would like to eat with him. Five minutes later they came back and escorted him to Brother Emilio.

†

Clement's heart was in his mouth, as soon as Marcus announced that Robert Fitzwarren was in his offices, demanding immediate access to his lawyer.

Would the man ever leave him in peace?

"Send him in," Clement muttered, through clenched teeth. He might as well get this over with as quickly as possible.

No sooner had Marcus left when the door, not yet fully closed, was yanked back open. Robert Fitzwarren in a furious temper filled the frame. Fitzwarren slammed the door closed. Clement jumped involuntarily. A satisfied smile twitched at the corner of Robert's mouth as he watched the lawyer cower on the opposite side of the desk.

"The de Bernay matter will take time." Clement's mouth had dried up, and the words squeaked from his parched throat. "The preliminary hearing was only last week, but I can assure you all the relevant papers have now been filed."

"That's not why I'm here." Robert cleared the end of Clement's desk of papers in a rapid sweep and perched on it, leaning forward.

Clement cast his eyes to the floor and let out a sigh. It was going to take Marcus an age to put them back in order. Robert following his eyes, swung his boot in the direction of two of the files that had not disgorged their contents. A swift kick emptied them, papers spilling from them in a flurry to join the rest of the mess on the floor. "My father is ill. He wants to sign over his estates to me to govern now that he is no longer fit. Can you do this for him?"

Clement nodded slowly. "I can do this. I would need to get from him details of his holdings and property and then we could draw up the relevant legal documents to pass control of them to you."

Robert's eyes narrowed as he realised there was a problem. Clement was not William's lawyer. Robert did not know the full extent of his father's holding's. "It is just the main property he wishes to sign over. Those are the main burdens upon him."

"I am assuming your father has his own lawyer? It would be wise to consult with him as well. It may be that he has many of the deed papers in his hands," Clement replied, his voice still trembling.

Robert shook his head. "My father has no great trust of lawyers. A sentiment I am beginning to share. He keeps deeds and papers relating to his properties close to him, so there is no other lawyer involved."

Clement wrung his hands together nervously. "I can call and see Lord Fitzwarren. We can draw up a list and from that a power of attorney for you to act and the terms of that power that he would like to apply."

"Were you not listening? My father is ill. He sits in a pile of his own shit and doesn't know what day of the week it is. There is little point in consulting with him." Robert spoke through tight lips.

"I would still need his signature. He would still need to have a witnessed signature on the document," Clement said, his throat still dry and his voice still sounding reedy and high.

Robert leant across the desk, bringing his face so close to Clement's that the lawyer could smell his fetid breath. "Prepare the documents and I will get his signature and you can take care of the witnesses."

Clement understood, and his head nodded quickly. At least he wasn't going to have to go to the Fitzwarren house. That visit would have twisted his stomach with dread for days.

"If you know the holdings that your father wants you to manage, then I can draft the documents you need," Clement conceded rapidly. It seemed to be the quickest way he could get Fitzwarren out of his offices.

A malicious sneer spread across Robert's face. "Good. Have them delivered to me this week at the London house." Robert pushed himself up from the desk using another pile of Clement's papers, sending them to land with the rest on the floor, leaving the little lawyer alone, in the middle of a spreading sea of files and papers.

Clement heard the door to the street slam, and a moment later Marcus was on the threshold of his office, his eyes taking in the mess he would have to clear up.

"Damn that family to hell," Clement said, with feeling. "Will they ever leave me in peace?"

✝

William knew Robert was back. He had heard Ronan's loud voice as he set them quickly to their tasks, then their footsteps as they ran to prepare rooms on the floors above him. William lamented that he was forgotten about. He might still be the lord, might still remain master of this house, but he knew it was in name only. The master the servants ran to obey was now Robert Fitzwarren. William sat and listened to the thud of feet on the boards in the room above, his temper beginning to boil. None of them would have dared make such a racket when he had control of the household. None of them cared now if his peace was disturbed.

It was an hour before the door to his room opened. Unannounced, and quite drunk, his son Robert entered.

William's face hardened. He waited for Robert to speak first, watching as he walked into the room, sat on the edge of the table, regarding his father through brown eyes hooded with slack lids.

"So, old man, you're still here," Robert slurred.

William regarded him coldly, but said nothing.

"I need to know something," Robert continued. He had a glass in his hand and in one quick motion he drained it. "Who else knows?"

William watched him put down the empty glass slowly on the table, Robert's eyes never leaving his father's face. "Tell me."

William, knowing to delay any longer would just raise Robert's temper, answered, "No one."

"If only I could believe you, old man." Robert paused before he continued. "You have too tight a hold on the purse strings. I think it's a hold you need to release. My lawyer is drawing up a covenant giving me control of your affairs so you need not bother yourself with the day to day running of the estates."

"I'll not sign them. Not while I've a breath in my body. Do you hear me?" William raged, disbelief on his face. With both his gnarled hands he tried to push himself up from the chair, managing to raise himself, his arms shaking, but when his useless legs felt the weight of his body they crumbled beneath him and William fell back heavily in the chair.

Robert howled with laughter. "How will you stop me? You cannot even stand."

"I will not sign away my life," William spat from the chair.

Robert slithered from the table top to the floor, leaving the empty glass and advanced on William, who glared up at him. "I'll have what's my due now. I'll not wait until your stinking corpse breathes its last."

"It's not yours to take!" boomed William.

It was the first time William had ever refuted Robert's birth, and it stopped Robert's advance for a moment. "Ill advised words, father. Ill advised," Robert said, menacingly. "If, in your dotage, you are to utter such ramblings then it is surely best for me to take over the running of your affairs? Juris has already attested that your illness has left you with less than a sound mind."

"Juris!" blurted William. Why would his own physician betray him?

Robert sneered and answered the question he could read on William's face. "Money. That's why Juris attested that you are no longer capable of running your affairs."

William frowned, seething.

"I have gone to a lot of trouble to secure this," Robert continued, through gritted teeth. "It would have been a lot simpler to just still your breathing."

Taking two more quick steps towards William, he dropped his hands over his father's wrists and pinned them painfully to the carved arms of the chair. Bringing his face close to William's, he said, "You will sign, and then you can live out your last remaining days like a hermit in his hovel."

William's mouth opened, then sense prevailed and he closed it immediately. Robert was drunk and dangerous. He knew him well enough to know that he wanted to exercise his temper; better that he did it on one of the servants than on William. So William just nodded, and kept his wary eyes on Robert.

Robert's mouth twitched into a smile, and, releasing his hold on William, he straightened. "So you can see the sense in that idea then. Good. Clement's clerk will have the documents for you to sign in a few days."

William was shocked, but not surprised, he supposed. It had not taken long for Robert to realise that he could easily take control of everything William owned without having to wait for his father's death. Whoever was his lawyer was probably the one to blame for this. William was fairly sure his son would not have had the insight to dream this up on his own.

What was William going to do?

William stared at the glass Robert had left on the table. The firelight glinted through the cut crystal. The decision, when he made it, was one he realised he'd known he would make for a long time. A withered hand reached for the bell chain on the table and Edwin, summoned from the corridor, quietly opened the door and stepped into the room.

"Come here, man." William beckoned the servant to him. Edwin moved towards him obediently. "Master

Carter, do you remember him you took a message to him before?"

Edwin nodded, remembering the message he had delivered the previous year.

"I want you to tell him to come and meet with me here. If anyone asks you about this tell them is it to order wine for my cellars. Do you hear me?"

Edwin nodded in silent reply

"I also want you to send a message for my lawyer, Gladstone, to visit me, after Robert has left. Mark my words. After Robert has left, so you hear?"

"Yes, my Lord, " Edwin confirmed, nodding again.

William waved a hand in dismissal and slumped back in the chair. He had tried once before to use his younger son to bring Robert to heel and it had failed. This time he was going to have to make the bait a lot more attractive. What other choice did he have?

Chapter 10

The Journey Begins

He was released the following day from the dark barrack room, emerging blinking into the harsh white light of the Mediterranean morning, the sun rebounding from the limestone walls and cutting harsh hard shadows where it could.

Brother Franco was there, unsmiling and sweating in the heat. "We will take you by ship to Malta. Your brother and sister, I have been assured, will go with you."

When they arrived on the Order's ship he was taken straight below the decks. The steps down to the cabins were narrow and steep. He waited until they were clear before he made his descent. Not, he noted, with the same speed and confidence displayed by the man leading him. A narrow wooden door was opened, and he was bid to enter. As soon as he stepped through, it was closed quickly behind him.

Lizbet launched herself at him, forcing him to stagger backward, her arms around his neck, her head pressed to his chest. "You fool, you bloody idiot, Jack. I thought they'd killed you."

It had never crossed his mind that they'd think he had perished after they had taken him from the room to the interview with Brother Franco.

"I'm still here." Jack wrapped his arms around her and looking over her head met the eyes of his brother sitting on a bed, his knees drawn up to his chest, regarding him darkly.

Jack gave Lizbet a squeeze and let her go, taking a seat on the edge of the bed next to his brother. After a moment he said, "I had no choice. You know that, don't you?"

Richard nodded, but his face remained expressionless.

Jack continued. "How are you feeling?"

Richard tipped his head back against the wooden wall and raised his eyes to the ceiling. "Like a fool's fool," he said quietly.

Jack switched his gaze to Lizbet. "How's he been?"

Lizbet paled. "I'm sorry, Jack, I didn't have a choice. I tried not to give him any but he was so bad and he started raving and saying things he shouldn't so I thought it best to quieten him down."

"It's alright, I understand," Jack said, although disappointment showed clearly on his face. "I found out Andrew is calling himself Fitzwarren, we suspected as much."

"What happened?" It was Richard who had spoken. "I've had my name stolen twice in as many weeks. You might as well let me know if I made a good account of myself."

Jack regarded him with cool blue eyes. "You gave me no choice. All I know is they are taking us to Malta, and there is a meeting with the Grand Master which I am not looking forward to."

"The current Grand Master is Claude de la Sengle," Richard supplied quietly, "a soldier at heart and a knight second. Appealing to his desire to ensure the Order remains at the top of the military tree should not be too difficult."

"It might not be for you," Jack said hotly, and then casting his eyes over the wreckage of his brother, he amended his words. "It might not have been too difficult for you once." Then to Lizbet, "how much have you left?"

"Quite a lot, he got me to buy more in Venice after he got the money from Chester Neephouse," Lizbet said.

Jack's face was grim, and he held out his hand. "Give me it here."

"Jack, you can't take it away, I've seen what he's like. Please," Lizbet said, her hand tightly wrapped around the jar. Jack's expression was enough, and sighing she dropped it into his palm.

"He gets half of what he has been having. Are you listening to me?" Jack said, and Lizbet nodded. "We can't get any more." Then turning to his brother, he said, "And you. If you press Lizbet for this, I'll throw it over the side of this ship. Do you understand?"

Richard nodded.

Jack could hear occasional shuffling footsteps that told him there was a guard outside their cabin. Done with pacing, unable to see much from the tiny window, he gave up and let the *Santa Fe* rock him to sleep. He was woken when the ship lurched. There was a creaking groan that seemed to run through the very core of the ship and then, leaning, the wind took her. The *Santa Fe* had been rowed from her berth by the galley slaves, now the canvas had been unfurled and the wind had caught the sheets, pulling her south.

Soon after this, the cabin door opened. He was collected by one of Brother Emilio's men whom he recognised, and escorted onto the deck.

The ship was fast, the crew experienced and skilled. When he asked, he was told it would take them only six days to sail the length of Italy, then another four to round the coastline and head past the Island of Sicily. From there it was a short journey to the rocky isle where the Knights had retreated to after their loss of Rhodes. There was always the danger of running into Turkish ships so they would sail close to land, the gleaming coastline of Italy remaining on their right hand side.

The *Santa Fe* was a military ship, and although Jack had never served in a standing army, he could not help but admire the brisk precision of the well trained men on board. Initially, he had not seen the connection between them. Some were on the decks working with ropes and ratchets, others sat astride the mast beams, others clung to the polished wood by their feet alone, leaving their hands free to work the ropes securing the canvas sails. The more he watched, the more he became aware that their actions were coordinated. An order to set the sails had a series of men all over the ship working in unison, often without being able to see each other. All striving towards a single task, a task that had to be timed precisely, with all their actions executed together, otherwise one side of a canvas sail would flap down while the other remained taut in its lashings.

Jack, standing alone with his thoughts, hands on the rail, did not initially hear Emilio approach.

"My men are to begin practice. I thought you might enjoy watching."

As Jack watched, a small area was roped off on the deck, and the *Santa Fe*'s shifting deck brought a whole new aspect to their arms training.

Jack looked on with interest. He was an admirer of skill, and of practice, keenly aware of the tight bond between the two. Often men spoke of talent. Talent was a concept he had mused on at length on occasion. He would freely admit he had none; all his skills were earned at the expense of time and practice. There had been no unseen gift of talent bequeathed to him. He'd seen men with a sword, men he would freely admit were better than he was. Was this the blessing of talent? Did that give them that advantage of extra speed? Did that ensure their blade was always set at the right angle? Did it bless them with a second sense to anticipate an opponent's next move? He had never thought so. These men he had seen worked hard, and outside of the melee, he'd seen them in the practice ring. All it had done for him was reinforce his conviction that if he out-practised his opponent, he would be better.

As Jack watched, he found himself becoming an engaged spectator. For an hour, his mind was released from the dread that filled him, of a meeting that was coming that he did not know if he was equal to. He traded comments with Emilio about the skills of the men they watched, and when the training was completed, and he was escorted back to the cabin, he was sad to leave. It had been a welcome release.

†

The next day when he was brought up onto the deck, Emilio invited him to join the men, not just watch them. This was an activity much to Jack's liking. The new game was balance. In the constantly shifting

Mediterranean Sea, the deck beneath his boots dipped and swayed, and when the wind caught the sails fast, the deck seemed to rush away beneath his feet. The weather had roughened the surface of the sea and the deck was slippery with salt water. Jack, soon in bare feet, skidded across the wood, and joined a sword school that was as dangerous as it was entertaining.

When the training was finished, Jack, his hands clasped behind his back, stared moodily over the side rail of the *Santa Fe*. She was still in sight of land and Jack's eyes were fastened on the coastline. He wished the ship would turn in and sail closer to the green line on the horizon that marked the edge of Italy. It was too far to swim at the moment, much too far. Jack would feel a lot more comfortable knowing he could make it to land. If she changed her course and hugged the coastline then he would be able to make the swim should he have to. Jack's preferred method of passage would have been to remain drunk for the entire time, however he'd not seen ale since he'd boarded the ship, and with his brother insensible half the time it didn't seem such a good idea joining him.

Jack's relationship with Emilio settled quickly into one of grudging respect. The man's ability to command the men beneath him was unquestioned. It was obvious that they both feared and respected him in equal share. He was a member of one of the most elite fighting forces in Christendom. Jack saw no reason to underestimate the man's training. Emilio was genuinely good humoured and if occasionally the eyes he laid on him were greedy ones, Jack had stopped caring overly. When Jack caught Emilio watching him at the end of a training bout, the look on the knight's face languidly desirous, Jack just laughed, and after a sorrowful sigh, Emilio joined him.

"How can you stand the man looking at you like that?" Lizbet said, coming to stand near Jack, close enough so her words would not carry. They allowed her out on deck for a few hours each day. Richard though stayed in the cabin. "It's a sin, and him a bloody member of the Order as well!"

Jack regarded Lizbet for a moment before he spoke. "God, I am sure, has little time to worry about Brother Emilio's tastes." Turing his eyes back, he regarded the coastline again. It was growing ever more distant. He'd drown before he got anywhere near it now.

Lizbet could see the look on Jack's face and misread it. "It'll not be your sin to bear. God will not judge you for it."

Jack heard her words but his attention was wholly on the retreating land. Turning his back on Italy and Lizbet, Jack leant on the rail, gazing down at the *Santa Fe*'s three hundred trapped rowers. He normally preferred to keep away from the pit in the middle of the ship where the galeotti lived and laboured. Standing now though, next to Lizbet, his eyes could not avoid gazing upon the backs of the men in the crammed deck beneath him where they lived chained to the benches.

Most were dark skinned Turks, Hospitaller prisoners. On their backs they were branded with the mark of the captive. A few were lighter skinned, and two were fair. God only knew what their crimes had been to send them to a life as a galley slave. Theft, desertion, piracy? It was, Jack mused, in many ways a harsher punishment than a sentence of death. At least an execution brought with it a certain finality to human suffering. The galeotti slaves were chained to their benches until they died, something that might very well take a long time.

When the breeze that drafted the *Santa Fe* shifted slightly, it brought to his nose the rank scent of decay from the deck beneath him. Jack's knuckles whitened on the guard rail. It was a smell that held a memory of Marshalsea. The aroma, ripe with the scene of sweat, urine, faeces, blood and rotten flesh, was an unpleasant reminder.

Christ! Richard, I hope you know what you've done.

Jack could almost feel a pull on his body dragging him towards the pit beneath him.

Brother Emilio joined him, his fine tanned hands resting on the guard rail just that bit too close to Jack's. Used to the attention now, Jack didn't move.

"Why so serious? Surely you do not feel sorry for those wretches?" Emilio ran his fingers across the whitened knuckles of Jack's left hand.

The touch, as unwanted as it was, he tolerated.

"How long do they live?" Jack asked, his eyes still fastened on the backs of the rowers.

Emilio shrugged. "Some, a few weeks, some of them last for months and the unfortunate ones live for years. The strong are at the inner ends of the benches and take the greatest strain, as the oars move the most for them. They have the job of keeping their bench rowing in time. Get it wrong and the oars will catch outside the ship with those in front or behind. Then the wooden shafts will be forced back into the rowing crews' heads. I've seen a man killed by the blow before. So the rower on the end needs to keep the rhythm going. The rowers closest to the hull have the easiest work, and they swap with others on the bench. So a weaker man will be nearer the hull so he does not jeopardise the lives of the other rowers. They are treated better than many prisoners."

Looking down at them, Jack found that hard to believe. They were all practically naked. Even from this distance he could see the sores on the men's feet. In front of each bench fastened to the floor was a raised plank. When the rowers were in action, their bare feet pressed against it, bodies braced, as they drove the oars through the water. Their toes, curled beneath their feet, had their skin ripped off where they pressed against the planking.

Emilio, seeing the expression on Jack's face, continued. "A galley master knows the value of the galeotti. If he weakens them, if he overly punishes them, if he does not feed them, he risks his ship. They govern themselves as well. When a man cannot take his place anymore, they kill him themselves."

"How very reassuring," Jack commented. He could see now that the rowers on the ends of the benches were indeed the biggest, strongest men. Roaming among them, unchained slaves carried water, filling cups held in outstretched hands. The *Santa Fe* rode the waves with her sails today. At the moment the oars were not needed. The men sat, some asleep, heads against the wood of the oars which were locked and lifted clear of the sea. Jack just hoped that he would not be joining them.

†

Lizbet had never given up talking to Richard, not when Jack was present, but when they were alone. If she was lucky, he would reply. Lizbet felt relief then, hoping he was coming back to them. Most of the time, however, he just ignored her.

"I wish he would try and keep this clean." Lizbet held up the doublet she had been rubbing vigorously with water. Inspecting the marks she was trying to remove, she grumbled and set to scrubbing them again. "It's no easy task when all you have is water. I keep telling him he needs to present himself at his best. But when did he ever listen to me?"

Lizbet knew she'd not get a reply, but she'd rather talk to herself than sit in stony silence.

"That'll have to do. When it dries it might look better." Lizbet angled the jacket towards the light from the window and frowned, adding, "Or not." She smoothed it out and hung it on the back of the bench to dry.

"Who is Jack meeting?"

"Lord! You made me jump. I thought you were asleep," Lizbet exclaimed, a hand on her chest.

"I could hardly sleep with you prattling on, could I, woman?" Richard replied.

Lizbet, hearing the croak in his voice, slopped water into a cup and took it to him. His eyes met hers as she held it out and she said, "It's just water." She watched him drink and when he returned the cup to her, she refilled it and gave it him back. Laying back, he wiped the back of his hand across his mouth and closed his eyes. Lizbet was about to leave him when he spoke again.

"Who is Jack meeting?" Richard repeated his question.

Lizbet shook her head. "Where have you been? I sometimes wonder if you hear anything we ever say to you anymore, and now I know you don't."

Richard opened his eyes.

"Do you know where we are?" Lizbet's stern voice enquired.

The look on his face was answer enough.

"We're on a ship bound for Malta. Your foolish brother has taken your place and your name. When we arrive, they are taking him to meet with the Grand Master. Days ago you even told him about de la Sengle. Don't you remember?"

Richard didn't answer, but she could see he was considering her words. Then he asked, "Why was he foolish enough to try and press for the deal on his own? They'll never believe him to be me. He doesn't know enough."

Lizbet was exasperated. "He wasn't foolish. He was taking us home, all of us. We were leaving Venice. He'd given up on you and your plans. Before he could, Gent arrived and the Knights shortly after."

"Gent?" Richard sounded confused.

"Yes, Gent. He'd tracked us down in Venice and Jack killed him. He killed him while you were laid on your back on the floor," Lizbet added unnecessarily. "The Knights arrived looking for you and he'd no choice but to assume your name for himself. If not, we'd have had a dead man on our hands and we would be sat in Venetian prison right now." Lizbet sounded cross.

"How long ago was that?" Richard asked. He sounded confused.

"Five days ago." Lizbet said, and then corrected herself. "No, seven days. We spent three days locked in the room in Venice before we boarded the ship and then we have been in here for four days."

Richard, lying on the bed, brought up both of his hands and held them in front of his face. Both were pale, thin and trembling. He closed his eyes and covered his face with them. "I didn't know."

"Well, you do now." Lizbet was still furious. "Not that there's anything you can do about it. If they might not believe him, they would truly laugh at you."

Those words hit him painfully, and she saw him flinch. Lizbet's eyes narrowed. She was not about to let him go. Fastening a small hand around one of his thin wrists, she made to pry it from his face. "Look at me."

Richard tried to wrench her hand away from his wrist.

Lizbet laughed at him. "Once you'd have had me on the floor over there by the wall, but not now." Violently, she tore his hand from his face and found herself looking straight into his dark eyes. What she saw there stabbed at her heart. "I'm sorry." Lizbet let go of his wrist. Sliding an arm beneath his shoulders and another behind his neck, she drew him into a careful embrace. Her head near his ear, she told him over and over the words she hoped he needed to hear, and she didn't stop until the ragged breathing of the man in her arms had lessened.

Chapter 11

A Unlikely Ally

Jack spent as much time as he could on deck, away from the confines of the cabin and the company of his brother. His presence on deck, amongst Emilio's men, was on the whole, welcomed.

Jack, hands on his knees, breathed heavily. He'd won the match, wrong footing the man who now sat on the floor in front of him. Jack extended an arm, pulling him back to his feet. "That was unlucky," he said clapping him on the shoulder.

"That was not bad luck," Emilio announced, coming to stand between them. Then to the other man, "Estrado, you are a clumsy oaf. If you let English here beat you, think what the Turks will do to you."

Jack looked hurt, Emilio grinned. "You have been taught well. But…"

" …But what?" Jack pressed, when Emilio paused.

Emilio sighed. "It may be different in England."

"It's not different, and you know it," replied Jack hotly. "Tell me?"

"You wrong-foot yourself constantly." He kicked Jack's left boot. "This foot is too far back, you've not enough weight over it. When you want to press forward you've not as much power behind the move as you could have."

Jack's brow creased. "Yes, but it's a compromise. If I need to go back then I'm balanced right."

Emilio shrugged. "As I said, maybe in England you have different ways."

"Anything else?" Jack pressed.

"Your grip is too far forward. You never take the time to vary it to suit the strokes," Emilio supplied, matter of fact.

"I do change my grip, you're not watching closely enough," Jack replied defensively.

"Perhaps," Emilio conceded.

"Is that everything?" Jack said, his blue eyes bright.

"Yes, yes," Emilio said, nodding, "apart from the angle you hold your blade when you attack."

Jack's eyes widened, the final slight was too much for him to ignore. He missed the fact that Emilio was grinning at him.

Emilio laughed and slapped him hard on the back. "It is too easy to raise your temper, Richard. And that truly is a fault. You have an admirable skill, but come and let me show you that if you place your back foot further forward it will give you a greater advantage."

Emilio selected two of the training swords, tossing one towards Jack. Then he ducked inside the ring, much to the delight of Emilio's men. Jack was utterly surprised when he found himself facing a man whose skill had a polish well beyond his own.

Sweating in the heat of the morning, both men were breathing heavily by the end of the bout. Emilio summoned one of his men to bring them water.

Jack emptied the cup quickly, holding it out for a refill. "Your skill is enviable."

"And so it should be," Emilio replied, accepting the compliment.

"Why do you say that?" Jack asked, confused.

"I was taught by the best. My father is brother to the Holy Roman Emperor, Charles V," Emilio supplied, as if this was explanation enough.

Jack didn't reply, but he knew the look on his face was one of open disbelief.

"You seem surprised? The Knights of the Order are drawn from the greatest families in Europe. De la Sengle himself is related, through his mother, to the royal house of Valois." Emilio sat down on the steps of the ladder leading up to the next deck.

"I would not have expected a man of your birth to be guarding a store house in Venice." Jack immediately regretted his words when he saw the Italian's face darken.

"I know, it is a constant annoyance. The Order expects proof of your skill many times over before they will recognise you with any advancement. It is even harder for me. I have to prove myself twice over, just to avoid any suspicion that my advancement is owed to my parentage," Emilio replied sourly.

Jack leant against the wooden panelling next to him. "Often our families are responsible for shaping more of our lives than they could ever know."

Emilio looked up at that. "Ah, so you are a man with secret troubles as well then?"

"Maybe," Jack conceded.

Jack was wearing nothing but a linen shirt. The cuffs, pushed back for the sword play, showed his scarred wrists. Emilio's hand reached across, his eyes on Jack's, tugging the material down to cover the rucked skin. "Those are the brands from shackles. I'd be careful who sees them." Emilio's hand ran lightly down the back of Jack's, his mouth twitched into a smile and his eyes locking with Jack's, he said, "Dine with me tonight."

Jack, hesitating for a moment only, gave Emilio a slight bow. "That would be a pleasure."

Jack watched Emilio leave to go below deck, suddenly very conscious of the scars on his wrists. His eyes travelled up the ladders and there they locked with a familiar pair of brown ones regarding him quizzically, Lizbet. Next to her, watching him carefully as well, was his brother.

✝

When Lizbet helped Richard back to the cabin, he sank into a chair at the table. His stomach felt as if it has been filled with acid and it burnt from within him.

Lizbet, standing back, hands on hips, regarded him seriously. "I'd like to tell you that you have looked worse."

It was warm in the cabin, stiflingly so, but he still felt so cold. The tremors began, sweat beading on his forehead. Richard wrapped his arms around himself to still his body, but it was of little good.

An hour later Jack arrived back, and agitated, he paced the room.

"What's the matter with you?" Lizbet asked.

"Emilio. He's invited me to join them for dinner," Jack supplied, stopping his pacing and staring from the window.

"Lucky you, at least one of us will get some good food tonight," Lizbet replied sarcastically. The food that had been delivered to them so far was basic at best.

"A high price to pay for a night in the company of Emilio and the rest of them," Jack grumbled.

Lizbet crossed the room and squeezed his arm. "School your thoughts, it will be fine." Then she added grinning, "Brother Emilio likes you well enough. If you don't come back tonight I will assume you have found a better bed to sleep in." Lizbet nudged him with her elbow, laughing.

Jack shot her a dark look. "Hush, woman. I can't offend him, can I?"

A serious look descended on her face. "Just be careful what you say."

†

When he was escorted to Emilio's cabin later that night, Jack was not sure what would be on the other side of the door waiting for him. His worst fear had been a dinner with Emilio and the other senior Knights onboard. His relief was palpable when the door opened and he found the cabin was empty apart from Emilio.

"Sit." Emilio indicated a chair opposite set near the table. "There is no need to look nervous."

Jack dropped into the chair. "A formal dinner was not something I was looking forward to."

Emilio looked delighted. "Good, then formal it will not be." Emilio already had a glass of wine before him. There was a servant standing at the end of the table. Emilio waved at him without shifting his eyes from Jack, a glass was filled and silently placed in front of Jack. When the servant had completed his task, Emilio spoke to him in rapid Italian. A moment later they were alone.

"I would wager you've not often been beaten in the ring with a sword," Emilio enquired once the door was closed, his fingers idly twisting the stem of the wine glass.

Jack inclined his head. "Not often."

"I can believe it. With your talent and my sword master's tuition you would have been…" Emilio paused for a moment, "an interesting opponent."

"And I'm not at the moment?" Jack said a little too quickly.

" Oh, you're interesting." Emilio grinned. "But a little tuition and you would be marked amongst the best."

Jack was silent; it was praise he had not expected.

Emilio laughed. "I didn't even want to learn to wield a sword. It was forced upon me by my father. You are lucky."

"Lucky," Jack echoed, confused.

"You had to learn your lessons well. I had to excel. If I didn't, I got a whipping," Emilio stated bluntly. Jack had already drained his glass and Emilio, leaning forward, refilled it.

"It has served you well," Jack replied. "You are amongst the best I have ever seen."

"You think?" Emilio replied, sounding unimpressed by Jack's praise.

"Yes, you are formidable with a blade," Jack replied, honestly.

"It is something, I suppose," Emilio said, then leaning forward, added, "and you are one of the few I have ever heard admit it."

Jack's face was serious. "You have a skill with a sword the like of which I've never seen."

"Practice, that is the price of it," Emilio admitted. "It has brought me here, and hopefully I can use it to make my way higher up in the Order. The Order is my family now." Then changing the subject, he added, "And you, where do you want to be?"

Confusion clouded Jack's face. Then he said badly, "I hadn't really thought about it."

Emilio placed his wine glass down squarely on the table in front of him and observed Jack carefully. "I find that hard to believe." Then, when Jack did not answer him, he continued, "You are travelling to Malta to meet with the leader of the most powerful military order in the Christian world. It seems strange for you not to have considered it. When I first went to Malta it was a matter of great moment in my life. I made a pilgrimage to where St Paul was shipwrecked. It is that saint who guides my life within the Order."

"You have no regrets?" Jack asked, trying to change the course of the conversation.

"Regrets? Not any more," Emilio provided. "My brother will take the titles and the land and have the ear of the Pope. If I had stayed and joined the Church, I would have just been a tool for my brother to use, like he uses everyone around him. He is neither a likeable man nor a good one. To have his shadow cast across my life was not something I wanted."

"I have a brother like that," Jack said. A vision of Robert, in an alleyway in London, wearing nothing but his shirt drifted into his mind.

Emilio's brow furrowed. "The man who is with you does not look like a threat to anyone."

"I have another brother, in England," Jack said, by way of explanation.

"Ah, and the one who is with you? Why do you travel with him?" Emilio asked conversationally.

"He's my brother." Then when that did not seem to satisfy Emilio, Jack added, "He has been ill."

"I can see that, and I can see why." Emilio said.

Jack could hear the distaste in his voice.

"It's not as it seems," Jack said, defensively.

Emilio inclined his head. "He is your brother, and you are right to defend him."

The conversation paused. Both men sat in silence as servants admitted themselves and food was laid on the table between them. Any qualms Jack had harboured vanished at the sight of it. It had been a very long time since he had seen food like this. The fact must have showed on his face.

"So, if I wish to woo you, then I simply need to use food. I do feel a little disappointed," Emilio said, smiling.

Jack was repressing an impulse to take some of the meat from the serving plate in front of him, but he managed to wait for Emilio to start.

"Richard, you have the look of a starving dog on your face. Here." Emilio, picking up a knife, served several slices of the thick cut meat onto the plate in front of Jack, before taking some himself. Then, waving his knife at Jack. "Eat, please."

Jack needed no further invitation. He might have been a little disconcerted had he known how closely Emilio was watching him. Emilio picked up the wine flagon, refilling Jack's glass when it slipped past the half way mark for a third time.

"So, did your sword master never outline your faults to you?" Emilio ventured after a while.

"He wasn't interested in me," Jack said, spearing another slice of meat from the serving dish and depositing it on his own plate.

"Ah, a poor tutor, the world is too full of men who can't succeed on their own merits, so they teach," Emilio said, sorrowfully. "I had a horse master I could outride by the time I was twelve, yet still he believed he had knowledge to impart to me."

"Oh, it wasn't that." Jack spoke through a mouthful of food. "He was Harry's tutor."

"Harry?" Emilio said absently.

"My cousin, if your brother is your cross then Harry was mine when I was younger." Jack supplied. "His father spent good coin on trying to turn him into something he was not."

"You must know Edward Fitzwarren?" Emilio placed the words with care into the conversation, lightly and with little emphasis.

"He's another cousin." Jack put down his glass again, the attentive Emilio topping it back up.

"He's one of the few English knights to make a name for himself in the Order," Emilio continued.

"What for?" Jack asked, pulling a hunk of bread from a loaf on the table and adding to his plate.

"He's led men against the Turks. An able commander, he is one of de la Sengle's trusted captains," Emilio supplied.

"It's been a long time since I last saw him," Jack provided.

Emilio sat back, his own glass cradled in his hands, watching the man before him carefully. "You will meet him again when we get to Malta, and you will be able to see for yourself if he has changed."

Jack's hand, reaching for the wine glass, stopped in mid air. His face paled, and his eyes, catching Emilio's, looked quickly away.

"You are indeed, as I told you earlier today, easy prey," Emilio said, the words spoken quietly, but edged with a threat.

Jack tried to recover his composure, taking the glass of wine into a tight hold. He refrained, however from saying anything.

Emilio put down his glass and steepled his fingers together, his face thoughtful. "So then, why would you not want to meet Edward Fitzwarren? He's Harry's cousin, and yours also. Maybe you had a childhood disagreement? Perhaps Edward would not remember you? Or then again, perhaps he would?"

Jack swallowed hard, the food before him forgotten.

Emilio tapped the back of his thumb thoughtfully against his chin. "So why would you not want to meet your cousin? Indeed, as he is well placed in the Order, he could, I have no doubt, further your cause. He would be a valuable ally, I would have thought."

Jack dropped his hands to his lap. Both were shaking.

"Unless of course, you are not Richard Fitzwarren."

Jack stared at the table. Taking in a deep breath, he lifted his eyes and found Emilio staring at him intently. The look on the Italian knight's face was no longer friendly.

"Who exactly am I taking to Malta?" Emilio's voice was cold, his dark eyes boring into Jack's blue ones.

Emilio let out a long and impatient breath. "Do I need to make everything so easy for you to understand?"

Jack remained silent.

Emilio leant forward slightly towards Jack. "Tell me who you are. Or I shall have to ask the question of those you are travelling with."

Jack looked at the table, considering his answer. He knew he would need to supply one now, the threat was clear. Squaring his shoulders, his blue eyes met Emilio's. Jack delivered his words bluntly. "I am Jack Fitzwarren, my brother is Richard. And, as you have seen, he is too ill to meet with anyone. So I took his name."

"Jacques Fitzwarren," Emilio repeated the name slowly, laying emphasis on the French pronunciation

Jack nodded.

"So, tell me, your brother, why is it he is so… unwell?"

Jack's mind raced. Why indeed was his brother ill? His eyes met Emilio's searching gaze and he swallowed hard.

"Your brother is a weak man? I can see what he has fallen prey to."

"No, he's not," Jack replied, suddenly, and then, "At least he wasn't."

Emilio refilled first Jack's glass and then his own. "Perhaps I should have been destined for a career in the Church. At least I would have had more experience of the confessional." Picking up his own glass, he motioned for Jack to do the same. "I will draw out the truth, no matter how long it takes."

After an hour Emilio called for a halt in the conversation, sending for more wine. Jack had no idea what would happen now. He felt strangely as if a weight had been removed from his soul now that another man knew his burden. Emilio had made little comment, keeping his words to simple questions.

There was a discreet tap on the door. Emilio rose and returned a moment later, with a full flagon. Dropping back into his chair, a smile wandered back onto his face. "I believe you. And I can understand your situation, your brother is… unwell."

Jack's face raced with confusion again. "I lied to you!"

"It was an expedient lie. In your position I would have probably done the same. Your brother has lost his wits. Let us both pray he recovers them before we get to Malta. We, however, can still be friends, I think."

†

"Where are you taking him?" Lizbet shrieked, hanging onto Richard's arm when two men came to take him from the cabin the following day. Jack was already above them, on deck, with Emilio.

One of them gave her a look of utter distaste, peeled her hand away, and with a brisk push, propelled her back inside. A moment later Lizbet was staring at the closed door.

They led him, between them, to a small room occupied only by Emilio, and lowered him onto a bench. When the door was closed, the Knight, arms folded, regarded him darkly.

"I know who you are. Your brother, I like well enough, I can understand what he has done," Emilio said, levelly. He moved to stand a little closer, looking down upon Richard, who was forced to tip his head back to meet his gaze.

"I know your cousin as well," Emilio continued. "He has made a significant name for himself within the Order. Grand Master de la Sengle relies upon his captains heavily and Edward Fitzwarren is one of his trusted men."

Richard remained silent.

"I would not have you shame him. When you arrive in Malta, it will become known that you are part of his family. Your brother cannot continue to protect you. He is not a man who dissembles well."

Richard dropped his gaze from Emilio's. "I know."

"Good," Emilio said, suddenly, "then we are in agreement."

Emilio's servant arrived, and the Knight left. With voluble distaste for his task, the man attempted to remove filth, lice, matted hair and soiled clothing. Richard did not resist his ministrations, the process taking place without engaging him at all. When the man finished, he left the scissors, knife and mirror on the table.

Cold, lethally pointed, the scissors lay on top of the Florentine mirror where the servant had placed them. A trembling hand reached for them, pushing them away from the silvered glass. Gripping the handle, Richard lifted the mirror. The face that stared at him was not one he recognised.

He put the mirror down with a clatter.

It was not one that could bring them safely from Malta.

The words of the priest rattled around inside his head. Chanting and repeating the penance. "Salutis et innocentum… salvation of the innocents."

Richard felt sick. It wasn't this time a nausea brought about by the opium either. They were going to Malta, all of them were going to that steel isle and the chances were high that none of them would be coming back. He had no idea what they would do with an unmarried woman who was carrying a child – his brother's child.

Christ!

"Salutis et innocentum…"

Richard's head rang painfully with the words.

He needed to get them from Malta as quickly as possible. That they were going there at all was a folly now. Andrew had won. He'd extracted his revenge for the sin he believed Richard had committed. The deaths of the children, of the villagers and of Mat clung to him like a noxious odour. Andrew's words, he was sure, were lies but somewhere a grain had taken hold and cracked open and spread through him until he had to consider that it might be a truth. If Elizabeth and Seymour were lovers, his actions for the last five years had been based on a hollow sham.

It wasn't the last five years that mattered now. It was the next few weeks. He had to save them from Malta, somehow.

When the door was opened to the cabin an hour later, Lizbet stared at him open-mouthed for a moment. He met her gaze and she dropped her eyes quickly. He knew what he'd seen written on her face – hope – and who was he to deny her that?

†

Jack lounged in the shade, watching two of Emilio's men spar on the polished deck. Suddenly there came a cry from aloft, quickly followed by another. Straining his eyes against the harsh sun, he could see the lookout, and the man's outstretched arm pointing towards the horizon. Jack could see nothing but sea. The sun was in that direction and he shielded his eyes against it.

"I can't see a damn thing. What's he shouting?" Jack spoke quickly to Emilio, who also had his eyes fixed on the blue horizon.

"Turkish ships. Two of them," Emilio replied, his voice a pitch higher than normal.

The ship suddenly seemed to erupt around him. There was sudden uproar, feet pounding on the deck. Breathless and excited, Emilio dived past him, bellowing commands to his men.

Jack looked around. Only minutes ago, the *Santa Fe* had been tranquil and quiet. He'd been listening to the sounds of taut canvas, along with the creak of stretched rope, as he'd stared at the disappearing coastline. Now the air resonated with orders, the sound of men running, appearing from below decks, manning their posts around the ship.

Emilio reappeared with his men at his back.

"Two of Dragut's ships. There… can you see them?" He pointed, but Jack could see little against the harsh bright sun.

"I'll believe you," Jack said, still trying to see them. "Just two? Are they coming towards us?"

"Yes, they are coming in fast, side by side. The Captain, he is experienced," Emilio supplied.

"Can we outrun them?" Jack asked.

"Why would we want to? The *Santa Fe* is one of the mightiest ships in our fleet. We do not turn our backs and run from the Turkish dogs." Emilio's voice sounded incredulous.

The two ships were closing on the *Santa Fe*. Jack made to step further towards the rail to get a better view. Emilio, a hand flat against his chest, stopped him abruptly.

"You need to go below," Emilio commanded." We will ensure your safety."

It was then that Jack realised, all of Emilio's men, rather than being deployed on the ship were instead standing close, and Jack realised why.

"I'll not hide behind your swords." Jack pushed Emilio's hand roughly away.

"You cannot fight with us." Emilio sounded aghast, standing now in front of Jack. "I am tasked with bringing you to Malta. Alive."

"Let me stay. Surely you'll not deny me that?" Jack's eyes flashed bright in the sun.

Emilio gave rapid orders. Two of his men moved to flank Jack. He was, it seemed, going to be allowed to remain on deck, and he grinned his thanks to Emilio.

Returning his eyes back to the incoming ships, he saw they had drawn apart, both heading straight for the *Santa Fe*. Their intention was now obvious. Both ships intended to pass close to her, one on her port side, the other to starboard.

"Christ! Are we just going to sit and wait for them?" Jack blurted.

"The Captain has her in hand. He will not bring her within range of the Turkish guns," the man to Jack's right replied.

There was plenty happening on the *Santa Fe*. Commands, which Jack did not understand, were being relayed, men obeying, shinning up the rope ladders, running along the decks, coiling ropes around the bollards. But so far the ship had remained set on its course. In the very near future it would pass between the two Turkish ships and be in range of their guns. The two men stood with him pressed him back so they were out of way of the sailors now all employed on deck.

"Their cannon are already out. Look!" Jack said, pointing. They could see the doors along the side of the Turkish ship off the *Santa Fe*'s port side open, ready.

The raised voices of those in command issued an order which was repeated along the length of the ship. There was a rumble that Jack felt through the soles of his boots, one that made the sweat run cold down his back. The canvas from the topsail was released, blocking the sun. Jack found himself suddenly in the shade. The hemp ropes cracked tight at the bottom and the white canvas bearing the cross of the Knights bellowed and then snapped taut in the wind. The sudden deployment of the sail made the masts creak as the rigging strained against the shackle blocks and chains anchored on the decking.

No one had told him to take hold of anything. Emilio's men were holding on and braced. Moments after the canvas took the wind, it felt as though the *Santa Fe*'s stern was lifted out of the water. The deck beneath Jack rose and he lost his balance, hands flailing wildly as he grabbed hold of the rail facing the galeotti to stay his fall. The wind drove her on and brought her in a sudden move straight into a firing line with the Turkish ship that had been about to run down her port side.

Below him, the ship emitted a fierce drumming. It was the sound of cannon wheels on wood, but sounded more like rumbling thunder, close and guttural and from the bowels of the *Santa Fe*. Jack was still trying to secure a good hold on a guardrail when the first volley of cannon fire left the ship.

The noise was cataclysmic.

"Jesus!" Jack swore. The deck shook from the blasts. The cannon recoiled, the ship dipping heavily against the blast, the firing side rising from the water.

"Hold on, there'll be a second as soon as the guns are lower." The warning came from Emilio, appearing suddenly at his side.

The smoke from the cannons had engulfed one side of the ship. The wind whipped it skywards to smother the deck, the acrid smell of burnt powder already reaching Jack's nose. Emilio was right, and this time Jack was ready. As the ship settled back after being lifted by the recoiling cannon, a second series of blasts rang out.

From where Jack was, he could see nothing through the smoke, and neither could anyone else on the deck. They relied wholly on information relayed from the men clinging to the masts above the smoke layer. There were calls from aloft followed by immediate orders from the Captain. Jack could hear above him the high pitched buzzing noise as rope reeled at speed through the wooden pulley blocks attached to the spars. Instinctively he took a step back but nothing fell through the smoke to the deck. The whirring whine stopped suddenly with a jarring clunk, the sails jolted the *Santa Fe* around, hauling her port side from the first Turkish ship and swinging her starboard side towards the second. Only half of the cannon had the target in their sights.

The first twelve of the *Santa Fe's* starboard guns fired. The recoil through the complaining timbers was less this time, the ship's deck not tilting skyward as much. The *Santa Fe* was still changing course when the second half of the gun deck came in range a moment later, and another volley of cannon balls left the ship. The deck was still shrouded in smoke. All Jack could hear was a steady stream of information relayed from above and the Captain's loud barked replies issued from the rear deck.

"What's happening?" Jack demanded, sliding down the rail towards Emilio.

"They have badly damaged the Turkish ship," Emilio supplied, and as the breeze cleared the smoke, he added, "Look, she is listing to the port side. The other is coming to her aid." Emilio's voice was breathless with excitement. The other Turkish ship was sliding through the blue waters directly behind its stricken sister, intent on turning its guns on the *Santa Fe*.

Emilio exchanged quick words with his second in command, ducked under the barrier and headed across the deck.

"Where's he going?" Jack grasped the soldier's arm, but his hold was briskly shaken off. Whatever liking Emilio had for Jack was one not shared by all his men, it seemed. A moment later he could hear arguing from the deck above their heads, then suddenly the *Santa Fe*'s sails turned to take the wind in full. Jack felt the tug beneath his feet. The *Santa Fe* was turning from the Turkish ships. Within moments she was out of range of the Turkish guns, and they did not give chase, the Turkish ship remaining to defend the listing one.

Emilio returned a moment later, his face serious and his expression dark. Behind him, attended by two of his men, came the Captain. The look on his face was murderous.

Jack straightened, preparing himself for whatever it was that was coming in his direction.

The Captain came to stand in front of Jack, eying him closely, taking in the stained and crumpled linen shirt, the unshaven face, and the grey boots with their frayed stitching.

"You have brought shame on the Order, on myself and on my men." His words betrayed a temper that Jack would rather not see released. "As you are such a precious cargo, you will stay below." Jack could tell that there was much more he wanted to say, but his next words were directed at Emilio. "See to it." With that, he turned on his heel and left them.

Emilio's face was a mirror of the Captains. "Below decks. Now!"

His men, as unhappy as their leader, prodded Jack hastily towards the door and the ladder leading below, and soon Jack was interred inside the stifling cabin with Lizbet and Richard. The key turning on the outside of the door made the final point that they were to stay put.

"What's happened? I thought we were about to sink," Lizbet said, standing quickly.

"We've been attacked by Turkish ships," Jack replied.

"Christ! Are we safe?" Lizbet said, taking a tight hold of Jack's arm.

"Yes, the *Santa Fe*'s guns ripped through one of the ships and the Turks aren't pursuing us. And now the Knights are acting as if we attacked their bloody ship."

An hour later, Emilio appeared briefly at the door. Richard and Lizbet watched the quick exchange before the door was closed again and the key turned on the other side.

"Well? What's he said?" Lizbet demanded.

"It seems we have brought shame on the Order. The Captain has never backed away from a conflict with the Turk, until today. Emilio's orders are that we must be presented to the Grand Master. No risk should be taken during our passage that will lead to us not arriving in Malta," Jack said bleakly. "We are to blame for the *Santa Fe* retreating from the fight. Every man onboard would happily see us beneath the waves for that. The guns hit the Turkish ship, and they could have easily delivered a final blow, but Emilio insisted the Captain follow his orders and they disengaged."

"Bloody hell," Lizbet said. "So are they going to keep us down here until we get to Malta?"

"There are a hundred men outside that door who would like to see you dead right now. So behind this door with Emilio's men guarding the other side is probably the safest place we could be," Jack explained sarcastically.

Chapter 12

A Role for Apate

It had been weeks now since Andrew's first interview with Brother Caron, the Grand Master's aide, The haste with which Andrew and his men had been transported to Malta had given him hope that the reception he would receive would be a favourable one.

After Andrew's brief interview with Brother Franco in Venice, they had been swiftly transferred to a fast caravel, which was about to make the return trip to Malta. Within a week, as the Mediterranean skies had turned an impossible blue, they had sailed into the harbour, past Fort St Angelo, and the construction site that was to be the matching fort on the opposite side of the inlet, Fort St Elmo. If Andrew had expected the name he had used, and the cargo and men he brought with him, to have afforded him some recognition on his arrival, he had been wrong. He had found himself stored, like a letter, waiting the attention of their master. Andrew was left in no doubt about the power and superiority of the Order, and of the Grand Master.

He was given good accommodation in Mdina, but it soon became evident that it was just a comfortable prison. After two days alone, pacing the rooms, he was interviewed by Brother Caron, a Knight of advancing years, who concerned himself with the administration of the Order on Malta, leaving its defence to his younger and more able brothers He had with him a brother acting as silent scribe, fastidiously recording Andrew's answers provided. When Andrew had asked where the rest of his men were, he had been told smoothly that they were billeted in accommodation fitting their rank. Andrew certainly got the feeling that he was supposed to be grateful for his cool, white-walled prison. The rooms gave him a view over a lemon garden and of the rocky expanse of Malta as it sloped towards the glinting sea in the distance.

Andrew's story was a simple one. He had the sense not to deviate from it, nor elaborate upon it. He had the weapons in England, but he carried samples with him and was more than willing to demonstrate their use. He also offered a new method of shot manufacture. He had with him a munitions manufacturer from Antwerp, formerly Head of Ordnance at the Tower in London, who possessed the knowledge to improve the recipe and usage of black powder. He stuck with the original story that he had used in Venice, that he was Richard Fitzwarren.

Andrew's gnawing worry was that his men had turned against him. He had growled at them on the caravel, before they landed, that if they ever wanted to get back off the burning rock that was Malta, then they needed to back him or they would be facing the legendary wrath of the Knights. However, he had not envisaged that he would be parted from them. Separated and locked away, with no idea where they were, or where the cargo he had brought with him had gone, Andrew found it difficult to believe that they seemed to have so little interest in him. Something had gone wrong.

His temper would have snapped had he known that what he offered was already being tested. The men had elected Froggy as their temporary leader. Under his guidance they had provided well-schooled and effective demonstrations of the flintlocks they had brought with them when requested to do so by their captors. Master Scranton had spent hours closeted with the most knowledgeable men the Order had on the subject of black powder, until they were in agreement and could report back that there indeed might be some worth in what the man had to offer. Soon he was working in the powder stores, setting up a workshop outside Mdina's bastion walls, to manufacture his new form of powder.

†

Master Scranton muttered under his breath and Froggy Tate continued to ignore him. Scranton had been set to work to produce his own recipe for black powder. At his disposal were the required ingredients, the quality of which Scranton could not dispute, but he lacked able hands. The quantity he needed to produce to prove the process was large, and Scranton, to his annoyance, was having to work rather than direct. Froggy Tate had some experience with powder, and so he had been drafted in to help, while the other men, Marc and Pierre, remained behind bars in Mdina.

"We'll be here for weeks before we have made enough," Scranton said, a little louder this time.

Froggy, casting a black look towards the little man, unable to ignore him any longer, replied through gritted teeth. "Then the sooner we make it, the sooner we'll be finished."

Scranton, a hand on his aching back, straightened. He glowered in the direction of their guards where they sat relaxed in the shade beneath a stunted pine tree. "If those men worked with us rather than just sitting and idly watching us then we would be finished sooner."

Froggy moved his head closer to Scranton's before he spoke. "They're Knights. They're not going to get their hands dirty doing this. Don't annoy them again. Remember what happened yesterday?"

Scranton opened his mouth to speak, then seeing Froggy's face harden, closed it abruptly. The day before, the disrespectful observations he had cast in the direction of the two Knights acting as their guard had led to a denial of water all through the heat of the afternoon.

Froggy was erecting the wood trestle tables they were to use to produce the powder on. At the end of each day they were sluiced clean of the charcoal dust and left on their sides to dry. The dust got into everything; every fibre of their clothing was coated with the fine black powder. As they ground it up to reduce it to the consistency needed, it made the air thick, the charcoal catching in their throats, making their eyes water and clogging their noses. The Knights posted as guards had wisely positioned themselves away from this hazard. They were working outside of the bastion walls on a patch of naked weathered limestone near the entrance to the catacombs. These had been requisitioned by the Knights for use as their own powder store and inside their black depths were the ingredients and the part-worked powder that Scranton was making.

"Here they come," Scranton remarked, as the two local Maltese he had been allocated to assist him arrived. There was a barrier of language and, Scranton insisted, of intellect. Froggy felt sorry for the two young men. They were trying their best and it was not their fault that they lacked clear instructions. The Maltese had their own language although they knew a little Italian, which was unfortunately more than Scranton did. Scranton issued his instructions in the form of hasty and impatient demonstrations with Froggy attempting to act as his interpreter.

"I'll go and bring up the casks we made yesterday," Froggy said, setting his step towards the entrance to the catacombs.

"Let them do it. I need you to help me with this," Scranton said, as he made a bad job of righting the last of the wooden benches. Then, turning to the two young men, Scranton pointed towards the entrance to the catacombs which lay at the bottom of a steep set of stone steps carved into the limestone. "Go on, get down there and get the jars." Scranton, grumbling, turned his back on them and made his way towards the Knights and the shaded tree where the water was kept. The men continued to watch Scranton's retreating back, blank expressions on their faces.

"Vesetti, vesetti," Froggy provided in Italian from where he knelt behind the table, pulling straight the wooden supporting legs. The two men smiled at Froggy in thanks and disappeared down the steps. No one saw them emerge a few moments later, collecting an oil lamp that had been used at night by the guards, and go back into the powder store.

The stone catacombs contained most of the blast. Scranton and the Knights were under the trees that gave them some protection from the falling stones when a section of the roof was blasted into the sky. Froggy, behind the wooden table, was blown backwards but suffered nothing more than bruises and a temporary loss of hearing. The two Maltese in the catacombs did not fare so well.

†

Shortly after the explosion, a letter arrived on Malta. A letter from Venice, telling the Order that Richard Fitzwarren, who had been delivered by the caravel, was perhaps not who he claimed to be. The Order had rapid communication lines, and Brother Franco's letter had been relayed along the length of Italy by riders. It had then taken the short sea crossing to Malta from Sicily, arriving before the *Santa Fe* and before Jack and Richard.

It had taken only a little investigation to reveal that the seal used on the letter Jack had written was the Fitzwarren seal. Andrew had already confirmed his identity as the son of William Fitzwarren. One of the Order's Langues in Birgu had a knight by the name of Edward Fitzwarren, cousin of the interred Richard. When the Grand Master's aide next questioned Andrew, he was attended by a Knight, who, had

Andrew known it, was looking at him very closely, but not for reasons related to his proposed deal.

†

Brother Caron, the Grand Master's aide, threw his hands up in the air. "I have no idea what is going on. There is a man here, claiming to be Richard Fitzwarren. He clearly isn't, but he has in his possession the flintlocks, or at least some of them. Brother de Bisset has been working closely with his powder expert and feels that there is indeed a process here that we should have control of. However, after the explosion at the powder store, they can do little more as all the supplies were destroyed."

"It is tempting to lay the blame for the loss on these men," Claude de la Sengle, the Order's current Grand Master growled. "But even de Bisett has told me that the fault of this lies with the control Brother Carew exercised over the men working for him. None of them should have been allowed near the powder store with naked flames. The fault of that lies squarely with him."

"It has left us though with poor stocks. More has been brought up from Birgu, but we cannot weaken our defences there overly, so the emphasis needs to be on rebuilding our supplies here at the citadel," Caron said, and then added, "and the cost will be considerable."

"I am aware of the cost. It was an unexpected expense we could have done without. The building program to make this isle a secure base will be a heavy burden on our coffers. But it will be worth it," de la Sengle commented.

"I can sympathise with Brother Carew. This powder expert needed help and Carew was forced to find men to work for him. There are few to spare at the moment, as you well know, so he gave him those whom he could afford to be without. All spare skilled hands are working to complete the fort, to protect the harbour. That was his only fault, that he gave Master Scranton fools. Scranton is an expert of some note, isn't he? Surely, he should have schooled those beneath him with the knowledge they needed to work with powder?"

"Where is this Master Scranton now?" de la Sengle asked, refusing to be drawn into conversation where the only focus was to allocate blame.

"We thought it wise to remove him and his processes from the close proximity of Mdina. He is working with our own powder experts to produce more near St Paul's Island," Caron supplied.

"And the flintlocks?" de la Sengle asked. "They were sent to our armoury. What is the conclusion?"

Caron smiled. At least on this point he had a definitive answer. "They are the missing Italian weapons. We are confident they are from the shipment Monsinetto took to England."

The Grand Master nodded. "And this second man? Also claiming to be Fitzwarren? What do we know?"

"Very little." Caron fished on the desk for the letter, a letter that had made it by land quicker than the *Santa Fe* had sailed around the rugged Italian coastline. "The second man claiming also to be Richard Fitzwarren is, in the words of the controller, on the way here from Venice." He paused while he scanned the letter. "Clothed in the rags of poverty, accompanied by a woman he declared as his sister and another man who is without his wits."

"How long behind this letter will they be?" de la Sengle asked, twisting the earthenware cup in his hand.

"Less than a week, if the winds are in their favour," Brother Caron replied.

"A week," de la Sengle repeated. "I will meet with the man you have here and see what he has to say."

†

Morley's eyes met Cecil's across the desk. Little usually shocked him, however this request was one that he had not seen coming. Mary's lust to prove her devotion to God had moved to a higher level, it seemed. Her new demand was one that even Cecil could not countenance.

Mary now desired that Kate Ashley, currently interred in the Fleet prison, be one of the next to burn for her Protestant beliefs. Even worse, that her sister, Elizabeth, should be present to witness the event. If Mary had been looking to gain attention then this proposal would most certainly obtain it, if not from God then definitely from the City of London.

"The Council are obviously against it. There is popular support for Elizabeth. To parade her in front of the City like this, to make her watch such a spectacle, will gain Mary little support. Indeed it will, if anything, strengthen Elizabeth's position. It is well known that Her Majesty has little liking for her sister and if she subjects her to this ordeal she'll find London will back Elizabeth. Martyring Protestants is not as popular as Mary wishes to believe," Cecil growled. He was agitated, a condition he rarely suffered, however he had received several demands that the Queen's desire be thwarted. If Henry had been stubborn, his daughter was even more so. Her father could be swayed by arguments of reason, but when it came to matters of religion, Mary would tolerate nothing but the exercise of her own will to serve the Lord. The eradication of the scourge of Protestantism was a crusade that she believed God had gifted to her, and there was nothing could deflect her from that path. Until now.

Cecil continued, "Have you found out yet who killed Mistress Haddington?"

For a moment a smile flicked to the corner of Morley's mouth as the obvious answer tumbled in to his brain. The reply that it was Mary who was responsible for Mistress Haddington's demise he quickly buried along with the smile. "I have a man for the crime."

"Well that's a start. We can build around that. Produce something to Her Majesty's liking and it may be that I can persuade her to keep Kate Ashley and Elizabeth's subjugation for the future, should everything not go her way. And Morley! It will go her way this time, do you hear?" Cecil barked across the table.

Morley nodded.

"Find someone else, close to Elizabeth that will satisfy Mary, someone who does not matter to the princess," Cecil commanded.

Morley left the interview shortly after, walking through the corridors. His mind on his current puzzle, he was little aware of his surroundings. Elizabeth was now at court with a small household. He had been pleased to find out that she was attended by none other than Catherine de Bernay. It was not long before his feet took him in her direction.

†

The trepidation Catherine had felt initially when she was forced to move to court with Elizabeth soon left her. The apartments at court afforded to the princess were dire compared to Durham Place, and the Princess was very rarely absent from them. On the few occasions when she had been required to attend court, the excursions had been brief, formal and had required little of Catherine other than for her to stand in silence obediently observing the floor.

Catherine had not seen Morley for months and her heart sank when she recognised him walking towards her. This fact obviously showed plainly on her face and Morley's smile widened.

"So sad? Maybe I am just passing by?" he said, coming up alongside her, gently catching her arm and tucking it into the fold of his own.

"We are, as you might have noticed, somewhat out of the way. Nobody, sir, passes by," Catherine observed coldly.

"A viper's tongue as ever," Morley said quietly as he leant close to her.

Catherine didn't reply but cast a sour sideways glance at him.

Patting her hand, he continued, "As always there is a dilemma. Mistress Ashley is in prison, as you know." Morley paused just long enough for Catherine to be reminded of how Kate had ended up there. "And now it seems that it is our task to keep her safe. After all, we both know how she got there, don't we?"

Catherine stopped abruptly, her arm tugging on Morley's. "How she got there?" Her voice was incredulous.

Morley smiling again, patting her hand. "Tides come in," he said, "and when they go out again, as they always will, they remove all the traces of our footprints in the sand."

"What's that supposed to mean?" Catherine replied hotly, her feet firmly planted on the ground, refusing to take another step forward.

Sighing, Morley pulled her gently to walk on with him. "It means, my dear, that the world is ever changing, and we must change with it."

"Ah, so now you'd rather Mistress Ashley was not in jail," Catherine replied bitingly. "Well, that is your fault. I don't think there's a lot I can do about it."

"You have the ear of Elizabeth I assume?" Morley said, and when Catherine just looked at him he continued, "It's Mary's wish to show the people that she will root out Protestantism, even within her own household. I am sure you heard about Mistress Haddington?"

"No, surely they wouldn't do that to Kate Ashley!" Catherine stumbled, and her face went pale.

"I am afraid so. As I said, you and I are now charged with keeping her safe," Morley said quietly.

"How?"

"Speak to your Mistress, tell her that there's a move to bring such a case against Kate Ashley. Tell her that any member of her household will suffice to take Kate's place," Morley said. "She can keep herself and Kate safe, and she can pass the message back to me through you."

Catherine's eyes were wide. "It's murder."

Morley's head twisted in a grimace. "A harsh word. I was thinking more that it is an expediency. Your mistress, I am sure, will understand."

When Catherine's head was reeling, and she thought the interview was finally over, Morley it seemed had one last question. "And Fitzwarren, have you heard anything from him?"

Catherine answered with a quick shake of her head.

†

At the back of the apartments, a small enclosed garden was available for the Princess and her household. It was poorly kept. The apartments far from the main court were used for minor officials and then only on an irregular basis, so routine maintenance was kept to a minimum. It had been a long while since they had been used for permanent occupation. Elizabeth, a book in her lap and with Alice Mayers sitting sewing next to her, looked up when Catherine's feet crunched on the gravel path.

Elizabeth must have read the look on Catherine's face. Alice found herself swiftly dismissed. This was a conversation that Catherine did not want to have, and her heart was hammering in her chest.

"My Lady, I have been asked to speak with you," Catherine said, and found herself shocked when Elizabeth quickly rose, and taking her hand pulled her down to sit next to her.

"Is it Richard?" Elizabeth said, under her breath.

Catherine quickly shook her head, launching in to her rehearsed speech. "The message is that there's a move to send Mistress Kate to be executed. Your sister wishes to make an example of a member of your household," Catherine's voice faltered, "and you have been asked to find another."

"Who sent the message?"

Catherine's hands clasped in her lap trembled. "I don't know who, my lady. That was just the message I was to pass on. He said he will find me again in a few days."

Elizabeth looked at her closely. "You've never seen him before?"

Catherine shook her head rapidly.

"Tell me again exactly what he said," Elizabeth demanded.

Catherine repeated her words, never straying from the story, never varying it, and knowing that her salvation lay in being the messenger only and not complicit in the crime. Eventually Elizabeth appeared to be satisfied that she had nothing more to gain by her repeated questions, although she kept Catherine close for the remainder of the day.

An hour later a letter was sent to Durham Place requesting the delivery to the apartments of more of her chattels. Catherine was horrified when she saw Lilly Walters arriving, delighted to have been invited to join Elizabeth at court and full of excitement. Elizabeth informed Catherine curtly of her arrival, along with the name she was to pass on when she was approached again.

†

Morley sought Catherine out the day after Lilly arrived, and she quickly supplied him with the servant's name. There was, this time, no conversation, no pleasantries. He simply paused as he passed her in the corridor, asked for the name, and Catherine answered him quietly. A moment later he was striding down the passageway, his boots clicking noisily on the tiles. Catherine walked on unsteadily. She took refuge in an alcove in the corridor. It held a semi-circular alabaster bench and in a niche a statue of a Greek goddess. Catherine, trying to settle her breathing, sat and returned the effigy's blind stare. The statue had one hand held out before it, palm open holding a flower. The figure's other hand was behind her back clutching a dagger. The white unseeing eyes belonged to Apate, the Goddess of deceit. Catherine's stomach convulsed.

A few days later, the Court was full of the news, that yet another member of Elizabeth's personal household had been interred in The Tower. A number of seditious Protestant writings had been found amongst her belongings. There was even a rumour that this particular servant had confessed to hiding her papers in Kate Ashley's private rooms. It was this action that had led to Kate's incarceration in the Fleet Prison, and not her own association with the Protestant cause.

Catherine had been in no doubt where the rumours had come from, sure it would also be the same person who was fanning the flames to ensure they made their way around the Court. Lilly Walters was the sacrifice. Kate Ashley might be in prison, out of reach of Elizabeth, but there was now a significant doubt that the crime for which she was being held was hers. In the face of such doubt, it was inconceivable that she would be dragged from the prison and paraded through London in her shift before being tied to the stake for a public burning.

Morley was indeed feeling quite pleased with himself. Cecil's approval, however, of his recent endeavours had been less than enthusiastic. It seemed the tide had lapped in again and changed the landscape of the political shoreline.

Bartlett Green, an eminent scholar from Oxford and known Protestant reformer, had been watched for months, his correspondence routinely intercepted, opened and read. He was an associate of Christopher Goodman, the exiled Protestant clergyman and outspoken critic of Mary. Like John Knox, Goodman felt Mary to be a double abomination to the natural order, being not only Catholic but also a woman. A supporter of Thomas Wyatt, he had been involved in the failed rebellion. From his refuge in Geneva, he continued to lecture and write articles against Mary's reign. Bartlett Green's recent correspondence, that had brought about his immediate arrest, was a letter to Goodman, in which he stated that the Queen was dead.

It had seemed that Green was involved in a plot against Mary, or at the very least was aware of one. He had been brought to the Tower, but this humble and pious man had not confessed. The lines in his letter were ambiguous, it could easily be interpreted that he was not referring to the current sovereign. The charges of treason had to be dropped. Cecil had known from the outset that treason was not the charge that should have been pursued, but he had not been consulted.

Cecil, however, was not about to let Green go. It would set a dangerous precedent to free such a man, an outspoken Protestant and a known associate of the radical Christopher Goodman. So the focus had changed from treason to his Protestant preaching, examined in Newgate prison by the Abbott of Westminster. As a result, he was condemned to burn at Smithfield.

Mary had been furious when she heard that the initial case against Green had collapsed. His release would have bolstered the supporters of Goodman and also those who had survived Wyatt's failed uprising. Mary wanted the message to be a clear one. Green would not go to the stake alone. He would be accompanied by a fellow clergyman and six other outspoken Protestants, each from a different parish in the City. The planned executions at Smithfield would have far-reaching effects. The names of the condemned and the parishes to which they belonged would be read out, and Mary's message would be clear. London was not a safe haven for the Protestant cause.

Morley's actions had lifted some of the taint of guilt from Kate Ashley. Lilly Walters' execution and Mary's desire to humiliate Elizabeth, for the moment, were put on hold.

†

Overgrown the small garden might be, but Catherine liked it. The ivy climbing the walls, the rose bushes in need of trimming, and the beds bulging with fragrant lavender reminded her of the small garden her mother had kept at Assingham.

At Assingham, there had of course been a kitchen garden with lines of regimented, awkward-looking herbs, all different heights, but to Catherine's young eyes they had not looked as interesting as her mother's small garden, with its rose bushes, rhododendron that produced enormous flowers that dropped to carpet the grass, and purple and pink lavender sprouting against the walls. Catherine could remember collecting all the pale fragile petals to make fragrant water. They had given it little scent, so she had set her sights on her mother's rose bushes, cropping off most of the red flowers to add to her bowl of water. That, she remembered, had earned her a thrashing from her father.

Catherine paused as she walked through the garden, pulling one of the flowers towards her nose. The aroma reminded her of the rose water she had made as a child; the petals had imbued it with a heady scent. She had left it on a step in the garden. When she had been allowed out of her room and gone back to collect it, the water had been spoiled, she remembered. The petals had shrivelled and darkened and dozens of flies, attracted to the sweet scent, had perished and now floated on the surface. The beating her father had given her had not made her cry, but the waste of her mother's flowers made tears course down her face.

Catherine released the flower carefully, and blinked away tears that suddenly sprung to her eyes at the reminder of her mother. Her poor mother, who had done nothing to deserve her fate.

Catherine had more time to herself now than when Richard Fitzwarren had first deposited her in Elizabeth's household. The day to day tasks were performed by Mary's staff, who cleaned and attended to the laundry. Catherine's role was now confined to waiting upon Elizabeth. That Mary regarded Elizabeth as beneath the status of most of her courtiers had become obvious very soon after their arrival. She was afforded no special treatment, and the poor apartments reflected upon her status at Court. They left the confines of the rooms Elizabeth had been allotted as little as possible. Elizabeth had attempted to have her meals brought to her, however her request was ignored, so the solution to their hunger was to attend one of the smaller halls with her ladies for meals. Elizabeth had no special place, and was forced to find herself space amongst the other attending nobles and courtiers. Flanked by her ladies, Elizabeth, her face set like stone, would sit with two on either side and avoid the eyes of everyone in the hall. That she was Henry's daughter and found herself supping with servants did not brighten her humour. Catherine, like her mistress, hated the necessary trips to dine, when the stares of so many would linger upon them, and the faces, when she glanced up, were rarely kind.

Elizabeth might look like she was reading as she sat on the cushion-clad stone bench in the arbour in the garden, but Catherine now knew better. The look on the delicate fine face and the furrowed brow told of a woman deep in thought. The book on her lap was not her focus. The sharp eyes flicked round at the sound of footsteps on the path and her gaze met those of the younger woman's. Without a word she beckoned Catherine over.

Obediently, Catherine curtsied and remained, head bowed, standing in front of the princess.

"Have there been any more messages?" was all Elizabeth said, her eyes locked onto Catherine's face, watchful for lies.

"None, my lady," Catherine replied, both quietly and truthfully.

Elizabeth let out a noisy breath. "Sit next to me."

Dutifully Catherine sat.

"I am trapped, just as you are. Neither of us currently has a certain future."

Catherine wisely remained silent.

"If you hear from Richard Fitzwarren… or his brother, you will tell me immediately."

Catherine nodded.

"He cannot be in England." Elizabeth spoke to herself. Her eyes wandered back to the book in her lap and then after a few moments she seemed to realise that Catherine was still seated close on the bench next to her. "Leave me."

Chapter 13

A Stormy Reception

It was Emilio who unlocked the door, his face bright and excited. "We're here. I have persuaded the Captain to let you all on deck so you can see the majesty of the Order in Malta."

Jack had no idea then how grateful he would be for Brother Emilio's pride in his Order. He followed the Knight up onto the deck, shielding his eyes against the Mediterranean sun as he emerged from the relative darkness. He had been below decks confined with the others since the encounter with the Turkish ships three days ago. It had been three days too long for Jack. Richard was still poor company and Jack's mood was dark.

Jack's first view of Malta was not one he had expected. Sun-bleached and gleaming, the angular limestone walls of the Knight's defences threw the bright light back in his face. The sun flung its rays towards the island, but the sky beyond was bruised with angry storm clouds, darkening the backdrop to that of night. The *Santa Fe* sailed in the bright sunlight of day and towards the safe confines of the harbour.

The opening was a wide one, overlooked by a newly built fortification on the right, scaffolding and builders ladders clinging to the outer walls.

"That's Fort St Elmo." Emilio proudly pointed to the building under construction. "The Grand Master demolished the watchtower on St Elmo's point and now we shall have this great fort. It is laid out as a star, each point making it the perfect defence for the harbour. "

Jack could clearly see the towering limestone walls, smooth and flush. Even though they were still being built, their height already looked unassailable. He'd seen nothing like it in England or even Europe before. It was built with one purpose in mind, and the scale of it made Jack stare at it in wonder.

"The lower bastion walls are all finished and the central fort is nearing completion. It will give us complete control over this entrance." Emilio waved expansively.

Jack had to agree. The guns from the fort could hardly miss anything coming into the harbour. On the opposite promontory was a watchtower.

Emilio saw the direction Jack's eyes were looking, and he continued in his role as guide. "That is Gallows Point," he grinned.

"Is that a threat?" Jack replied dryly.

Emilio laughed and clapped him on the back. "There is just a watchtower there now. Why would we want to do such a thing to you?"

"There is a phrase, isn't there – never trust a knight?" Jack's tone was still flat.

"Surely, that is one is for ladies who court non-chivalric knights. The Order of St John is a Holy Order, we are…"

"Chaste monks?" Jack leant his head close to Emilio's. "You should thank me for keeping you that way."

Emilio smiled, providing an equally quiet reply. "God, in his way, has placed you as a temptation. It is not you who has kept my vows intact."

"Aye, I'll bet." Jack words were laden with sarcasm, but his attention was being drawn by the black backdrop that Malta now wore like mourning weeds haloing her bright white countenance. Jack felt the first breath of wind, heralding a change in the weather. His hands tightened on the rail he held.

God, he hated boats.

At least he was back within swimming distance of the shore again. As he watched, the flat water before the *Santa Fe* crested and rose, as the wind whipped the surface, and in moments the slight breeze had became a forceful wind. Above him he heard shouted orders as the ship's sails felt the first lick of the gales. She was coming into the harbour under oars but the main sails bearing the crest of the Order were lowered. In the breathless summer air, they had not felt the tug of the wind. Suddenly the canvas flapped violently then cracked taut, the wind pulling the *Santa Fe* to her port side.

"That's a bad storm coming in. Do you get them often?" Jack felt the deck dip beneath him as the boat heeled to the pull of the wind.

"Around the feast of Santa Maria, we always have bad storms. Jack, you look worried. We will be docked soon and you can kiss the ground and give praise for a safe passage."

Jack shot him a dark look. "That, I will give praise for."

Moments later his attention was caught by a splatter of water on his face. Turning his head, he looked for the source without realising that it was rain. As they watched, a curtain moved towards them, black, blocking out the vision of the land and in its centre something Jack's eyes could not even believe. A column, a black funnel of water was coursing across the harbour towards them.

The main sail, filled now with the force of the swirling gale, was pulling the ship further round, as the crew on the deck and above him fought to take the sail down. But every rope, every pulley, every chain was taut and fast and the *Santa Fe* continued to lean over to her port side.

The *Santa Fe* heeled even further to the left in an abortive attempt to move from the path of the incoming water-born tornado. Such was the change of course, Jack felt his feet sliding on the deck. Screaming came from the crew, orders relayed now by raised voices.

Jack read panic in their faces, and for once, open uncertainty on Emilio's face.

"What is it?" Jack took hold of his arm in a vice-like grip.

"I don't know." Emilio stared transfixed at the black mistral headed towards the ship.

The wind had arrived with force now and whipped the deck in a gale. Canvas was grabbed by her pull and the *Santa Fe* already in a tight turn was pushed over even further, the starboard side rising out of the water. A bucket cannoned across the deck, narrowly missing Jack and disappearing over the side into the black angry water.

"Christ! It's going to go over!" Jack yelled. The noise around him was enormous. The spout had veered away from the *Santa Fe* and towards the land, but the ship was still caught in her vicious swirling skirts. The wind was driving her mercilessly on, in the direction she wanted to go, but in a turn too tight for her. Masts wearing full canvas were tipped to such an angle, the sailors trying to furl the sheets were now hanging on for their lives, their tasks forgotten.

There was a scream from above. Jack looked up. A sailor, half of his grip hopelessly lost, was holding on with one hand thirty feet above him. There was a second scream as his hand slipped from its precarious hold, ending when he landed with a sickening crunch on the guardrail before rolling over into the sea.

The screams from the galleoti were even louder. The oars on the starboard side were now raised at such an angle, they were no longer held by the locks. Thirty seasoned oak shafts slithered through the sea of flesh, their journey halting when they battered into the portside inner hull. Slaves, chained and captive, clung to the benches. As the angle increased, some lost their hold, swinging on their chains and dislodging others.

A moment later the sea licked at the open doors of the port side gun deck, and the *Santa Fe* was doomed. The water had a hold on her now, and she would not right again. The main mast gave way and ripped a splintering gouge through the deck, collapsing across the stricken ship and bringing with it a tangle of ropes, canvas and men. Like thunder beneath him, Jack could feel the starboard side guns rumbling and then crashing into their counterparts on the port side, further weighing the *Santa Fe* down.

A sailor falling to the steeply angled deck rolled into Emilio, taking the knight straight over the guardrail and into the sea. Jack made a grab for him. Emilio was falling too fast. Jack's hand slithered down his arm until he had hold of nothing. His eyes were not fastened on the startled face of the Knight, but on his chest.

Jesus Christ! He's wearing a bloody cuirass.

Jack took one quick glance over his shoulder, at the chaos on the ruined deck of the *Santa Fe*, then followed Emilio into the sea.

The Knight had landed on his back. For a blessed moment the billowing robe of the Order kept him afloat. Then, as the fibres sucked up the sea, and borne down by the weight of the cuirass and sword, he began to sink helplessly. His mouth opened to scream and salted water, cold, harsh and choking closed his throat.

Emilio's body convulsed, as a knife bit painfully into the flesh covering his ribs. The leather straps holding the metal plate in place were slashed and the cuirass fell away. It was a firm and ungentle grip that propelled his head back to the surface. Emilio's starved lungs tried to gulp in air but they met only the water still choking his throat. For a moment he might as well have still been beneath the surface, as his own body forbade him the air he needed. Eyes bulging, his vision closing, his body expelled the water and let in the air, first a little making its way to his lungs, then a little more.

"Come on." Jack's voice was desperate. He had a tight hold on Emilio's shoulder and he was dragging him backwards. A second later Jack's head hit something hard behind him. It was the top half of the mizzen mast which had snapped away and was floating surrounded by the billowing canvas sheets. Emilio wrapped his arms around the wood, his face white with shock and beyond words.

"She's going down. Look." Jack could see the *Santa Fe* behind Emilio. On her side now completely, with the stern already well below the water, as he watched, the prow raised high out of waves. If Richard and Lizbet were on the deck he could not see them.

"Christ! Tell me you can swim." Jack had a hold on Emilio's arm. "The mast is still roped to the ship. She's going to pull this down as well. Get that bloody sheet off you and let go of the mast or you'll be going with her."

Emilio's robe was already sliced through on one side where Jack's knife had cut the cuirass away and with help he pulled it free, leaving him in hose only. Jack's nails bit into his shoulder, and he shouted, "Kick, breathe evenly and if you bloody panic I'll let you go. Do you hear me?"

Emilio didn't answer, but Jack took his shaking nod as acceptance.

All around them was the tangle of rigging and canvas, all carnage now, and lethal traps just beneath the surface ready to snare a leg or arm. The labyrinth writhed on the wind beaten surface. Jack couldn't even see the shore through the rain. It seemed that there was as much water coming down upon them as there was below them. Even the stricken remains of the *Santa Fe* were stolen from view, the cries of those on her ripped away quickly by the elements.

It was a luzzu that found them eventually. A small painted local fishing boat which had also been struggling to make a safe return to port when the storm hit. Emilio was draped over the floating remains of a smashed barrel that had been jettisoned by the sinking *Santa Fe*. Jack had one hand firmly under his arm, holding him up and he was towing them slowly through the water, praying he was not heading out to sea.

The fishermen hauled Emilio up into the boat and he dropped onto the floor of the boat, his head banging heavily off the wooden hull.

The people on the boat were speaking, someone holding out a bladder to him. Jack couldn't understand what the words were, but their intent was clear. The man knelt before him had a face that looked as if it was made from screwed up leather, it was so dark, creased and wrinkled. He poured water from the bladder into his own open palm, drank it, and then quickly poured in more so Jack could see what it was. The bladder was full of water. It was warm, but it was water, and they sensibly wanted him to drink.

Jack nodded and cupped his hands. The man grinned broadly, placing into Jack's hands a wooden cup into which he poured a steady stream of water.

Jack washed the salt out of his mouth then drank quickly. The warm water purged the last of the salt from his mouth and throat and he knew it would, in time, rid him of the pounding in his head. He drained the cup and held it out for more. The second cupful went down just as swiftly as the first. He met the man's eyes and was holding the cup out for another fill when he realised that Emilio was laid out cold on the boat floor.

Scrambling from his seat, shakier than he would have ever liked to admit, Jack dropped to his knees next to the Knight.

On any other day he could have bodily picked him up and shaken him, but after the seas ordeal he could do little other than rock his shoulders. Jack was rewarded with a groan and the relief was palpable that he still lived. He could elicit little else from the Knight and in his own exhausted state was forced to sit back and let the fishermen take them ashore. He tried to ask them if others had escaped from the ship but his enquiries in whatever language he placed them were met with blank expressions and he was forced to give up.

It was dark when the fishing boat reached the rocky Maltese coast. There were shouts from the land and replies from the boat, excited voices, and Jack realised they were the reason. Emilio still lay in a stupor.

Helping hands grasped his arms and steadied him as he clambered over the boat sides and onto the rocking quay. It was a support he needed. On land, his weight back on his feet, he soon realised his legs were not going to support him. Only the grasping hands, holding his arms, prevented him from sinking to his knees.

He couldn't understand the fishermen's their language, but the faces were friendly and the voices equally so. It was now the blackness of night and not of the storm that stole the light from the land. The fisherman had poor torches and used these to light the way from the boat to their huts. Clasping hands helped guide him up the rocky steps. The chattering voices seemed to be aimed at him, although Jack could not understand a word. They held him, guided him, stopped him from tripping and eventually led him through a low stone doorway and into a badly lit room smelling overly of fish.

   The fishermen lived away from their families and the cave, not too distant from their boats, was home. Nets sat in folded heaps, a cooking pot leaked a noxious smell from where it sat on a shallow fire. Jack allowed them to lead him to one of the benches hewn out of the limestone wall and he dropped gratefully onto it and watched as Emilio was carried in and laid carefully on the white dusty floor.

   Jack rubbed his hands with care over his face. His lips were blistered from the salt and his eyes, gritty and watering, could focus on very little in the gloom. They brought him some more water for which he was grateful and then exhaustion claimed him and delivered him to oblivion. His final thoughts were a desperate hope that Richard and Lizbet had freed themselves from the sinking *Santa Fe*.

✝

When he woke, he could hear Emilio's voice shouting.

God! Why did the bloody man have to make such a noise!

The piercing sound seemed to split his skull in two. The pain rattled inside his head. Jack raised his hands to his ears to block the sound. The cooking fire was out, and the cave felt cold. Jack lay on the floor, arms tight around himself, trying to stop the shivers that ran through his body.

"Up, Jack, come on." Emilio's soft Italian voice cut through his mind.

Jack let them help him, and stooping, men on either side of him, he staggered on unsteady feet from the cave and into the hot white light of the Mediterranean sun. His eyes clamped shut as the pain sliced through his head.

"Be careful with him!" Emilio shouted in Italian, as they hefted the unresponsive form of his rescuer onto the back of the cart they used to take catch to the market.

Emilio laid a warm hand on Jack's shoulder. "Soon we will be with my Order. You will be well, Jack."

Jack wanted to tell him there was nothing wrong with him, but he couldn't.

†

The *Santa Fe* served her crew and passengers well, remaining afloat long enough for their rescuers to take them ashore, along with much of her cargo. Richard and Lizbet had made it together into one of the small boats and through the storm to the safety of land. From there they were taken to the island's capital, Mdina.

Riding in the back of the jolting cart, Lizbet and Richard could see the citadel in the centre of the island long before they arrived. Perched high up on hill, the white bastion walls reflected the sun, the fortifications looking formidable. Inside those vertical stone walls was the Order's Grand Master, and soon there would be a meeting that neither of them were looking forward to.

One of Emilio's men, whom Richard recognised, pulled his horse level with the cart.

"Is there any news of my brother?" Richard asked quickly.

"I've heard of your brother's bravery," the Captain replied, slowing his horse for a moment, keeping it level with the cart. "There are men searching the coves. If there is news we shall have it soon. It was a godly act, and we shall pray for his soul."

"I doubt very much if Jack would take any solace from that," Lizbet said, quietly in Richard's ear.

They did not have much longer to worry. A messenger made it to Mdina the next day with the news that the missing Knight, Emilio, was safe, along with his rescuer. Both were bound for the Order's infirmary at Birgu.

Chapter 14
The Reckoning

The men who had brought Richard to Mdina hung back. The Grand Master stood on one side of a makeshift desk and opposite was a man in dusty apparel, sleeves rolled up to his elbows, pointing repeatedly at a diagram laid out between them. Finally there came a break in the conversation. The dusty man, replacing a worn cap on his head, walked away muttering, a plan rolled up and tucked under his arm.

One of the men who had escorted Richard from Venice walked towards the Grand Master. He bowed, and spoke quietly before indicating towards Richard who stood behind him. De la Sengle straightened and cast a dark assessing gaze over Richard, before issuing short orders. As Richard was taken from the room, de la Sengle returned his attention to the table and the curled plans, held down with lumps of dusty limestone, one in each corner.

Richard, obviously dismissed, was taken through Mdina's narrow streets to one of the Order's houses, and there left, under guard, awaiting the Grand Master's pleasure. If he had thought he would find out news of Jack, or Andrew, soon after arriving in Mdina, he was going to be disappointed. Richard waited in quiet solitude until the light was beginning to dim in the sky. Then the door to the spartan room opened and he was beckoned to follow the Knight who was stood on the threshold.

"You have, it seems, a cousin in the Order," the Knight said. "For us the Order must come first, but we do not overlook family ties."

If Richard was confused, it did not show on his face.

"The Fitzwarren name is a respected one on Malta. Your cousin is a serving member of our Order," he continued, reading the expression on Richard's face.

Richard nodded. "It has been a long time since I last met Edward Fitzwarren."

"My name is Brother John. I am a close friend of your cousin. It is ten years, he tells me, since he last saw you," Brother John agreed.

Richard inclined his head, accepting the words, and added, "At least."

"He is posted in Fort St Angelo, but the Grand Master has summoned him here and explained your situation. It seems you have found yourself an unlikely sponsor."

"My situation?" repeated Richard carefully.

Brother John smiled, his eyes holding Richard's for a moment. "I have been told why you are here, and that you are assisting the Order with your ordnance skills and that your ship was wrecked on the journey, leaving you with only what you stand in now." Brother John led him to another room. Opening the door, he moved to one side to admit Richard, closing it behind him leaving the two men alone.

The Knight who had stood before Richard now, was not the Edward Fitzwarren he remember. This was a man hardened by the tough discipline and exacting standards the Order demanded. A scar, a pronounced white line on his tanned skin, ran from the corner of his eye across his cheek bone ending on his jaw. The frame that filled the jack he wore beneath the Order's surplus was a solid muscled one and Richard had no doubt as to the level of the man's skill. The Order's reputation was not based on the size of its ample coffers alone. It was the premier fighting force in Europe and that fact was based on the skill of the Order's members, who came from the elite, drawn from all the ranking houses in Europe.

Edward Fitzwarren didn't smile. He shook his head slightly as his eyes ran over the man stood before him. "Richard Fitzwarren. What a sorry state you appear to be in."

Richard inclined his head and folded his arms before him, and returned Edward's gaze in equal measure. "Times have been better."

"I've seen galley slaves with more meat on them." Edward hitched himself up onto the end of the table. That he was a man at ease with his surroundings and used to the role of command was evident. "My father still writes on occasion. I've heard you were disinherited some years ago, wanted for treason and murder no less."

"Treason can be a crime wiped clean by the passage of time," Richard replied carefully.

Edward grunted. "And murder? Is that a crime that lessens with time as well? How England must have changed since I left."

"That crime lacks a trial, so I'd have to argue it is not one I bear a conviction for," Richard replied coolly.

"Yet!" scoffed Edward, then changed the subject. "You and my brother have a lot in common. He's spent his life avoiding being brought to book for his ways."

Richard met his gaze. "I saw your brother earlier this year."

"Harry!" Edward replied loudly. "I don't suppose he was doing anything that would make our father proud."

The look on Richard's face was answer enough, but he said, "He is little changed."

Edward regarded him for a long moment before he spoke again. "I have been told you have come to Malta to offer some service to the Order, but have somewhat fallen on difficult times on the way." Edward's eyes took in the oversized clothes, the unstitched boots and the spare frame of the man who stood before him. It was a long time since he had seen him. Had he not been told that this was Richard Fitzwarren he would have passed him in the street.

Richard spread his arms wide in acceptance of the words. "It has not been an easy journey."

"And you travel with your bastard brother? I remember him, one of Harry's servants. His birth and bearing make him not fit to break bread with. You keep poor company," Edward spoke scathingly, watching Richard carefully.

"I choose my company well," Richard replied, his tone hard.

"Perhaps, in your poor eyes, but not in the Lord's." Edward delivered the rebuke and continued to stare at Richard. "I don't know if you even know where you are, or who you are going to stand before. I would guess not. As a member of the Order, I have little. But I would not see a Fitzwarren, and a cousin of mine, stand as you do now."

"Your charity is appreciated, and undeserved," Richard replied.

Edward snorted. "Undeserved is right. Shortly you will stand before The Grand Master and make an account of yourself. I'll not help you save your neck, but I'll not have my name tarnished by the sack of shit you look like at the moment. You are my cousin, remember that. It would please me if you would act with humility and reverence before the Grand Master."

Edward pushed himself up from the table and left Richard alone. Richard remembered him well enough from his younger years in England. Edward, older than

Richard by half a score, had been a man when he was still a boy. His Uncle's eldest son, and the heir, it had been a family scandal when he had declared he was to join the Order of the Knights of St John. Richard remembered clearly a heated conversation between his father and his uncle as they planned to try and stop Edward from leaving.

Joining the Order was a commitment for life. It also committed his inheritance as well. His Uncle's estates, lands and property when they finally vested in Edward would be passed into the care of the Order of St John, and his family, his brother Harry and any remaining descendants would be left impoverished. The Order were not known for leniency when it came to enforcing their fiscal policy. Edward had joined anyway and some sort of trust, if Richard remembered rightly, had been concocted to protect Edward's father and his family from any property claims the Order lay upon them. Harry squandered his father's money and his father let him; it would, Richard reflected, have been little loss if the Order had taken it.

He was not alone for long. Within the space of an hour, Edward's own servants had provided him with new clothes that fitted, under strict orders to make him presentable. They did not however treat him well. Edward had left them in no doubt that the man they were to deal with might be related to him, but he had little liking for him. They made clear Edward's dislike with their shoves, jabs and pitiless jeers.

✝

It had been a relief when she had first arrived, but it had been one that was short lived. Assured that she was being found suitable quarters in the citadel, Lizbet had been immediately escorted, upon her arrival, away from the Master. She had fervently hoped that the meeting he was about to have would set her world, and his, back to rights. Lizbet held the simple hope that if Andrew was exposed for what he was, then the Master would be back in charge, and they would be back in the position they had hoped to be. Any misgivings she had about whether Richard was equal to this task, Lizbet had tried not to dwell upon. He had remained withdrawn, but during the journey to Malta he had stopped taking the opium and his senses had returned, even if he was not overly communicative. She had not thought that they would be separated. Lizbet fervently hoped it was not going to be for long.

Mdina was a tight-walled city, high on a rocky hill, surrounded by closely-packed terraces. The bastion walls were enormous, and those that had faced her when she arrived at the citadel seemed unassailable. They had entered through a side arch, a wooden ramp leading up to the gateway, one that could be removed in times of crisis. It was then, travelling through the arch, that Lizbet fully realised how thick the walls actually were. The passage between the outer and inner gates would fit five men lying head to toe, and at the end of it was another huge wooden gate clad with iron panels. It had stood open, but if it was closed she could not see how anyone could make an assault on the two doors and enter Mdina. Looking up in the passageway between the two doors, she had seen the opening above. The defenders, could rain down all manner of objects on the assaulting troops' heads from the safety of the room above.

Soon after she arrived, Lizbet was escorted to a wooden door, large, with a polished marble step. Upon entering, a smiling nun, in the habit of a Benedictine, guided her quietly to a garden that Lizbet could not believe existed inside that small packed city. The noise from the town outside was excluded. The ring of shod hooves on the stone cobbles was banished by the stone walls of the building. The tiny, well-kept garden was peaceful. She was left alone and found a bench in the shade of two elderly lemon trees, the plump yellow fruit weighing down the branches. In the middle of the small garden, a cooling pond with a constant trickle of water from an upturned urn was the only real noise.

Lizbet waited.

And waited.

Expecting Richard's meeting to be over in a few hours, Lizbet had thought she would be soon collected from the care of the Benedictines and not left here. When the heat of the day began to wane, she was beckoned silently from the garden, to follow a short stooped nun into a long cool shaded corridor. The floor, tiled in brown ceramics, led into the house. Lizbet contained her impatience, forcing herself to walk slowly behind the old lady's shuffle. Coming to a door, the elderly nun pressed it open. Stepping into the interior, she tripped on the bottom of the doorframe.

Lizbet's quick grasp at the woman's arm saved her fall. "God love you, woman! You nearly ended up on your backside!" Lizbet exclaimed in her native English, loudly as she wrapped a supporting arm around the woman and pulled her back upright.

The look on the old lady's face was one of stricken horror. Her mouth opened and watery eyes regarded Lizbet with something akin to terror. Feeble hands tried to push away the supporting hold.

A nun, wearing the same black habit and with a white apostolnik on her head, sat at the desk in the room and rose suddenly. "Sister Agatha!" She spoke in soft Italian, and provided another pair of strong hands,

hands that were more acceptable help than Lizbet's, to guide the old woman into a chair.

"I will find out who sent you on this errand," the nun said, letting go of Sister Agatha. A strand of wispy grey hair had escaped the old lady's wimple. Tenderly, the nun smoothed it straight, and tucked the straying hair away again, smiling. "There we go. You sit there while I get you a cup of water."

Lizbet stepped back and watched as the nun held a cup of water to the lips of the aged lady, her Italian was thankfully slow and measured and Lizbet's sharp ears followed her words. The hands that she tried to grasp the cup with were clawed, the nails turned in and the fingers folded and bent back, rendering them practically useless.

"Please, wait with Sister Agatha while I get someone to take her back," the nun said, and in an efficient flurry of black serge, she was gone and Lizbet was left alone with the old lady. Lizbet tried another bright smile, but she could read only uncertainness in the woman's face and still a trace of fear.

Lizbet decided to venture a few words, this time in her halting Italian. "My name is Lizbet. Sorry if I scared you."

The old lady looked around the room as if seeking help, and then biting her lip with her top teeth pushed herself hard against the back of the chair.

Lizbet reverted to English, and took a step forward, her hand out in a gesture of friendship. "Please, don't be afraid."

There was a choked whimper from the lady and at that moment the nun, attended by two younger women, appeared at the doorway.

"Sister Agatha is scared of her own shadow," the nun said, soothingly in Italian. "Your voice, your accent is all too unfamiliar for her." Lizbet did not fully understand her quick Italian and looked confused, and the nun added more slowly, "Sister Agatha may be an old lady, but she has the mind of a child." Then turning back to the elderly lady, she helped to lift her from the chair. "Come on, Agatha, the sisters will take you back to your cell. Find out who sent her."

Lizbet watched as the other two nuns took an arm each, easing the little lady from her chair and guiding her from the room. The nun watched her departure with a grim expression on her face. "Someone has been cruel to poor Agatha."

Lizbet waited and watched while Sister Agatha and her escorts left. The nun quietly closed the door, gesturing to the seat recently vacated by Agatha. Lizbet, hopeful of good news, sat down turning an eager look towards the nun who seated herself at the desk opposite from her.

"It seems you have been left in our care for the moment," the nun said, smiling slightly.

"I am sorry," Lizbet said, shaking her head in halting Italian. "I understand only a little Italian."

The nun sat at the desk looked at her thoughtfully. "You will learn more while you are with us no doubt. I will show you to your room."

"I won't need one," Lizbet said, rising suddenly, a look of panic on her face. "I'm not stopping for very long, just today, I would think."

†

The call of Monsinetto's cargo was too much for the normally patient Grand Master, but with many pressures on his time, it was late evening before he could interview the new arrival to Malta. Richard was shown into a room where the Grand Master was sluicing the dust from his hands into a bowl held by a serving brother. Sat on a chair against the wall was Lizbet, her eyes wide. As he entered, she made to get to her feet, but a command barked at her from the man stood at her side made her sit down heavily again.

De la Sengle took his vows seriously. The food laid at his table was simple, sufficient and not at all flamboyant. The Order could easily afford tableware that would surpass the best the Kings of Europe could lay on any table, but de la Sengle's table was humble. And this austerity showed that de la Sengle represented a power that needed no ostentation to underline its position in the world. The Order of St John needed to woo no one, elicit favours from none of the powerful European houses and sway no great leaders with shows of worldly wealth. De la Sengle's simple pewter plate, the cut bread resting on a wooden board and his earthenware cup were the statement of poverty and a military might that did not need to be proved. De la Sengle was one of the most powerful men in Christendom and Richard knew it. Christian Carter had warned him to take care, and if there was a moment when that advice applied it was now when Richard was stood before the Grand Master.

"I can assure you that your brother has been found safe. He is in our infirmary at Birgu, but he has suffered no lasting injury and he will soon be in Mdina." De la Sengle cast disapproving eyes over Richard. "It seems he is a man of some courage. Brother Emilio owes his life to him after the *Santa Fe* was hit by the storm."

There was relief on Richard's face, a fact noted by de la Sengle. His tone changed abruptly when he delivered the next sentence. "Have you any idea of the shit you are in? What kind of wastrel are you?"

"I am hoping to prove to you that you might have a use for this wastrel," Richard said calmly.

De la Sengle flung the loose drops of water from his hands and took the proffered towel from the serving brother, and passing it back to him dismissed him from the room.

"Two men, both claiming the same name and both claiming the right to trade in stolen arms in as many weeks. You, however, have an advantage."

"How so?" Richard asked, carefully.

"I know that you are in fact Richard Fitzwarren. Your cousin has confirmed as much." De la Sengle sat, leant back in the chair, regarding the man before him. He had already read a communication from Emilio and knew the man before him had been ill, and the signs of it he could see plainly stamped upon his skin.

"Explain your current situation to me," de la Sengle said, and then added slowly, "And I would advise you to use more than a sprinkling of truth." He cast his eyes towards Lizbet, and the threat was clear.

Richard was not afforded a chair, and holding the Grand Master's gaze, he began, keeping his hands behind his back to disguise their slight tremble, that Lizbet, seated behind him, could see only too clearly.

The account, when he was finished, was a more than accurate description of the trials of the last six months along with an honest confession of his own failings. If de la Sengle was surprised by anything he heard, it did not show on his face.

"It seems a punishment has already been meted out for your impudence," de la Sengle said, at length after he had considered the younger man's words. "And you travel with your bastard brother and a woman. I am told she is also one of your father's by-blows." He cast a disparaging look in Lizbet's direction where she sat immobile. "Am I to envisage that this is some kind of charity on your behalf? Or do you collect bastards, sir, like some collect hounds?" de la Sengle's words were not kindly put.

"I could not leave her in England, and I had not intended to bring her this far. However, my circumstances changed, and I could not abandon her," Richard replied.

"From the sound of it, this was quite the reverse. You are perhaps lucky she did not abandon you."

"I owe her a debt," Richard confessed. Still standing, he shifted his weight slightly, the strain of remaining immobile apparent on his face.

"Duty we owe our family, but it should never be a debt," de la Sengle observed coldly.

Richard took the rebuke in silence.

"It seems you are surrounded by family trying to save you. Emilio has also told me of the shame that led your brother to assume your place. He did so, I believe, to shield yourself and your sister. He is a man of some honour, I am told."

"Both of them are here because of my actions. Their fate was not of their making," Richard supplied quietly. "I would ask for an assurance of their safety, if that would not be an impudence."

"It would," de la Sengle replied curtly. "Would it ease your soul if you knew that their fate was no longer tied to yours?"

"It would," Richard conceded.

"Your brother is owed a debt by the Order. He has some knowledge of the powder processes it seems, so he been despatched to work with Master Scranton. Your sister will stay with the Benedictine Order, here in Mdina," de la Sengle supplied, matter of fact.

"Then it remains only for you to mete out your punishment against me," Richard said, his eyes meeting those of the Grand Master.

"That might be so, however that does rather miss the fact that you are privy to a great deal of information regarding Monsinetto's missing arms shipment. The papers that accompanied the man who came to me first to strike a deal confirmed that," de la Sengle replied, turning the conversation back to the cargo he was interested in.

"It is true. They are in London," Richard provided.

"Can you send for them?" de la Sengle asked. "How did you intend to bring them to us?"

"I would have returned to England then arranged a shipment aboard a merchantman. There must be a safe port in Europe where we could have transferred them to one of your ships." Richard said.

De la Sengle rose from his chair. Walking to the door, he opened it. A moment later, a Knight entered carrying some of the flintlocks Richard had brought with him from England. The noise of them being laid on the wooden table made Richard's nerves jump. Beside them, they laid his notes and the mould he had made that could produce countless musketballs in a day. Two more men, finely dressed, entered as well and took seats next to de la Sengle, at ease and casting enquiring looks at Richard. Both were wearing the insignia of the Order and one of them Richard recognised instantly as Edward Fitzwarren, but there was no friendly greeting written on his cousin's face.

"So where shall we begin," de la Sengle said, retaking his seat. The man to his left had taken one of the flintlock pistols from the table and was busy examining the mechanism. Edward Fitzwarren, his feet crossed and arms folded across his chest, leant back in his chair. The eyes that regarded Richard Fitzwarren standing before them were those used to assessing the worth of men.

Richard shifted his weight again, wondering with academic curiosity how long he would be able to remain standing. "What I had to sell was not the flintlocks, but the knowledge and the expertise I brought with me."

"I have heard this already." De la Sengle reached for the notebook, pulling it towards him and flipping it open. "Your writing?"

Richard nodded in acceptance of de la Sengle's words. "I recorded as much as I can of Master Scranton's process plus the results of the tests we carried out with the bombard."

The interview continued relentlessly. Questions followed, discussion ensued. The notes and calculations were assessed by the three men, whose skills in the art of the war were amongst the finest the fighting world had ever known. None of them doubted the advantage this could provide. If the firing range of weapons could be increased then this would give the ships in the Order an incredible advantage. They could turn their guns upon the Turks and keep their galleys and men out of firing range.

The questions continued.

Did it diminish accuracy? How many tests had been carried out? Was the powder stable? Did its effectiveness reduce over time? Did the pellets crumble? What storage conditions were needed? How long did the manufacture process take?

Richard answered the questions honestly.

"Did you test this only with the one bombard?" de la Sengle asked. Turning his eyes upon Richard, he frowned as he watched the man stood before him sway on uncertain legs. There was, however, little compassion in his voice. De la Sengle turned to Lizbet, who still sat quietly behind them. "Bring him your chair. I have not finished with him yet and I would rather not have to talk to him laid on the floor at my feet."

Lizbet was up in a moment, the chair in her hand dragging noisily behind her. "Can't you see how unwell he is?" Her voice was loud in the small room. She said to Richard, "Here, the chair is behind you," and with her arm firmly on his, she helped him lower himself onto it. Richard's hands, held clamped behind his back, had gone numb and it was with difficulty that he placed his weight on the chair arm.

"Yes, madam, and we are also aware of the cause of his illness," de la Sengle said, addressing her directly for the first time.

"That was not his fault." Lizbet's temper, contained for hours, as she had listened to Richard's interrogation, snapped. "And it doesn't mean you've the right to treat him like an animal."

Richard tried to reach for her to still her words, but he missed her arm. Lizbet took a pace towards them. "You might be the messengers of God but you act with cruelty."

It was Edward, on de la Sengle's right, who stepped forward and struck her with the back of his hand sharply across the face. Her reaction was immediate and quick, but Richard's was quicker. Leaping out of the chair, he threw his arms around her and stopped her advance.

"Bastards and curs to a man," Lizbet screamed at them, her arms pinioned to her sides by Richard.

"Get her from here!"

The guard at the back of the room took a savage hold on Richard's arm and dragged Lizbet from his grasp, pushing him hard into the chair so that it rocked back as he landed. Lizbet, freed, turned round and her nails gouged three red lines across the man's cheek.

"No!" The shout came from Richard. Rising, he tried to get between her and the guard.

Edward, moving quickly forward, delivered an abrupt kick to the back of Richard's legs and a moment later he was on his knees on the floor.

Lizbet had turned at the sound of his voice. Dropping to the floor, she flung her arms protectively around him. "Leave him be!"

"I said get her out of here," de la Sengle growled.

Lizbet was dragged from Richard and then from the room. All of them could hear her sobbing in the corridor even when the door was closed back in the frame.

On his knees still, Richard spoke. "Show her some kindness, damn you."

De la Sengle ignored his words and continued as if Lizbet had never been in the room. He addressed Richard where he knelt still, one hand palm down on the floor supporting his body. "Did you only test this powder on one piece?"

"Show her some mercy, please," Richard said, ignoring the Grand Master's question.

"How she fares rests very much in your hands, do you not think?" de la Sengle said. His voice bore a hard edge.

"Get up off the bloody floor, and answer the question, damn you," Edward Fitzwarren commanded.

Richard, using the chair as a support, made it back to his feet, and returned to stand and face them, his hands once again behind his back. His face was ashen, his body shaking, but his voice was once more under his control. "We only had one bombard to use. You will have a wide range of ordnance. It had been my hope to demonstrate the powder here, using your guns."

De la Sengle turned to the man on his left. "The powder manufacturer they brought with them, has he produced any more of this yet?" His finger stabbed at the notebook on the table.

"We have removed Master Scranton and his assistant to a more remote location. Powder production is a hazardous process. The method that Fitzwarren has brought to Malta might not be one we can trust. It seemed wise not to risk a second explosion. I have not had a report that he has produced more yet."

De la Sengle looked directly at Richard. "We lost not only the powder your Master Scranton had made in that explosion, but also our own stock for the defence of the citadel." After a lengthy pause he added, "You wish for my gracious wishes and goodwill, Fitzwarren?"

"I do, sir," Richard replied, his eyes holding de la Sengle's intense gaze.

"Mmm... So tell me, what makes you think I should give it? So you have access to all of Monsinetto's cargo? Remind me of what this comprised."

"I believe you are well apprised already of what was included," Richard replied.

"Don't try and play games. Tell me what there is," de la Sengle stated, bluntly.

"There are thirty cases of flintlocks with fifty in each case, five cases of pistols with one hundred in each case, all the weapons matched. Seven cases of crossbows, with thirty in each case. In addition there are ten cases containing two thousand rods for the muskets and one thousand for the pistols. So there are sufficient for each gun plus spares. There are two cases of powder holders, one for each gun plus another two hundred spares. For each flintlock there is a hand mould plus another fifty additional ones. There are three cases with spares for the muskets and flintlocks, with one hundred of each of the moving parts, hammers, frizzens, and triggers and then fifty sets of spares for the muskets. And I wish nothing more for it than the freedom of my men," Richard finished, holding the Grand Master's gaze as he delivered it.

"You have a good memory. And so do the Italians," de la Sengle replied, sarcastically. "What makes you think that they will not take this cargo from you?"

"Simply because no one knows where it is," Richard replied, honestly.

"Everyone, it seems, had an interest in the whereabouts of these arms, and unfortunately for you it has long been assumed that they have found their way into my armouries. So if we accept that you have them, where are they now?" De la Sengle pressed the question.

"I would respectfully ask that I keep that location to myself. It would not take long to bring them into the safe keeping of the Order," Richard replied, guardedly.

"You think I would let you leave here, after your outlandish promises of free weapons? I would wager you would soon disappear," de la Sengle scoffed.

"I would not want you to let me leave without a sizeable escort of your men, to ensure the safe passage of the weapons to your armoury," Richard replied. He stood, ignoring the chair, his hands behind his back, but despite his best efforts, he could feel his balance beginning to evade him.

"You do realise that by standing before me and bartering in stolen goods you are willing to wager your life?" de la Sengle said, observing him quietly over the rim of a cup he had just taken from the table. "So perhaps not only impudent, but a fool as well."

"I would try to change your mind," Richard said. "I have also a group of men. I am sure they are in your keeping. They are well trained in using these weapons. They can train your men and share their skills."

"These were your men. Now another claims their leadership," de la Sengle said, closely watching him. "Perhaps we have already tested them. You do not have much of a bargain to strike."

"The bargain I wish to strike is a cheap one for the Order. The arms, all the knowledge I can offer, in exchange for the freedom of my brother and sister."

De la Sengle dropped back in his chair, tapping his fingers on the arm for a moment, before he answered. "That all depends on whether we judge if you have, or have not something to trade with."

"I will share as much knowledge as I have with you," Richard said. His voice was quiet now and was edged with tiredness.

De la Sengle leant forward and flipped the notebook closed. "We have your notes, we have your expert. The question that remains, at the moment, is whether indeed we need you?"

"I wish only, sir …"

"To trade in stolen goods," de la Sengle cut in.

"I'd argue that they are not stolen," Richard replied, quickly.

"Hah, well I think with some certainty that they do not belong to you. Is this impudence all of your own unfortunate making?" de la Sengle asked.

"The impudence is of my own making," Richard said, levelly.

De la Sengle nodded. "You have a very short span of time, so make good use of it. I want to know where these arms are. I suggest you tell me exactly where they are, and how they managed to disappear for nearly three years."

"Sir, I will gladly give them to you, but I ask only…"

"You are in no position to ask for anything. We have your brother, your sister and your men. Before you leave this room, you will answer the Grand Master's questions," Edward Fitzwarren said, his voice threatening.

It took another hour of close questions before Claude de la Sengle was satisfied he knew as much as he was likely to ever know from Richard Fitzwarren. By the end of the interview it was plainly obvious that the other man laying a claim to the Fitzwarren name was of little use to them.

Richard finally found himself dismissed, and in silence they led him from the room, down the narrow hall and into the blinding white light in the narrow Mdina street outside. The interview had run through the night and the morning sun was now cresting the hill behind Mdina. He was taken for another interview with Brother Rodrigo, the order's Ordnance expert. Suffering another three hours of questions, it was midday before they were finished with him.

The heat in the room had been tolerable, but outside it was as if he was warmed by a fire from all sides at once. With the sun blazing down from overhead, ridding the streets of shadows, the island's inhabitants had long since taken shelter from the hot rays, dozing until the worst of the summer heat had passed. Wordlessly he was shown into another room, where the walls, bare of plaster, were cream limestone, cool to the touch. The only furniture a bed, a small worn altar, and on the wall, painted on cracked wood, a picture of the Madonna.

The door closed. There was a keyhole. Richard didn't hear the lock turning, but he had more sense than to try the door. He had been told to wait, and wait he would. He was housed comfortably, that he could not dispute, and his welfare was obviously of some concern as he was allocated a serving brother whose permanent home was usually the infirmary in Birgu.

Brother Augustus had introduced himself sourly, his dislike for his task evident in both his speech and his manner. Richard attempted to refuse Brother Augustus's examination, and found himself moments later, pinned to the wall by two of the physician's assistants. The incident left him with bruised ribs and a split lip. He was forced to undergo a dispassionate review and answer Augustus's searching questions. The experience taught him that there was little point in resisting and that compliance with the elderly man's wishes and requests was a less painful route. Augustus, who never smiled, remained in Mdina, with the sole purpose of restoring the health of his unwilling patient.

Chapter 15
Trial by Lawyer

Within a week, Robert had the papers he had demanded Clement produce for him. The document, Clement assured him, would give him authority over any of his father's stewards and retainers. And importantly, access to his property and control of the rents and dues. It seemed the only thing that Robert could not do was dispose of any of his father's lands. The last point had come as a blow to Robert. The house in London and the Sussex Manor Robert had every intention of keeping, but William Fitzwarren had acquired wealthy tracts of land from Henry VIII after the dissolution, when he had paid a low price for them. Although they provided a good income, he planned to sell them off and use the money for his own purposes. Robert had never even laid eyes on the land, and had little interest in his father's investments.

Robert currently received a stipend from his father. In addition, he had been granted a manor of his own near Chichester when he reached his majority. However he never visited, deeming it too lowly a place for his accommodation, preferring his father's manor in Sussex, or when in London, his Town House. William had given the Chichester manor into the keeping of one of his stewards, the lands were rented out and the property maintained with a minimum of staff. The income from this Robert received, but his eyes were now on his father's title and all the money that went with it. The London and Sussex houses, plus the money from the sale of the monastic parcels, would supply Robert with full coffers and sufficient money to allow him to do as he pleased. Or so he thought.

☦

William knew why he was in the room as soon as he walked through the door. The sheaf of lawyer's papers in his hand and the evil smile on his son's face told him of Robert's excited anticipation.

"I want you to read these, old man. I want you to know what you are about to lose." Robert strode across the room and put the papers on William's lap.

"I have no need to read them," William said, his voice surprisingly steady and his temper in check. "You give me no choice. Know this, Robert, that what really saddens me is that you have not the wit to do anything with it."

In a quick movement, Robert retrieved the papers from William's lap, slapping his father hard across the face with them. "Old man, remember who you are talking to."

William's temper snapped. "You owe everything you have to chance! To a mistake! To my mistake. Oh yes, I recognise my folly now."

Robert's eyes widened. "How can you say that! I've met that cur you threw from your door, remember that. Richard and that dog tried to murder me in the street, that's the kind of men they are. Gutter shit."

"Better gutter shit than what you have become," William replied, his temper flaring and the skin on his face colouring to a mottled red.

"What have I become? Go on, tell me," Robert blazed. "You've tied me to you with the promise of being your heir. But you've never thought to fulfil that, have you? You keep me on a tight leash, old man, and that is about to change."

"You'll do nothing with it. At least Jack looks like a man who can handle a blade. Look at you? What are you good for?" William, hands on the chair's arms, he leant forward and spat the words at Robert. The fact that William had met Jack was something that Robert had been unaware of.

Robert held up his hand. "What did you just say?"

William grinned, letting himself back fall back heavily against the chair. "Aye, that you didn't know, did you? I've met him. He's the image of Eleanor. I'd have recognised him as her son anywhere."

"When did you see him? Did he come here?" Robert's mind was seeing his plans fall into tatters around him.

"It appears he's left the country with Richard," William said, satisfaction in his voice. "So you've nothing to fear from that quarter. Give me your papers. I'll sign them. Take what you can from them, while you can."

"What have you done, old man?" Robert growled.

"Nothing. You know Richard well enough. He'll be back and he's got Eleanor's son with him. Ask yourself why he keeps him close," William said, as he began to unroll the papers in his lap.

"He's wanted for treason and both of them are wanted for murder, Richard twice. He'll not grace England's shores again unless he wants to face the rack," Robert said with certainty.

"That might be so," William said, but his tone told Robert that he thought otherwise.

"Sign! Sign!" Robert almost screamed in his face. "You'll not taunt me any more, old man. The next time I see you will be when they nail you in a coffin and may that be very soon."

Robert was shaking with rage as he watched. William, slowly and painfully added his name to the sheets, where the blank lines had been left for his signature. When he had finished, Robert snatched the papers and without another word, stalked from the room.

†

Christian Carter had been surprised when he had received the message, delivered in person from Edwin. Carter knew that if a lord wished for your presence, you did not decline, whatever misgivings you might have regarding the meeting. Christian could think of only one reason why he was being summoned – Richard. It had been six months since Christian had last seen Richard, their last meeting being in the middle of the night in his kitchen. Richard had been battered and filthy and had presented a plan to sell the flintlocks Christian had in his possession to one of the most notorious forces the world had ever known, the Knights of St John. Christian had feared from the beginning that this was a fool's mission. However clever Richard was, trying to broker a deal with a group who saw most European crowned princes as beneath their contempt, was one Christian could never imagine going well.

So it was sooner than William Fitzwarren could have hoped for, that a soberly dressed merchant called at his house, requesting to see the Lord. There was a moment of confusion when Ronan informed Christian that the Master, Robert Fitzwarren, was currently absent. Christian pressed his case, assuring Ronan that it was Lord Fitzwarren who had requested that he visit. He was here to discuss a wine shipment that had just arrived, one that Lord Fitzwarren wished to use to restock his cellars. It was unusual for William to see anyone but his physician, but the issue was finally resolved when Edwin, William's servant, appeared and confirmed that it was the aged lord who wished to speak with Master Carter.

Edwin opened the door and showed Christian into William's downstairs bedroom. The room was overly warm. Outside, the evening was still pleasant, but a fire burnt in the hearth. William saw Christian cast a glance towards it. "I feel the cold. It is the curse of old age." Then to Edwin he said, "Damn you, man, get him a chair."

Edwin picked up one of the heavy high backed chairs and hefting it across the room, he placed it close to his Master.

"Sit, sit," ordered William, when the chair was placed where he wanted it, a gnarled hand pointing towards it.

William observed his visitor closely before he spoke again. The same age as his son, he looked at ease despite the mysterious summons that would have unsettled many men. But then he was one of Richard's friends. Whatever else his son might be, he was no fool, and he was unlikely to choose men who lacked wit to associate with.

"You knew my son, Richard, when you were at University?" William said, at length.

Carter nodded in acceptance of the words. "We shared lodgings when he was at Cambridge."

"And now you are a wine merchant, I hear," William continued.

"Indeed," Carter accepted, but added nothing else. He seemed happy to wait patiently for William to get to the point of the conversation.

"And a man of few words as well, it seems," William said dryly.

"I'd rather not waste them, my Lord. Until I know why you wish to see me I do not know which ones to choose," Carter provided pointedly.

William raised his eyebrows, but chose to ignore Carter's impudence. At the moment he needed something from the man. "I am trying to trace my son."

"I've not seen Richard for quite a while, I am afraid," Carter said, truthfully.

"When did you see him last?" William asked, his nose wrinkling to shift his spectacles closer to his eyes.

"In February," Carter replied.

William, watching him closely, could read nothing on the merchant's face.

"Perhaps you know where he is?" William asked, his eyes not leaving Carter's.

"I am afraid I don't know," Christian said, honestly. "As far as I know he left the country and where he is now I could only guess at."

William regarded the younger man through his spectacles. "You know he is wanted for treason and murder?"

Christian inclined his head slightly. "I had heard that there was a warrant for his arrest, yes."

"Some would say that you do not choose your friends wisely," William commented slowly. "You have a good reputation and a solid business. It surprises me that you would risk it by associating with such a man as my son has become."

"Isn't it said that misfortune tests the sincerity of friendship?" Christian replied, coolly.

"Ah, so you don't believe he has been justly judged then?" William asked, quietly.

"My lord, I have no details of how he came to be branded a traitor. We have known each other a long time. I am proud to count him amongst my friends." Christian supplied the pronouncement dryly.

William settled back in his chair and regarded his visitor closely. "And what sort of man is it then, that you count yourself fortunate to call a friend?"

Carter suddenly seemed wary. "Surely, my Lord, you know your own son?"

"Sons are often not what they seem." William sounded distracted, and there followed a long silence.

Carter spoke quietly, breaking the silence. "If I should hear from him, is there is a message you would like me to deliver?"

William's eyes fluttered open. "Tell them, tell both of them, I want to see them." William's right hand pulled the cord, the bell rang and a moment later Edwin, who must have been on the other side of the door, appeared. "Show Master Carter out, then come back in here and help me to bed."

☦

Mistress Harrington's sufferings might have finally been brought to a quick end, but Morley's it seemed, were just beginning.

"Some fool told her Majesty about it, so now she wants to repeat the process all over again. She is adamant that whoever shot Mistress Harrington has robbed God of his rightful vengeance," Cecil stormed, pushing his glasses back up his nose.

"Someone saved the woman from a last minute of torment, that was all, and all the rest of them suffered at the stake," Morley said, defensively. "You were there. Was that not message enough? Did Mistress Harrington's execution achieve nothing?"

"Well, that act of mercy is about to cost the Protestants dearly. There'll be another pyre to attest to Mary's devotion to the Lord," Cecil replied. "Green has been condemned and Mary has demanded that he be accompanied by members of each of the largest parishes in London and the man who fired the arrow!"

Morley rolled his eyes. "All it serves is to harden the city against her."

Cecil agreed wholeheartedly, however it was not a debate he was about to have at this moment with Morley. "Her Majesty wants another proclamation nailed to the city's gates and doors by the end of the week, detailing those who will be brought to justice for their Protestant perversion."

"A week?" Morley protested. "It took me nearly four weeks to prepare the cases against those who accompanied Mistress Harrington. Obtaining confessions, getting the court paperwork for their judgments takes time."

"Well, this time you have a week. And don't forget Her Majesty would like to feature amongst their number whoever it was who delivered the arrow to Mistress Haddington's neck," Cecil instructed. "She would show the city that her justice will not be subverted. And Morley," Cecil added, staring at him over the frame of his spectacles, "the judgment is secure against Green. Just find these other eight to accompany him to Smithfield."

Cecil slid a folded sheet towards Morley who took it and opened it in a quick movement, his eyes flicking back up to meet Cecil's immediately. It was a list of names, Protestant names.

"Green tied to the stake for his Protestant beliefs and another from each of the larger parishes in London. Hopefully this will appease her Majesty and deliver her message to the city," Cecil supplied, reading the look on Morley's face.

"A week?" Morley repeated quietly.

Cecil nodded and Morley wearily pushed himself from the chair.

"There is much to do if the city is to hear the warning that it is not safe to adhere to the Protestant faith," Cecil said. "Go, you are right. A week is not long."

†

Straight after the burnings, Morley's men had combed the building where the arrow had been fired from and had found little. There were several windows the shot could have been made from, but whoever had been responsible had long since made good their escape. The building was a wheelwright's shop and it had been vacant and locked on the Sunday when the executions took place. A forced wooden door to the rear leading into an enclosed yard, showed how they had gained entrance to the building and this was also the likely direction of escape. The yard was surrounded by a high wall against which were stacked finished wheels, piles of staves, spokes, barrels and crates, affording the escapee an easy route. Once over the other side of the wall, they were in the back streets of London, where they could easily disappear into the filth and sprawl of the poor houses beyond. This was not an affluent area of the city.

It was a hopeless pursuit and Morley knew it. His archer would have to be provided from one of the city's gaols. In the meantime warrants were issued for a number of outspoken citizens whose fate was soon to be shared with that of Green.

Morley applied his usual thorough approach to the task at hand. Any personal dislike for his work did not interfere with the execution of Cecil's orders. Very soon he had an unwitting victim for the shooting, extracted from a London gaol and moved to the less pleasant confines of the Tower.

†

Edwin had been instructed to bring William's lawyer straight into his room the moment he arrived. Edwin was a little perturbed when the lawyer arrived accompanied by no less than three of his staff. William had already sworn Edwin to secrecy regarding the lawyer's visit and Edwin had sense enough to admit them all promptly to the room. He closed the door quickly and stood with his back to it, waiting for orders from his master.

"My lord, you are looking well." Master Luttrell, robed in black, stepped towards where William was sat. Without being asked, he dropped into the seat that Edwin had placed close to William earlier for his visitor. His staff remained quiet and looked towards the floor at their feet.

"Master Luttrell, you are a liar and you know it," William replied, regarding the lawyer over the top of his spectacles.

"We are growing old together. I leave my practice to younger men in my chambers now. I'm here only because you are one of my firm's oldest clients," Luttrell replied.

It was a long time since William had seen his lawyer face to face. He could see that the man's clothes hung on a spare frame. Grey whiskers and tufts of white hair escaping from beneath his cap told of an age that matched William's own. "So you've broken your retirement for me then?"

Luttrell nodded. "It's a pleasure, as always to serve you, my lord."

William sniffed loudly, and leaning forward, said quietly, "What I have to say is for your ears alone."

A moment later and Luttrell's staff were dismissed to wait in the corridor outside the room with Edwin.

"There has been a change in my family circumstances. I wish for you to deal with the legalities of the situation," William pronounced, once the door was closed.

"Of course," Luttrell said. "Please tell me what you want me to do for you, and I can advise."

It was a tale William did not want to repeat and he kept the details to the minimum. But he told Luttrell enough, so that the lawyer knew that Robert was not the heir and that his first born, John Fitzwarren was. William wished to recognise him as such, and the legalities of this he wished Luttrell to deal with. He also confided in his lawyer the details of Robert's attempts to remove his authority and deal with this property on his behalf.

Luttrell was quiet for a few moments, considering the problem that William had set, before he pronounced the words his client wanted to hear. "It will take me only a few days to have these documents drawn up for you. Will you want to retain them yourself once they are executed?"

William shook his head.

Chapter 16
A Truth Revealed

Jack heard the door close along a corridor and propped himself up on one elbow. His stomach grumbling, he hoped the noise was the herald of the arrival of food. The thin soup and unleavened bread they had given him the night before had left him feeling hungrier than before he'd started. The infirmary in Birgu was busier than normal, he was not the only one to have found themselves in the water after the storm.

It was not food.

Jack grinned when he recognised Emilio and pushed himself up on the bed.

"Well, now you are here, you can get me out of this bloody place before I starve to death," Jack said, happily. "Where's Richard?"

Emilio returned his warm smile. "In Mdina, with your sister. He's met with the Grand Master, I believe, and his cousin. I am sure you will see them both soon." Emilio's face clouded. "The *Santa Fe* was a great loss, thirty-eight men lost their lives. If it had not been for you, I would be among them."

"Christ! Thirty-eight?" Jack repeated.

Emilio nodded. "None of the men below decks made an escape. She turned on her side so fast there was no time for them to get out. It was only those on deck who had a chance."

"We were lucky," Jack agreed. "I have you to thank for wanting to show me the forts, otherwise we would all have been below deck as well."

"It was not luck, Jack, it was God's will. He has a purpose for you," Emilio said, gravely.

"Well, his purpose will not be served unless I get some food." Jack swung his feet down from the bed. He was dressed in nothing but a shift. Jack looked directly at Emilio, and when he spoke his voice was quiet and serious. "And my brother, can you take me to him? He might need my help."

"I will ask," Emilio replied.

Jack, however, was not taken to meet his brother. He spent another two days in the infirmary at Birgu before being taken to the capital Mdina. If he had hoped to meet with his brother once he was there he was to be disappointed. He wanted to know how the meeting with de la Sengle had gone, and more than that he wanted to know where Kineer was and the rest of the men he had brought to Malta. Any questions on that score that he asked were not answered. Soon after his arrival in Mdina he met with a member of the Order, Brother Rodrigo, who had asked him some pointed questions about powder production. These he attempted to answer as well as he could. Then it was announced he would be taken to meet with and assist Master Scranton.

✝

Brother Caron had been responsible for interviewing the first man who lay claim to the name Richard Fitzwarren, so it was natural that he should also question the second. It was on the third day in Caron's company that they arrived at a series of questions Richard had no desire to answer.

"Your cousin tells me you were banished from your father's house. Disgraced, after an incident involving Henry's daughter, Elizabeth." Brother Caron repeated the facts he had been told by Edward Fitzwarren. Before him he had his own notes and to his right, one of the Order's novices was acting as his scribe for the interview.

Richard's eyes met those of his interrogator. "I don't think that is of much relevance to the current situation. I will answer any questions about the arms and the powder manufacture that you have."

"Brother Augustus has told me you can be… reluctant. Surely, you do not want me to use the methods he has had to avail himself of, and not for such simple questions?" Brother Caron's threat was quite clear. "Brother Augustus also tells me you are in no condition to resist. He has also kindly asked me not to increase his workload. So please, answer my questions and let me keep my fellow brother happy."

If Richard thought that they would be satisfied with a general description of the event and its subsequent effects upon him then he was wrong. The interview lasted three hours, and at the end of it Richard's head swam. However, the fog of confusion and uncertainty Andrew had cast over a past incident had cleared. Caron's detailed and thorough questioning had made Richard face his past. Under Brother Caron's cold and dispassionate analysis he became aware that what Andrew had suggested was a lie. His mind ran on to the time before Seymour had forced himself upon Elizabeth in the garden: a time of friendship, of shared thoughts and of confidences given and received. To his own shame, he realised the fool he had been, to allow Andrew's doubt to take root and grow.

"…did you hear me?" Caron repeated, his scribe at a temporary halt, looking up as well and staring at the man seated opposite him.

"Sorry, it's been a long afternoon. Please, put the question again," Richard replied, his voice tired.

"No. Perhaps you are right, it has been a long afternoon. We can resume again tomorrow," Caron accepted.

†

The heat was making it hard to breathe. Jack decided that whoever had the idea to make the trip during the day had been mad. Jack hadn't seen his brother since he had arrived in Malta. Richard had remained in Mdina, and it was Emilio was taking him to meet Scranton. They had left Mdina early, on horseback. The journey was a scant six miles, but as Jack was starting to learn, six miles on Malta took the same time as twelve miles anywhere else. The track was a narrow one of pock-marked rock, winding between the poor terraces that were built onto every available scrap of land. The iron-shod hooves of the mount they had given him rang out like the sound from a cracked bell as they clipped the limestone rock.

Most of the time they were forced to ride in single file down the middle of the track. The soft limestone path bore worn ruts from the carts that were dangerous traps for the horse's hooves. Jack saw little to endear him to this rocky isle that the Knights had been gifted. The population, who had to eke out a subsistence living from the poor rocky ground, were no different to those in England, except the quality of the soil and the heat were most certainly against them.

They finally crested the ridge between Mdina and the next valley. Jack, glancing behind him, could not believe how close the citadel still was. On this terrain there was little safe opportunity to raise the horses to more than an occasional brisk trot. Jack was beginning to think walking would have been quicker and more companionable, as they would have at least been able to talk to one another on the journey.

Descending into the next valley there was a brief opportunity for Emilio to draw his horse level with Jack's before the track narrowed again. He had told Jack why, after the incident in the catacombs, that it had been felt wise to relocate Master Scranton some distance from the citadel.

"Your brother looks like a man with much on his mind sometimes," Emilio said conversationally.

Jack considered Emilio's words. "He has lost his purpose, and no longer seems to have any liking for what we're doing."

"This bargain could make him a wealthy man," Emilio pointed out.

"I think if we escape here with our lives I'd be more than happy," Jack replied candidly. "I don't think he cares any more, and if I search my own heart I don't find I care overly either." Jack sounded morose.

Emilio leant his head close to Jack's so only he could hear his words. "You could always gift your wealth that your brother hopes to make for you to the Order. That would be sufficient, I would imagine, to secure you a place amongst our ranks."

Jack turned to look at him squarely. "You would not want an ungodly soul like mine."

"It's wasn't the quality of your soul I was thinking of," replied Emilio, shamelessly.

Jack ignored him, and asked instead, "Where are we headed?"

"That's where we are going." Emilio pointed across the valley to a rocky outcrop on the other side, a little higher up than they currently were.

Jack couldn't see anything. One piece of sun-scorched hillside covered in scrub looked just the same as the next piece. Emilio pressed his horse closer to Jack's until the sweating flanks touched. Then reaching an arm across, placed it around Jack's shoulders, turning him in the direction he was pointing.

Jack, taking his eyes from the rocky valley, looked straight at Emilio. "You really do not miss an opportunity, do you?"

Emilio looked hurt for a moment, then a smile spread across his face and white teeth glinted in the sun. Leaning towards Jack, he said conspiratorially, "You would expect nothing less of me!"

"I should make you confess that you have desires other than those of the Order," Jack said, amused.

"They would take one look at you and forgive me my sin," Emilio said, gravely.

"Really?" Jack said, sounding dubious.

"Well, no. They would cast me from the Order. Then you would never be free of me," Emilio replied, grinning.

"Well, that's a threat I shall heed," Jack replied.

"Or a promise?" Emilio shot back.

Before Jack could reply the path had narrowed and Emilio had pulled his horse back behind Jack's again.

☦

Master Scranton was sullen and unresponsive. The sea voyage had been a longer one that he could ever have anticipated, the weather was too hot, and his near demise when the catacombs had blown up had finally convinced him that whatever this venture was, it had certainly not been a good idea. Master Scranton was homesick. When Andrew Kineer had taken the reins, he had hoped that soon he would be returning to Antwerp, but instead he had found himself incarcerated on a ship, subjected to an inquisition by the Knights and instructed to prove his methods, none of which had been done politely. Scranton was a man who was wishing very much that he had never set his eyes on Richard Fitzwarren. It seemed to him a very long time since he agreed to trade his services across a table in Antwerp.

It was an encounter that Jack was not particularly looking forward to either. Master Scranton had never held Jack in any high regard. Jack also knew that what would have been said about himself and Richard after they had parted ways would have been less than complimentary. Kineer would have done as much as he could to turn them all against them, of that Jack was sure.

Jack heard Master Scranton before he saw him. His shrill voice rang out from above them. Jack gathered his reins, pushing his horse to the front. It stepped carefully up the steep white path towards the terrace where Master Scranton was shouting commands.

Rounding the last corner, Jack found his horse drawing level with a white limestone rubble wall. As the horse stepped further up the hill, Jack rose higher until he could see over the wall. Scranton!

On the other side of the wall, Master Scranton, leaning over a long tray and berating his workman, came into sight as Jack's horse brought him further up the hill. It took another half dozen steps before Scranton became aware of his visitors. Hearing the tap of hooves on stone and the jangle of tack, he turned to find he was staring straight into the unsmiling face of Jack Fitzwarren.

Jack did not remove his eyes from Scranton's, relishing his horrified expression as he dropped from the saddle. Stepping up through the gap in the wall onto the flat terrace where Scranton had his stock in trade laid out, Jack, unsmiling, faced the little man.

"Master Scranton." Jack stood, his arms folded, enjoying the expression on the little man's face.

Scranton opened his mouth to speak, but no words emerged.

"It is so good to see you." Jack smiled maliciously.

Scranton's eyes flicked between Jack and the Knight who had arrived with him.

"Surely you are pleased to see me, whole and well?" Jack said, making Scranton's eyes widen even further.

"Of course, Master Fitzwarren, I am heartened to see you. Andrew did indeed gain the favour of the Knights then on your behalf?" Scranton replied, his voice high pitched and a little shaky.

"Something like that." Jack regarded him with cold crystal blue eyes. "So tell me, Master Scranton, what has been happening since we parted?" Jack crossed the short distance between them and stood close to Scranton. That the proximity made the little man nervous was plain and Jack let him suffer. Refraining from speaking, Jack began to inspect the wooden trays on the trestle tables that Scranton had set up in the shade on the olive trees.

"We've been working here for two weeks. There was some slight incident with the powder…" Master Scranton hesitated. "…and it was felt a more remote location would be suitable."

Jack's eyebrows raised. "I'm not sure if blowing the roof off the catacombs and sending several men to Hell can be really described as a minor incident."

"That was not my fault!" Scranton's voice had gone up in pitch.

Jack held his hand up. "I'm not here to judge, or fight with you, Master Scranton. For once, we are on the same side." Then Jack put the question he very much wanted an answer to. "Andrew, have you seen much of him since you left Mdina?"

Scranton shook his head. "I've not seen him since we arrived on this godforsaken island. I was brought here two weeks ago, and I've been lodging in the village below. Have you seen it? Fishing hovels. I, sir, have been sleeping and eating amongst the fishing nets and pots for two weeks now."

Jack took a comedic step back, grinning. "That's apparent from the smell."

Master Scranton's mouth opened wide, but he shut it again quickly, swallowing the complaint he was about to make.

"We were a little delayed, but I'm here now, Master Scranton. Please take me through everything you have been doing since you arrived." Jack had finished inspecting the tables and wooden constructions around the terrace.

"They gave me idiots to work for me. The powder store in the catacombs was perfectly placed. Why they thought to use exposed oil lamps, I have no idea. If they had taken complete casks in and out then it would have not happened, but the fools opened the casks and decanted the material. It was the dust." Scranton looked at Jack's uncomprehending expression. "The dust. They opened the kegs and the powder dust rose into the air. The exposed oil lamps ignited it. That was the primary explosion and the secondary one of course was when the kegs themselves ignited. We lost four of our own kegs."

"And how many men?" Jack asked coldly.

"There were two of the fools down there. A few more minutes and myself and Master Tate would have been inside as well."

"Tate? Froggy?" Jack said, quickly.

"Aye, the same, and I nearly got blown to kingdom come as well." It was Froggy Tate, dressed in hose, with a grubby grey linen shirt stuck to his sweaty body, emerging from a set of rocky steps behind Scranton.

Jack strode straight past Scranton and flung his arms around the little man, giving him a ferocious hug.

"Get off me, you great lummox." Froggy, grinning, fought free from Jack's tight hold.

Jack had a warm smile on his face, and there was genuine relief in his voice. "It's good to see you, Froggy."

"I am pleased you caught up with us. I'd have thought you would have made it here before now.

We've been up here nearly two weeks. How long have you been on Malta?" Froggy asked. He had a cloth in his hand and wiped it across his sweating forehead.

"My throat's fair parched." Jack's eyes connected with Froggy's. The message that he didn't want to speak more in the present company passed wordlessly between them.

Froggy's eyes flicked between Jack and the Knight who stood close to him, then he said, "If you follow me, I've a flask of something that'll sort that out."

Jack clapped brother Emilio on the arm. "I'll leave you with Scranton. It seems Froggy has better employ for me." And laughing, he followed Froggy between the gnarled olive trees and up a short set of steps carved out of the rock. They emerged a moment later back into the bright sun. Before them was a flat dusty limestone track and on the opposite side, a wide shallow cave offering blissful shade. Inside there were boxes, plate, cups, a water skin and bedding roll. It was obvious that a man was living in here. Froggy saw Jack looking around the small cave.

"Aye well, it was either sleep here or share one of those shacks near the sea with Scranton," Froggy provided by way of explanation for his humble accommodation.

"I can see that would not be a difficult choice." Jack sat on a carved ledge that ran along the side of the cave.

Froggy dropped to sit cross-legged on the floor. He produced a worn-looking earthenware bottle and pulled the stopper out. He didn't take a drink himself but he passed it to Jack.

"What is it?" Jack sniffed experimentally at the contents.

Froggy just shrugged.

Jack took a swig and gagged. Standing, he banged his head off the cave roof. He spat the mouthful out, flinging the bottle back at Froggy and wiping his hand across his mouth.

"That wasn't funny!" Jack said furiously, rubbing gingerly at a cut on his head.

"Oh it was," laughed Froggy, slapping his hand off his leg. "They make it from cactus and olives apparently."

Jack sat again. Reaching for the water skin, he poured some into the cup and rinsed his mouth out. Froggy watched, still amused.

"Well now, how about you tell me what happened since we left you?" Jack asked as he pushed the leather stopper back into the water skin.

The humour left Froggy's face. He cast a quick glance outside before he spoke. "Kineer came back and told us you were a few days behind and that the Master had told him to carry on and that you'd catch us up. We made it to Venice and he went to see someone, came back and said he had instructions from the Master to take the men to Malta and you would meet us here. We arrived here weeks ago. Kineer arranged for us to demonstrate the muskets we had. I had all of them unpacked, and between us all we gave a good account of them."

Jack interrupted. "And where was Andrew during all this?"

"Not with us, he was lodging elsewhere. We've not seen him since we arrived," Froggy said. "After we'd demonstrated the muskets, Scranton was to make his new powder. I was helping him and it was just two days later the catacombs blew up. Before we had time to say a hail Mary, we were bundled up and dumped here."

"The rest of the men? Marc and Pierre?" Jack asked.

"As far as I know they are in Mdina," Froggy supplied, then asked, "What happened after we left?"

"A lot, Froggy. All you need to know is the Master is back, and Andrew Kineer is no longer in charge." Jack hoped he sounded more confident than he felt.

"What happened… it was Kineer, wasn't it?" Froggy said, at length.

"Why do you say that?" Jack asked.

"The lass. She has a shrewder head on her shoulders than we give her credit for. She told me Andrew lied to you. I knew that the wagon that killed poor Mat was left on the flat. There was no way that was going to roll down the hill from where we left it. Then there was the powder store. There was a guard on it, Jack. No one got past it. Except Marc later told me Andrew relieved him for an hour in the afternoon and sent him on an errand. That'd be long enough to take two of those kegs and stow them in the church."

Jack's face was dark. "You have most of it. I know we can count on you."

"And on the rest of the lads. I didn't keep any of that to myself ,you know. They're not stupid, Jack. By the time we got here and you and the Master had not arrived, they all started to see what he was trying to do, especially after Dan did not come back."

"And what was that?" Jack asked, pointedly.

Froggy leaned forward and said, "Take the Master's place. You can't blame us. There wasn't much we could do. It's been like trying to pick our way through a field of shit ever since we got here, especially after Scranton blew the powder store up." Froggy leaned closer to Jack. "They don't like us. Treat us little better than the islanders. For God's sake, I'm living in a bloody cave!"

"I was despatched here to see if Scranton had redeemed himself. The Grand Master wants to find out if there is some truth in what he says he can do. I've not seen Richard since I got here or the rest of the men," Jack admitted.

"So the Master is in Mdina then?" Froggy asked, sounding relieved.

Jack nodded slowly.

Froggy grinned. "He'll have them eating out of his hand soon, you'll see."

There was concern on Jack's face. "I wish I could believe you, Froggy. It wasn't an easy journey."

"It's not been easy for any of us," Froggy said, his face clouding.

"And they've taken Lizbet as well," Jack said, morosely.

"Good God! You brought the lass to Malta as well! What did you do that for?" Froggy gasped.

"We couldn't leave her. Andrew left us with little enough. Anyway she's safe where she is now," Jack said, grinning.

Froggy's face fell. "Go on, where is she?"

"There's a Benedictine Order of Nuns in Mdina," was all Jack said.

Froggy's eyes widened. "Oh I'd like to be a fly on the wall in there!"

Jack couldn't help himself. "I hope for her sake it's not a silent order."

Froggy guffawed with laugher slapping his hand off his thigh. "Well, if it is it won't be any more! Jack, it's good to have you back again," and then he put another question, one he feared he already knew the answer to, "And Dan?"

Jack dropped his eyes to the floor. Without saying anything he pulled the knife he had taken from Gent out of his belt and held it out for Froggy to see. "I took it from Gent in Venice."

Froggy's shoulders slumped, and reaching over, he took the knife into his hand. He met Jack's eyes and asked, "And Gent?"

Jack reached over and reclaimed the blade. "I used Dan's knife."

Froggy's mouth was a thin line. "When he didn't come back I knew Kineer had killed him."

They sat quietly for some time. It was Froggy who broke the silence, asking, "So at the moment our best path off this overheated rock is Master Scranton and his powder expertise?"

Jack nodded. "I think it might be. So I need to make peace with Master Scranton, and make sure he doesn't blow anything else up."

"He's a nervous man, and he's not working well at the moment, Jack. It's taking forever to get this powder made," Froggy said, gloomily.

"We need to get Scranton finished here, and back to Mdina to show the worth of his powder process. The sooner we do that, the better," Jack said, then hands on knees he pushed himself back up. "Right, time to talk with Scranton and find out how long this is going to take."

Master Scranton was in conversation with Emilio. Jack listened for a few minutes before moving in a little closer. The munitions manufacturer was running through a seemingly endless list of complaints.

"I shall have enough made in another few weeks," Scranton provided. "The problem you see is the heat. It is drying everything too fast and it bakes it to brittle cakes. Apart from the fact that this makes it dangerous to handle, we can't form it into pellets."

"But you have found a way around that?" interrupted Jack, a little impatiently. Emilio had listened to enough of Scranton's gripes and left them together.

Scranton's eyes narrowed. The little man's nerve and temper were being sorely tested and Jack's manner was not helping. Jack saw the reaction on the little man's face that his words had produced, and chose his next ones with more care. "Master Scranton." Jack addressed him formally, his mocking tone now absent. "It appears we are in firm agreement that leaving Malta as soon as possible would be a benefit to us all."

The little man looked up at him and then seeing Jack's frank, serious face, he nodded.

"Good, then I suggest that we work together to bring this about as soon as possible," Jack concluded.

"I was telling Brother Emilio but a moment ago…"

Jack interrupted. "The Brother has no working knowledge of powder. I propose you tell me and let me see if we can provide a successful demonstration and get us all out of here. Agreed?" When the munitions manufacturer did not reply, Jack continued, "I can, when occasion demands, Master Scranton, be as capable as my brother. So are we agreed?"

"Agreed," Scranton said, and then as if to add weight to this he added, "Master Fitzwarren."

Jack smiled and clapped Scranton on the arm, making the little man stagger. "Good man, now show me where you are and what progress you have made. Can you see that brother from the Order over there?" Jack nodded to where Emilio, attended by two of his serving men, was enjoying a cool drink beneath a carob tree. "He is sending a full report back to de la Sengle on our progress, so arm me, Master Scranton, with what I need to know."

Jack was heartened to find that his idle brain had retained more than he had thought possible about the process. Richard, who was interested in everything and anything, had been fascinated by how varying production methods could result in the charge sending the projectile much further. Jack recalled he had listened under sufferance, however he was able to ask a few sensible questions, surprising not only himself but Scranton as well.

"There's much left to do. It just takes time and I'm afraid to admit that myself and Master Tate have tried our best, but without skilled hands to aid us, we have many days of work left."

"How many?" Jack asked. From what he could see, there wasn't that much left to do, but Scranton couldn't resist being as bleak as possible.

"At least ten days, maybe more," Scranton said, forlornly.

"I'm advised we have less than a week. De la Sengle wants proof swiftly, I'm afraid," Jack said gravely.

"But without more assistance, Master Fitzwarren, we aren't going to manage," Scranton's high pitch voice complained.

Jack held out his hands. "They may not be skilled hands, Master Scranton, but under your direction they could be useful." Jack made a mental note to make his brother pay dearly for this.

"You'd help?" Scranton blurted, shock on his face.

"If it helps move me closer to Italy, then yes, I am at your disposal," Jack said, seriously.

"Well that would be a help. With both you and Master Tate, we might be able to make some progress." Scranton sounded heartened.

Jack was only wearing a linen shirt and began rolling up his sleeves.

"Surely, sir, if you are to toil for the Master here, you'd be better off without your shirt on?" Brother Emilio called, resting his back against the carob tree and smiling broadly at Jack.

Emilio had spoken in his smooth native Italian and Scranton looked between the pair, confusion on his face. "What's he saying?"

Jack held Scranton's eyes and said quietly, "He's saying we'd better hurry up, the Grand Master is not a patient man."

Jack matched Emilio's smile and replying in Italian said quickly, "Only if Master Scranton here works without his shirt as well?"

Emilio's face twisted in revulsion, and waving a hand at Jack, he said, "If that is your condition, then keep it on!"

Jack worked alongside Scranton and Froggy all afternoon. Master Scranton remained difficult. He complained endlessly and refused to answer any of Jack's questions about how they could speed up production.

"Master Scranton," Jack was finally forced to say, "we just need to complete these tasks as soon as we can and that will hopefully lead us from this island. Does the thought of leaving Malta not please you?"

"I find little to smile about. It's taken nearly three months to arrive here. I've been shot at, nearly killed in my bed, almost blown up and suffered endless insults. I'm regretting very much the folly of ever being a part of your brother's scheme," Master Scranton spat back.

"Well that may be so, but I would keep your regrets close, Master Scranton, for we're now not at our journey's end but at its beginning," Jack advised, wishing very much that Richard was here to handle Scranton.

"Its beginning? What do you mean?" Master Scranton said.

"Your journey is just about to begin. We are on Malta, and now, sir, is your opportunity to show the world what you know. You are surrounded by the Knights of St John and I can, with some certainty, say that at the moment you've probably never been safer," Jack stated, waving in the direction of Emilio and his men.

Master Scranton grunted.

"I can't be held responsible for your earlier error of judgment, if that is what you are thinking. My brother placed a bargain before you, Master Scranton, and we have finally arrived at that point of reckoning. Your journey starts here. Later you are to meet with the Order's head of munitions. I strongly suggest that you make yourself extremely useful."

Scranton took the rebuke silently.

†

Even though they worked in the shade cast by the trees, sheltering them from the worst of the sun's heat, it was still painfully hot. Sweat ran in a constant trickle down Jack's back as he helped to grind the ingredients into a malleable and even paste. The liquid used was urine. When mixed with this, unlike water, it prevented it from drying out so quickly and gave the paste a sticky consistency from which they could make the pellets. Once the paste was formed into even pellets, they were left to dry for another short while and then packed, under Scranton's watchful eye, in earthenware casks which were stored in the shaded caves.

Jack straightened his back and stretched, his muscles complaining from being hunched over the tables all afternoon helping Froggy produce the smooth paste. The once-white linen of his shirt was now blackened with the charcoal and damp with sweat. Jack rubbed the back of his hand across his forehead and delivered another dark smear to his face. The smell from the black powder also transferred itself to him, the acrid smell of strong urine mixed with the noxious odour of sulphur, a sickening aroma that pervaded the whole working area. Emilio had complained bitterly about the smell, relocating himself further away to sit and watch them work.

"How much more do we need?" Jack said, addressing Scranton after he returned from taking another batch of dried pellets to be stored in the earthenware casks.

"Five more to fill, then we will have enough," Scranton said, coming to stand next to Jack. "If they had given me more men, we would have had this finished days ago."

"They did," Froggy said, matter of fact. "If you remember, they blew themselves up."

Scranton scowled at Froggy. "And the blame of that was not mine."

"The poor buggers didn't know what they were doing, did they?" Froggy continued.

"If they gave me idiots to work for me, what can they expect?" Scranton said hotly.

Jack held up his hand. "Please, we've enough problems and I'd rather we completed this task without blowing ourselves up."

Scranton continued to scowl at Froggy but did not say another word. Instead he collected another tray of pellets and made his way back towards the caves.

They worked until the light failed. There was no way they could continue safely after dark. Sensibly, Scranton would not allow a lit torch anywhere near the work area. They left everything where it was, covered in animal skins soaked in more urine to keep everything moist until they returned in the morning.

Scranton made his way down the hillside to rest for the night in one of the fishing shacks on the shoreline, and Jack declared he would stay in the cave with Froggy. Emilio's men had rigged him a hammock between the trees and Jack had to admit that it looked much more comfortable than the dusty cave floor that Froggy had on offer. They passed Emilio's temporary camp on the way back to Froggy's cave.

"Don't come any closer," Emilio said, taking two precautionary steps back as Jack and Froggy approached.

Jack grinned and took a step towards him. "Make your mind up."

"You smell worse than the fires of Hell," Emilio said, his nose wrinkling in distaste.

Jack followed Froggy back to his temporary accommodation, taking with them provisions that has been delivered from the village: coarse bread, an acid cheese and freshly cooked fish.

Chapter 17

An Unexpected Arrival

Jack awoke early having slept well after the previous days exertions, despite the discomfort of the cave and having to use his boots as a pillow. Sitting in the entrance to the dim interior, he pulled on his boots and looked out over the bay. He could see the narrow entrance of water from the sea and the small fishing boats that were already heading out towards the deeper water to cast their nets. On the opposite side of the bay, the rocky island rose again, green tufts of course scrub and stunted carob trees clinging to what little soil they could find.

Jack turned and called back over his shoulder, "Are you coming?"

There was an affirmative grunt from Froggy Tate. Jack sat on the threshold of the cave and waited for him. As he turned back, he saw a scratched picture on the flat stone slab to his right. Raising his hand, he traced over the lines in the stone. It was a rough drawing of a galley. It seemed to sit low in the water, the oars drawn by the slaves showing clearly along the sides of the ship, two high masts rising high above the deck. It was not dissimilar to the *Santa Fe*.

"That's been there a long time," Froggy said, joining him. "They must have been able to see it from here down in the bay."

"The bay doesn't look deep enough," Jack said, observing the shallow tract of water.

"They don't draw much water. As long as it stopped in the centre of the bay down there it would be safe from beaching. And the waters here are so still. Look at it down there. It doesn't even seem to be moving. Have you ever seen the seas around England look like that?" Froggy pushed past Jack, emerging into the light of the new day.

"I've seen rougher lakes in England than that," agreed Jack, rising and stretching. "Come on, I want to get this over with as soon as possible. Scranton's endless complaining is why this has taken so long. Yesterday we made as much as he had in a week."

Froggy nodded. "I know. The man is no doubt good at what he does, but he never stops moaning. The pellets are too small, the wrong shape, the wrong weight, too dry, too wet. I've had weeks of stinking like a piss house and I'll be glad when we're finished."

"That's no hardship," Jack said. "You always smell like a piss house." Ducking, he avoided the swipe Froggy aimed at his head, and set off back to the production area.

They worked for as many hours as the heat and daylight would allow and by the fourth day they had nearly finished. In the pleasantly grey dawn, Jack and Froggy were back combining the powder and producing the paste and pellets hours before Scranton made his way wearily up the hill.

"I cannot stand another night here," Scranton complained as soon as he was in earshot of Froggy and Jack.

"Here we go," Froggy said, under his breath.

"Master Scranton," Jack said, sounding overly cheerful.

"The sooner we get that last of this made the better," Froggy muttered.

Scranton had his hand pressed to the small of his back. "One more night on the floor and I shan't be able to get up again."

"Let's get that last cask filled then and Brother Emilio can take us back to Mdina," Jack said, pausing in his work for a moment. "We started early, please check what we've prepared so far. If it is good enough we can start making it into pellets."

Scranton, still grumbling, advanced to the bench where Jack and Froggy had been labouring for several hours already. The paste was fine and even. Jack knew perfectly well it was as good as any Scranton himself had supervised the production of. After four days of working with him, Jack had a familiarity with the process that even Richard would have been proud of.

"It's a little coarse," Scranton finally declared, after he had rubbed some of it between his thumb and forefinger. "It needs to be a little finer, another hour and it will be good enough to use."

Froggy was about to say something, but Jack kicked him hard in the shin. "Another hour? Good, I thought it needed a little more work. It is good to have your expertise on hand. There is bread, cheese and ale, Master Scranton, over near Brother Emilio."

The little man inclined his head and shuffled off, a hand to his aching back.

"I'm not doing another hour's work just so he can say he was right. There's nothing wrong with it the way it is," Froggy complained hotly.

"I know, and we are not going to do it either. Scranton will not quickly return here, and we'll tell him, when he does, that we re-worked it as he directed. Then everyone will be happy," Jack explained, smiling.

"Everyone but me. We'll have just had to waste an hour to keep that bastard happy," Froggy said, groaning.

"We are not going to re-work it, you fool. We'll make the pellets, set them to dry, and then I am going to see if I can get this stench from my skin," Jack said, setting his blackened hands back into the paste on the trays on the table.

"My brother used to work in a tanner's yard and even he didn't smell this bad when he'd come home. It doesn't seem to bother Scranton. I can only suppose that after being round sulphur and piss his whole life his nose doesn't work anymore," Froggy said laughing.

Jack was right. Scranton made no haste to return to the tables where Jack and Froggy were working. When he did join them, the sun was high in the sky and Jack's stomach was telling him it was time to find out if Scranton had left them any bread. When Scranton made a brief visit back to tell them that they were working to his specifications, Froggy hid a sour expression and Jack kept his words civil.

☦

Finally they were finished. The last of the pellets had been made, dried and packed into the earthenware pots. Jack left them to pack away the camp and prepare for their return to Mdina. Sitting on the rocky shoreline, Jack shielded his eyes against the glare from the sun on the sea and looked out across the bay. The small huts the fisherman lived in behind him were empty, the only noise coming from the crickets buzzing in the carob trees. Jack dipped his hands into the water and watched some of the black dusted charcoal wash from his skin.

He was covered in it, and the smell of sulphur lingered on him as well.

Standing quickly, he pulled the filthy shirt over his head and, stripping naked, he walked into the sea, letting the warm water lap around him. Ducking beneath the surface, Jack stood, watching as the fine black dust from his hair washed down his chest.

Froggy Tate was stained black with the charcoal, the creases in his face lined with it. Tate, though, had been working with the damned stuff for weeks. Jack hadn't realised that he too was just as black, even after just four days of working on Scranton's powder production.

Lowering himself into the embrace of the blissfully cool water, Jack set out to swim to the other side of the narrow bay. Halfway across, he stopped, turning onto his back and looking up at the craggy hillside pockmarked with olive trees and sparse scrub. Up there he knew Scranton was working, but from this distance he couldn't see or hear him and Froggy. Lazily, he swam slowly, intent on making it to the opposite side of the inlet.

Looking towards the open sea, at the end of the bay, he could see a small island. It looked close enough to be connected to the mainland. But when Emilio had pointed it out, he had told him it was accessible only by boat. The channel between Malta and the rocky outcrop was a deep one. The island had offered sanctuary, so it was said, to Saint Paul. The Apostle was shipwrecked off the Maltese coast when he was being transported to Rome as a prisoner. From where Jack was now he could see a small rocky cairn on the top of the island.

The day after they had arrived at Scranton's temporary work place, Emilio had told him about the small island. It was a point of pilgrimage, not only for the islanders, but also for the Knights. Emilio himself had crossed to the small island several years ago, holding a vigil for the island's saint. Emilio had gone on to extol the virtues of Paul, telling Jack how he had delivered Christianity to the rocky island in the few months he was there.

Jack had then told Emilio that the local population must be easier to convince than he was. That had raised the Italian's temper, much to Jack's amusement. Emilio had continued to lecture Jack. It was Paul's calm persistence, Emilio insisted, that had won over the island. Dressed only in rags and with no earthly possessions, Paul had only the power of the Lord's words to arm himself to further the cause of Christianity. Emilio's tone had been one of rebuke as he recounted the tale of Paul's humility to the Lord. Jack, not about to be brow beaten by the Italian, had laughed and reminded the Knight of his sin against nature. The Italian's face had darkened then and he had avoided Jack's company for two days.

Jack had regretted his words. Emilio was, in general, good company and had a set of skills that Jack was openly envious of. He enjoyed his good humour and Emilio's endless store of tales about the Order. Most of them were embellished, Jack had no doubt, to favour the reputation of the Knights. The Order was a formidable force and the premier military might in the Christian world, and Emilio, took extreme pride in being a part of it. The Knights might have had a tarnished reputation in some quarters, but their military proficiency was rarely called into question. After two days, Emilio, looking pale, had admitted himself to Jack's company once again, treating Jack with a new reserve. Jack rightly guessed he'd spent the time on his knees in repentance and he found himself working hard to regain the Italian's former easy friendship. Scranton had watched Jack's efforts with disapproving eyes, especially when Emilio found it impossible not to laugh at Jack's advances.

Jack continued to drift towards the far shore on his back. He had no need to rush back. Scranton was supervising the packing of the black powder and Jack had no desire to handle any more of the stinking stuff. As he drifted further towards the opposite rocky shore, he realised he could see more of the channel between the tiny island and Malta. As he watched he saw something in the inlet. Something brightly coloured. Something red.

Jack was vertical in the water in a moment, droplets showering around him. His heart was racing.

Between St Paul's island and Malta, in that narrow channel, was a ship. The prow, jutting forward round the rocky promontory, bore a blood red flag with a simple crescent. It was the flag he had seen before, on the two Turkish ships that had turned their might against the *Santa Fe*, on the journey to Malta.

Jack launched himself back across the bay. He raised his head twice as he swam to see where the ship was. They could not see him at that distance, but the galley was turning as it exited the narrow channel, navigating into the small bay.

☦

Jack, his clothes still clinging to his wet body, made it back up the rocky hillside at a run, despite the incline and the heat, worried that the galley had not been seen and that Emilio was still lazing in the shade. However, before he made it back to the terrace, where Scranton's stock in trade had been laid out, he could hear Emilio's raised voice and those of his men.

Emilio's excited voice greeted him, "There are two. The man I posted on the other side of the hill saw them round the point and cut through the channel into this bay. They are far enough from the capital here to know they will not meet any resistance and if they are close to the island, they regularly take slaves from the fishing villages and anything else they can carry away."

"We need to return to Mdina," wailed Scranton, appearing suddenly from one of the caves.

"Two of my men will take Scranton back and the powder. They are leaving now. The rest will remain." Emilio's eyes were bright. "I've already sent a man back to the capital on the fastest horse. They will send a force to guide the powder in."

"Two men? You cannot surely guarantee my safety with just two men?" Scranton's voice rose a pitch.

"They have not even landed men on the shore yet. You've time to get well on your way to the citadel. There will be eight of us left and they will not put more than a dozen ashore," Emilio informed Scranton curtly.

Seeing that Emilio was not going to help him, Scranton turned to Jack. "We need to go, Master Fitzwarren. Brother Emilio's men have secured the powder in the cart, but the horses will be slow. We must make haste."

Emilio shouted orders quickly over his shoulder to the two men preparing to take Scranton to safety, before returning his attention to Jack. "Will you scuttle back then with Master Scranton, or remain?"

Jack grinned. "I'll need steel."

In a moment Froggy was standing at Jack's shoulder. "I'm not leaving Jack on his own, so he can scold my ears with tales of this for weeks to come."

Emilio nodded. Behind them Scranton wailed, but the men with him had their orders. A moment later he was bundled in the direction of the packed cart. Soon his shrill complaining voice was gone.

"That's a relief," Froggy muttered.

One of Emilio's men came running down the steps to the terrace and he delivered his message breathlessly. There was a third and a fourth Turkish ship behind the two they had already seen breaching the channel into the bay.

Emilio's face hardened. "Four ships will carry over two hundred Turkish soldiers. Not enough to invade Malta, but a lot more than eight members of the Order of Saint John can cope with."

"Don't worry, a Knight of the Order is equal to a hundred Turks, or so Emilio keeps telling me," Jack said to Froggy, giving him a nudge.

Froggy, who had a real sense of the danger, was not sharing Jack's amusement. "Let's hope we don't need to find out," was all he said in reply.

"Arm them," Emilio shouted, at one of his captains, pointing to Jack and Froggy. Then he moved briskly to the edge of the terrace, watching the first galley slide through the bright blue water to the head of the bay.

Jack, buckling a sword belt on, came to stand next to him. "The cart is going to have to cross that track along the edge of the beach. They won't miss it."

Emilio nodded in agreement. "We are going to have to hold their attention until that cart passes them and makes it to the road on the other side of the bay."

"How do you propose to do that?" Jack enquired. The belt was tight and he pushed Dan's knife behind it, next to the scabbard.

"We ride down, taking the shore path to the left. Then we go up the hill, past the fishing huts." Emilio was heading towards the horses his men had all saddled and ready.

"You think that will work? Surely, they'll know you are drawing them away from the cart?" Jack asked, following him quickly.

"These are Turks. Nothing in that cart could be as precious to them as the prospect of holding as hostage eight Knights of the Order. We will offer ourselves as a prize they cannot resist." Emilio smiled as he swung himself up into the saddle.

"When that happens, you'll be sure to tell them we're not part of their precious Order, won't you?" Froggy Tate said, caustically, in Jack's ear.

Within minutes, the group were mounted and forcing their horses down the crumbling roman road kicking up rocks and dust , the iron shoes ringing loudly on the stone path. Froggy and Jack were at the back, the Knights wearing the cross of the Order, rode flanking each other so they were as conspicuous as possible to the men on the ships.

"It's just occurred to me," shouted Froggy, riding next to Jack, "that being at the back is not such a good idea."

"I was just thinking that as well." Jack pressed his horse on to close the gap between himself and the rider in front. They could see men spilling from the side of the ship and wading to the shore. Soon the Knights would have passed them, their horses set on the track leading up the hill in front of the fisherman's shacks. Then, Jack was fairly sure, he and Froggy would find themselves at the rear of the troop and closest to the Janissaries.

The first horses made it to the bottom of the hill and set off up along the track in the opposite direction to the cart.

Jack shouted a warning. "Froggy, keep up!" As he had thought, they were closest to the Turks. The first of the Turks, wading up from the water, were intent on breaking the line of horses heading up the hill. Jack had his sword clear of the scabbard, the reins tight in his left hand.

Emilio and five of his men made it clear past the foot soldiers. The rest of them were faced with a vicious line of curved blades advancing straight towards them, intent on cutting them off from their leader. Jack gave his full attention to the man coming straight at him. The Turk had angled his blade high, setting it for a swing that would slice into Jack's horse's throat. Digging his heel hard into her left flank, hauling hard on the reins, Jack pulled her exposed neck away from the glinting blade. He didn't quite get her far enough out of reach. Razor sharp steel cut a neat slice into her withers, the blade stopping when it hit the saddle, the leather saving Jack's knee that was directly behind it.

Jack's foot, out of the stirrup, kicked the blade back into the Turk's face. The mare, startled and hurt, reared. Jack slithered off her back. For a moment she was between him and the Turk. Jack had the time to pull Dan's knife from the belt. When her flanks were clear, he faced his opponent, with steel in both hands.

The Turk's blade ran with the mare's blood. Jack's sword, longer than the Janissary's scimitar, gave him the advantage of distance. The Turk, flanked now by two more of Allah's faithful, had the advantage of numbers. The curved blade sliced through the air towards him. Jack deflected it, the steel of the weapons clashing together with a searing squeal. The Turk's yatagan sword lacked a cross guard. Jack's blade continued on down, cutting into the leather covering the back of his opponent's hand. Not a crippling blow, but the Turk jerked his arm back from Jack's steel. His undefended right side took the full force of the knife in Jack's left hand. It ripped through the flesh of his upper arm, carving a deep gouge across his chest.

Froggy, still mounted, brought his horse between Jack and the other two Turks, who were for a moment forced back. The command he gave the horse was for a courbette. If executed on a good mount, both Turks would have been faced with flailing hooves. The horse beneath Froggy lacked training, obeying him only by turning her hind quarters towards them. His purpose was served though. The mare split the two men apart and his blade engaged with that of the man on his right. Jack took immediate advantage of the improved odds, setting his sword toward the second.

By necessity, the blow Jack delivered needed to be debilitating and quick. The Turk's face screwed up in pain as Jack's sword bit into the bone of his left arm. Withdrawing the blade quickly, Jack move backwards. Behind the injured man, another three were leering at him, moving up to take his place.

Christ!

Jack tightened his grip on the hilt in his hand.

"Jack! Come on!" screamed Froggy, his horse behind Jack.

Jack knew if he turned to mount behind Froggy, they would be upon him. The infidel had badly wounded two of their crew. Their eyes told Jack he would not be spared.

The thunderous pounding of hooves drew all their attention for a second. Emilio's horse, followed by of two of his Knights, careered into the three Turks. One man went down screaming, trampled beneath a horse. A second, buffeted hard, lost his balance, flung to the rocky ground landing on his back. The final attacker took Emilio's sword full in the throat, dying gurgling and spluttering before he was released from the blade.

Jack needed no invitation. Moving quickly alongside Froggy, he mounted a moment later and rode behind him. The little man turned his mare up the hill, Emilio letting him pass, before the three Knights closed ranks behind them.

The Turkish foot soldiers quickly gave up chasing the horses up the hill. Soon they reached the crest of the hill between the two bays, halting when Emilio raised his hand.

"Christ, that was close!" Jack, breathing hard, muttered in Froggy's ear.

Below them they could see the shore party of a dozen armed men. They were talking rapidly and pointing to where the Knights were.

"They think we are cut off from the capital. The track runs down the other side and to the bay. If they landed enough men here then we won't be able to make it back," Emilio stated.

Even Jack knew that there was nothing that offered sanctuary on the north of the island. The only strong hold was Mdina, and that was now on the other side of the Turks, who were beginning to empty from the ships.

"There must be a way back?" Jack asked.

Emilio nodded, then pointed with his blooded sword. "We need to move quickly before they move up the valley. If we go along the ridge, then drop down, we can get across the valley before they cut us off."

Emilo turned to his men and, his intentions stated, the horses set off at breakneck speed. They were heading towards the wooded crest of the hill, below which were the bee hives and the terrace where Scranton had been working for weeks. What looked like a rocky track soon showed itself to be a treacherous limestone wasteland. Pock-marked with holes, the uneven ground was filled with traps for hooves, disguised by the poor scrub that clung to the top of the ridge.

Froggy's horse, with a double burden, lost its footing twice but recovered. The second time, Jack was flung so hard against Froggy's back, he nearly unseated him. One of Emilio's Knights fared worse. Riding too fast, the black gaping hole of a punic tomb, carved out of the soft rock, forced his horse to leap the gap. Landing badly, a rear hoof sliding into the void, both horse and rider rolled to the ground. The mare was quickly on her feet, but the rider lay unconscious, blood pouring from his mouth.

Jack's mouth twisted at the sight of the man, knowing for sure that his ribs would have splintered when the horse landed on him, forcing their way into his innards. Emilio wheeled his horse back round. It was clear he would not leave the man behind.

Jack detached himself quickly from the back of Froggy's horse. "I'll take his horse. Put him behind me."

Draping the dying man over the rear of his horse and lashing a securing rope around him to his saddle only took moments, but it was time they could ill afford. The longer they lingered on the crest of the hill, the more time the Turks had to fill the valley below them, cutting them off from the citadel.

Mounted again, they cleared the exposed limestone crest and fled into the trees that dominated the remainder of the ridge. There was a narrow path and they rode along it in single file, the riders hunched over their horses avoiding the branches from the Aleppo pine trees. Emerging into a clearing, they could see a track leading through the trees back down into the valley. Emilio though, ignored it, pressing his sweating horse further along the ridge.

"We are not far enough along yet," Jack heard Emilio shouting.

The trees thinned and Jack saw the terraces leading down to the valley, and between them a winding dusty track. He could also see something else. The red of the flags, streaming from the poles held aloft by the Turks as they moved up the valley below them. Scranton's cart was nowhere in sight. He must have made it across the end of the bay, over the ridge on the opposite side of the valley and onto the track to Mdina.

"If we ride down there now, will we cross before they arrive?" Froggy said, pulling his agitated mount next to Jack's.

"It's going to be bloody close," Jack said, holding the horse next to Froggy's.

"It will be even closer if we don't move," Emilio announced. Pressing his heels hard into his horse, he led the charge down the hillside. He left them little choice but to follow. Emilio's horse breaking from the cover of the trees marked their position, so they either followed him or made a rapid retreat.

Jack's horse, carrying a double weight, sank towards the back of the pack. He pressed her on hard. As she raced towards the flat valley floor, Jack could see the men on foot, running to intercept them.

It's going to be more than close!

Emilio, blade drawn, had known they were going to have to fight their way across to the slope on the other side of the valley. There were a dozen men in the lead, running swiftly, and behind them the same number again. If the first force could delay them for only a short while, they would be vastly outnumbered. Sheer weight of numbers would lead to their defeat.

Jack wondered why the troop behind the leading men had slowed. He knew the answer soon enough, when a barbed arrow whirred past him, rattling off a limestone rubble wall.

Christ, archers!

The man behind him was dead, Jack was sure. The body was bouncing on the mare's hind quarters. A knife to the rope bindings released the dead weight. Jack felt her pace strengthen, now that the uncertain burden was removed from her back.

Emilio's shouted order to join the road immediately reduced their profile to the archers. The track was wide enough to ride side by side, the Knights taking to the side closest to the Turks. Froggy and Jack found themselves on the inside, shielded from the archers.

Two more arrows, missing their marks, hammered into the tilled earth on Jack's right. The next buried itself, head and shaft, into the flesh of the horse on his left. Crumpling her legs beneath her, the horse tumbled to the rocky road, pitching her rider forward to roll on the track. One of the Knights pulled his horse to a jolting halt, his arm extended for the fallen man to take. Jack and Froggy were forced to a stop as their route became blocked by the unmounted man and his rescuer.

Jack heard the arrows again. Reaching over, he grabbed at the bridle on Froggy's horse, urging her past the standing horse.

"Go on, ride. Don't stop," Jack yelled.

An arrow embedded itself into the back of the man reaching for the offered hand. Surprise showed on his face for a moment, the force of the blow pressing him forward, stumbling into horse and rider. A second arrow cut through his leather doublet, the barbed head parting flesh and muscle.

"Ride. He's dead. Ride!" Jack shouted, his horse alongside the man offering help. Waiting no longer, and hearing the shafts of two more steel barbs clattering off the limestone wall he pressed his horse on down the track. As they neared the small valley floor, the path levelled out. Jack could see Froggy, Emilio and five of the leading men about to career headlong into the running line of Turkish troops. They had no choice now but to halt the foot soldiers advance, holding them back until the straggling riders caught up and passed them. Even if it was only for a short moment, the confrontation was still going to be lethal.

Emilio's sword flashed in the sun. Raised behind him, he brought it in a huge sweeping arc into the soldiers. Jack's horse trailing behind was only yards from him when Emilio and his men brought the fight to the Turks.

The arrows had ceased. They were now too close to the Turkish troops for the archers to aim cleanly anymore. One of the Knights was being hauled from his horse, screaming in defiance, his boot grasped from below.

"Ride! Ride!" The command was Emilio's.

The fallen Knight disappeared into a sea of vicious blows. Emilio, wheeling round, applied his heels to his horse, and the Knights, blades still in their hands, disengaged. This time it was Jack and Froggy in the lead, the remaining five Knights bringing up the rear.

They didn't have to ride far to outrun the troops on foot, but they needed much more distance to avoid the arrows the archers began to loose at their retreating backs.

They slowed the horses as soon as they reached the crest of the valley on the opposite side. finally out of range of the archers. Emilio had lost three men, and the horses were lathered, their sides heaving. Emilio's eyes were bright with rage. There were now only four of his men left.

"We need to get to the Citadel. Make sure Master Scranton has made it safely there with the powder." Emilio spoke between ragged, heaving breaths.

Jack nodded. The only safety for them now was in Mdina. If they remained outside of the walls, the Turkish troops would catch them. They were still advancing quickly across the flat valley floor, and soon they would begin to mount the slope where the riders were watching.

With much more haste than when they had ridden down the track two weeks ago, they cantered the tired beasts through the midday heat, towards the white walls of Mdina on the crest of the next hill, standing shimmering in the sun. Within a short distance, they saw the cart with Master Scranton bouncing uncomfortably in the back, and soon caught up with it. The ride was silent and difficult, the riders pressing the horses over the rough terrain faster than they would like, and the cart bouncing over stones and rocks with Master Scranton wailing in the back.

Scranton had tears streaming down his face. He was being flung painfully from side to side in the back of the cart. His small wiry hands clung to the boarded sides, but as the cartwheels dropped into another sudden hole, he found the wooden side wrenched from his grip. Scranton either found himself pitched off the seat, rolling on his back in the cart, or flung over the sideboards, in danger of falling from the cart. The black powder was tied securely, Scranton had overseen that job himself, and despite the best efforts of the man driving the cart, the casks remained securely fastened.

Scranton let out another cry as the cart bucked and pitched up into the air, shaking his hold loose again from the wooden side. Scranton missed the seat and fell yelping as one of his wrists clattered painfully off the side of the wooden seat. The cartwheel chose that moment to splinter. In another half a rotation, the rim split and the spokes buckled one after another. Scranton screamed and rolled sideways as the cart collapsed, the left side of it being dragged along on the remains of the hub.

The cart, the slowest vehicle in the group, and carrying the most valuable cargo, had travelled at the front of the fleeing group. Froggy, riding behind it, pulled his mare sideways, avoiding the carnage of shattered wood sprayed towards him from the collapsing wheel.

Scranton was already on his feet in the back of the tipped cart, shouting at the driver when Emilio pulled his horse up next to the remains of the cart.

"Enough! It has happened." Emilio's voice cut through Scranton's complaining wail. Emilio's tone even bore an edge that obtained Jack's instant attention. "Strip the powder out. We can't leave it."

The earthenware jars, packed round with straw and stinking animal skins, had, thanks to Scranton's fastidiousness, remained intact. It took four of them to lift down one of the powder jars, such was the weight. In a moment it was evident that it was too heavy for them to lash to a horse.

"We need to leave it, they'll be upon us." Scranton could not contain himself.

It was a mailed fist that took hold of a good portion of Scranton's jacket and the skin beneath and pulled him forward. Emilio spoke not to Scranton, but to one of his men. "Lacon, get him to Mdina and take these two with you."

Scranton was dragged forward, treated like no more than a sack of grain and hoisted up to ride behind the Knight, Lacon.

"Jack, take your man, ride with Lacon. He will see you safely back in Mdina." Emilio was turning back to his remaining men, his face grimly set.

"Damn that," Jack exclaimed, dropping from his horse.

Froggy, cursing, looked skyward.

Emilio cast his gaze over Jack, and said quickly, "You're staying?"

Jack grinned, "I want to see how good you really are."

Emilio's eyebrows raised. He shouted a hasty order at Lacon, who immediately divested himself of his cuirass and held it out.

Emilio took it a shoved it towards Jack. "I want you to live long enough to see just how good we really are."

"Jack!"

Jack turned to the sound of Froggy's voice.

"This is a bloody fool's mission, it's not our fight," Froggy called down from his mount.

"Go, make sure Scranton gets back to Mdina. Tell my brother you left with my blessing." Jack wasn't looking at Froggy, his hands busy buckling on the cuirass.

Emilio's men had stripped the earthenware jars of their protective bindings and the damp animal skins and they were set next to each other, the exposed black powder glistening in the sun.

"Are we fighting or blowing ourselves to the hereafter?" Jack asked, moving to stand next to Emilio.

"We have nothing to use as a fuse. This must not fall into the Turk's hands. They would use it against the Citadel and there is enough here to bring down the bastions. We will take as many with us as we can," Emilio stated simply.

"As far as plans go, this might be one of the worst I've heard," Jack muttered, watching one of Emilio's captains lighting a small fire some way distant from the black powder. "Why not set the fire next to the jars and then run. If we judge it right, it will take them out as they advance. They have no idea this was the cart's cargo?"

Emilio shook his head. "They could put the fire out, and then we have handed them a weapon to turn against the Order. We fight, and we either repel them or we set a torch to the powder."

Chapter 18

A Fighting Chance

The man sat next to Richard pulled the notebook closer, so he could better read the figures listed there.

"What do you think, Rodrigo?" de la Sengle asked, the Order's head of Ordnance, for the second time.

Rodrigo shrugged. "Without testing this, it is hard to say. Here." He jabbed a blackened finger at the notebook. "This shows that the projectile reached another forty-five feet. And the second test a little further at seventy-five. But there are so many other variables, I cannot commit without testing this myself."

"Could you follow the process?" de la Sengle pressed.

Rodrigo shook his head and flipped a page. "It is detailed here." He tapped his finger on the page. "And I can follow it through, but the method and some vital information about quantities is not complete." Fixing his eyes on Richard, he asked, "You write here to hold back a quantity of the charcoal for inclusion later in the process, but it does not say how much and in what form?"

"Master Scranton, as you can imagine, has kept some of the details to himself," Richard replied, honestly.

"We will have to wait until this man, Scranton, has made more," Rodrigo replied, sounding disappointed. "I cannot make this. I am told that he should have his powder ready for us to test soon."

The answer was not satisfactory, but de la Sengle understood the truth of it, and nodded. "We should be able to test it this week."

"If the powder store had not been…"

De la Sengle held up his hand to still Rodrigo's words. "Do not remind me again about the powder store. Brother Caron, I am sure, has barely slept since the incident, worrying about the cost of it. And I have now had three delegations from the Mendoni family, who are convinced that we are set to blow them all, and their city, to the heavens."

"It was unfortunate," Rodrigo agreed, nodding and returning his attention once more to Richard Fitzwarren's notes.

Edward Fitzwarren sounded bored. "Talk will not prove the method. Only action will show whether this is effective or not."

Rodrigo said in agreement, "There is nothing in the theory I can refute but we need proof…"

They heard the noise in the street first. Men's raised voices and a moment later there was the clatter of boots on the tiled floor in the corridor outside. The knock at the door was a cursory one that did not await an answer.

"Grand Master, Turks have landed in the bay near St Paul's. Four ships in total, and they have a raiding party moving inland." The message was delivered breathlessly by the rider Emilio had sent to Mdina.

De la Sengle was on his feet in a moment, any interest in what they had been considering banished immediately, in the face of the threat. Edward Fitzwarren pressed his questions to the man who had delivered the message and Rodrigo and Richard, still seated, were forgotten.

Richard, rising, hands flat on the table, added his voice. The tone cut through the heated and urgent conversation and gained de la Sengle's attention. "Test me. I have men. Arm them now. Let me show you what we can offer. The perfect opportunity has been presented to you. Test me."

"Arm you? Are you mad?" It was Edward Fitzwarren who spoke.

De la Sengle held up his hand to silence his captain. "Test or trial then. Let us see what you can offer us."

†

The wooden door to the yard was flung open. From where they were seated in the shade, two men stared, wide eyed, at the figure standing in the open doorway.

"Gentleman, you have but one opportunity to free yourselves from this isle and it is here and it is now. We fight and we win. Are you with me?" Richard Fitzwarren announced to Marc and Pierre.

"Fight who?" Marc said, as he stood.

"Who cares, if it gets us out of here?" Pierre pushed passed Marc, and was hard on the heels of the Master who was already turning to leave.

†

Scranton no longer had full feeling in either his legs or his arms by the time the horse he was seated pillion on made it through the city gates. He was dropped, disregarded, in the open square just inside the gates. Around him, shouts for arms were already being obeyed. The little munitions manufacturer, holding what he believed to be a broken wrist, flattened himself against the wall and watched as the Knights he had arrived with relayed the seriousness of Emilio's situation to the garrison commander.

He screamed again, jumping further backwards into the doorway, when a firm hand grasped his arm and a familiar voice spoke in his ear. "What's happened? Where's my brother?"

Scranton shook all over. "We were attacked…" he stammered, "…a raiding party."

"Where? Where did this happen?" Richard's voice was insistent and the grip on Scranton's arm tightened.

"Where we were making the powder. I came back with the cart while they led the Turks away and we met back up on the road to Mdina," Scranton managed, still shaking.

"Where are the rest of them?" Richard pressed.

"Some were killed. Then the wheel came off the cart with the powder in. Emilio sent me back with Lacon and the rest are with the powder." Scranton wrapped his arms around himself to still his shaking.

"And Jack?" Richard put the question again.

It wasn't Scranton who answered him, it was Froggy Tate's voice from behind them. "The fool stayed with them."

Richard whirled around to face Froggy. "And you didn't?"

A moment later Scranton was forced to take further refuge in the recessed doorway as the square was filled with horses. A force of twenty fully armed Knights, astride eager horses, accompanied by Richard Fitzwarren, and three of his men, took off through the arch from the city. Heading towards the ridge, where Emilio and his remaining force were waiting for the Turks to form an advancing line strong enough to attack. Scranton, his hands pressed over his ears, let out a fearful cry as the sound of the steel clad hooves echoed through the high narrow streets, like a hammer on an anvil.

†

From their position, they did not have the best view of the valley below, but the vantage point did afford an excellent view of the near ground and any approach the Turks might make. The five Knights were spread out in defensive positions behind the low terraces. All of them were wary of the Turks' archers.

"How many do you think?" Jack said, quietly.

Emilio to his right replied, "Twenty, maybe a few more."

"Nice odds," Jack said to himself sarcastically.

"They'll not expect to find us here. Rather they would expect to be chasing us all the way back to Mdina," Emilio replied.

"I agree, and if it weren't for Scranton's bloody powder, I'd be there now," Jack said, then his eyes caught movement below him. Between the rows of olive trees there was a sudden flash of red.

"There!"

Emilio had seen it as well, and he tightened his hold on the hilt of the sword in his hand. As they watched, Jack saw that Emilio had been right. The men advancing towards them through the hillside scrub had no idea that six pairs of infidel eyes were watching them from the top of the ridge concealed by the low rubble walls. There were four men in the lead, walking up the track where the cart had shattered its wheel, two more walking further to the right, up a thin dirt path along the side of the terrace wall.

Six they could take. Six was not a problem.

Jack's eyes narrowed as he looked beyond them to the other ten men a short distance behind. These were the problem. If they hesitated, if they did not make their weapons strike true, they would be outnumbered in a matter of moments.

Emilio signalled to the two men on his right to move towards those coming up the dirt path, leaving three Knights and Jack to deal with the four men coming directly towards them. They needed the Turks to remain unaware that their passage up the hill was being so closely watched. A slight breeze was thankfully taking away both the smell and the wisps of smoke from the small fire set ready to light the powder.

This would be no fair fight. They would attack when the Turks were almost upon them. With they had no chance to defend themselves, the advance line would crumble, and the real fight could be taken to the ten men coming up the hill behind them.

Jack could feel the sweat on his hand gripping the sword hilt, readying to move the moment the Turks were close enough. Hesitating for a moment, he loosened his grip, dried his hand quickly on his sleeve and took a firm grasp once again. Concealed behind a wall and two thickly leaved fig trees, the Turks could not see them. Their eyes were cast down at the rocky steep path they were walking up.

Jack swallowed hard.

The man to his left nudged him in the arm and in a quiet whisper said, "Take the one on the far right."

Jack gave a quick nod and fastened his eyes on his quarry. When they broke from their cover, Jack would have the furthest to go to engage. He needed to cover the distance before the Turk drew his yatagan, which currently swung at his waist. The group continued unawares up the hill. Jack's eyes widened as he heard their voices drift though the warm Mediterranean air towards him. He heard laughter as well. Jack's prey was clearly the subject of the joke. As he watched, the Turk threw his arms wide in a gesture of helplessness and his fellows laughed again.

Then the man took out a knife.

Jack's body stiffened, the arm clutching his sword beginning to tense. The gloved hand of the Knight to his left placed a hand on his wrist to stop him.

The Turk with the knife in his hand was not pointing it at Jack. He'd not seen the men concealed on the hillside; instead he waved the knife threateningly at his companions. Jack could not understand what he was saying. There was no trace of mirth in his voice, and his companions fell silent, turning their heads away from him and back to the track they were walking up. Jack would have sworn one of them was staring directly into his eyes. The Knight still had a restraining hold.

Jack risked a glance to his right.

The men approaching Emilio and his companions were on the same level. That was good. When the attack came, it would be at the same time.

"Wait," came the command from his left.

Christ, how close does he want them to get?

Jack's mark was no more than five paces from him.

If they left it any longer, he would not be able to get in position in time.

The man beside him must have sensed Jack's body readying to act, and held onto him for one more vital moment.

Emilio shouted. The hold was released. Jack's sword flew neatly up, and in a pace it had found its mark. The front line of Turks, taken by surprise, unaware of the hidden assailants, crumpled onto the rocky hillside, dying. The ten behind were a different matter.

While their companions had been attacked, they had had time to draw their swords. The group split into two, moving on the two positions held by the Knights.

Withdrawing his blade, Jack stood shoulder to shoulder with men whose skill at arms was unquestioned. The Knight beside Jack dragged him back. They would make the Turks step over their own dead before they could level their blades at the Knights. The hillside was steep enough to give them an advantage, and Emilio's men needed every one they could make.

Five of Emilio's men were left. The ten Turks advanced, blades drawn and with blood lust in their eyes. Behind them, moving quickly to defend their comrades, came another line of twenty Turks.

The Turks to his right had stepped quickly over their dead, and Jack heard the sound of blades engaging. A moment later the Turkish line near him pressed their attack. Coming towards Jack was not one, but two silvered and shining blades with red silk hilts, making them look as if they already streamed with blood.

Jack became unaware of anything but the need to stop the steel. A hard lateral swipe with his own blade severed the yatagan nearest him, a move which risked breaking his own blade, but the odds demanded higher risks. Taller and broader than both his opponents, Jack knew of the target he was offering them. A moment later, the razored point of a Turkish blade scythed across the front of his thick leather cuirass. Jack recoiled, unharmed, from the impact.

As he stepped back, his eyes caught the closing row of Turkish reinforcements, now no more than fifteen paces beyond. A second later he cursed himself, and his lack of a buckler, as he was forced to deflect a blade with his poniard. The impact numbed his arm and the blade was jarred from his grasp.

How long would Emilio leave it before he ignited the powder?

Not long!

Jack brought his sword up automatically to protect his chest, blocking the scimitar, the lethal arc rattling down the length of Jack's blade. At the same time, the Turk with the broken blade thrust his shortened weapon straight towards Jack's exposed left side.

The shattered blade never made it to him. The expression on the man's face turned from a vicious leer to one of sudden shock. Eyes widening, the scimitar tumbled from his opening grip. He caught the attention for a moment of his companion and that gave Jack the opportunity to land a blow. Not a lethal one, it lacked the velocity for that, but the cold steel bit into the fleshy shoulder of his attacker who emitted a howl of pain.

Jack took two brisk paces back.

The Knight to his left had a man down and was engaged with a second who suddenly fell backwards, arms flung wide and mouth open in a howling scream. A red plume was opening on his chest like a flower.

He'd been shot with a musket ball. Jack recognised behind him now the unmistakable sound of flintlocks being fired in unison.

The line behind the front row of attackers had stopped its advance. Some of their number were already down, and the line, now broken and uncertain, faltered. A moment later it crumbled and broke as de la Sengle's force from Mdina showed themselves on the ridge.

Then he heard a voice he recognised.

"Jack! No one told me you had been recruited."

Jack spun on the spot, his eyes scanning the ridge behind him, where he found faces he recognised. Marc, Pierre, Froggy, and next to them, a flintlock resting on his shoulder, his brother. Jack was about to speak when a hand in the back pushed him hard towards the top of the hill.

"Move now! They are bringing their archers up."

Jack ran to the top of the hill, his breath coming in ragged gasps. If he thought the fight was over, he was wrong. Froggy clamped a flintlock against Jack's chest.

"They are re-forming their archers just beyond that line of trees," Richard said, coming to stand next him and pointing towards a sparse row of Aleppo pine.

"We need them closer." Froggy was reloading as he spoke.

"At the moment, they don't know what attacked their front line, so we expect them to press forwards," Richard replied, then to Jack, "We are on display it seems. Can we repel fifty men with five flintlocks?"

"I bloody hope so." Quickly he had his weapon primed and ready to fire.

Richard settled himself next to Jack. "Acquit ourselves well and we might have a life outside of Malta."

"And if we don't?" Jack was busy ramming home a musket ball.

"You might learn to like boats!" his brother supplied, quietly as he hoisted the flintlock to his shoulder. Then to the whole group, he said, "On my orders, fire and reload."

"On your orders," Jack muttered under his breath, suddenly realising what his brother had meant about boats.

Richard had been right. The few deaths they had delivered with the musket balls had not been attributed to firearms and the Turks pulled forward a line of archers, far enough away to avoid physical contact but close enough to land lethal arrows into the line at the top of the hill.

The first shots rang out in unison. A slight breeze took the acrid smoke blessedly behind them and the firing line remained clear. Each man lowered their weapon, and reloaded. Their actions were matched, the pace measured. Then as one they lifted the flintlocks, picked their marks and fired on the order, attention immediately returning to the reloading process.

Shot dropped in the barrel.

Rod to press it home.

Hammer back.

Powder added to the frizzen.

Mark selected.

Wait. Wait. Wait.

Fire on command.

Jack selected the third musket ball. It had been a long time since Froggy's training at the camp, but the actions, the timing were all still second nature. After five rounds, Richard held his hand up and stood. Their targets had retreated, and the rocky hillside had another six bodies to add to the total.

Without a word Edward Fitzwarren took the flintlock from Marc's hands and facing Richard, said, "You will bring me these. All of them."

"All of them," Richard agreed.

✝

The Knights gave chase, picking off more of the Turks as they retreated towards the boats while Richard and his men were returned to Mdina with an escort.

Jack watched his brother closely throughout the ride to the Citadel. He rode in front of Jack, who could see only his back and little else. When the track allowed, Edward Fitzwarren pulled his horse level with Richard's. It was obvious that he was placing a series of questions, and Richard, turning his head to reply, was answering them. Jack was too far back to hear any of the words but Richard sat straight in the saddle and was, it seemed, providing coherent and reasonable replies to Edward. He'd been provided with good clothes and wore a dark doublet over a white linen shirt. But it was still obvious that the man beneath them was painfully thin. However Richard had, it seemed, thankfully recovered his wits.

Jack remembered Edward Fitzwarren well. He had little liking for him. Cast very much in the same mould as Robert, he was vicious, violent and had treated servants with little more than contempt. Jack had been on the receiving end of his temper many years ago, before Edward had left England to join the Order. It had been during a hunting expedition when he was carrying Edward's hawk. A beautiful goshawk named Mardy. He'd known the hunting was to be in the forest and the shorter winged goshawk was a better bird to fly in the woods. The goshawk was the lesser bird by far than the long winged peregrine. Edward, feeling shamed at the bird Jack had offered him, beat him senseless for the mistake. Jack doubted that Edward had changed much; the members of the Order were not known for their generosity of spirit and kindness despite the tenets that they declared they lived by.

    Jack had no opportunity to talk to Richard on the ride back to Mdina, and once there Jack found he was escorted to where Marc and Pierre had been kept during their time in Malta along with Froggy Tate. It did not seem like he was going to be admitted to his brother's company any time soon.

Chapter 19

The Queen's Crusade

Cecil was not present when Green's sentence was carried out. Morley, for once, was harbouring bitter thoughts towards his employer. His mood was not helped by the weather. Storm clouds had gathered over London. It had rained heavily over night and the ground around Smithfield was mired. Ponds gathered in the ruts and holes left by cartwheels and hooves, and the air was still laden with a fine wet mist. Water dripped in a constant stream from the front of Morley's hat.

Morley had difficulty believing that the idiots of the borough, charged with this task, had left all the kindling and boughs exposed overnight to the torrent from the Heavens. The chances of them raising pyres from the wet branches were fairly poor. He needed to find out who was in charge and make sure this did not happen again. It was a difficult enough task to organise the victims for these public executions, and to have the end result marred by such poor organisational planning was unacceptable. Morley had no doubt that if the day was not a success then Cecil would be laying the blame for the failure squarely at his door.

Then there was the matter of the crowds. There weren't any. Smithfield would normally be a packed mass of Londoners, but not today. He doubted it was just the damp weather that was keeping them away. After Mistress Harrington's execution, it seemed the city had little stomach for watching more of its citizens writhe in agony and beg for mercy. Today there were only a few dozen present. Many were workers from the stalls set up on the staging around the edge of the open space, selling food and wares to those attending the execution. London's merchants, keen to make the most out of the event, selling to the assembled onlookers.

Today's burnings had been organised to send a message to the city. Mary would not tolerate the Protestant subversion of the Catholic faith from any strata of society. Apart from Green and the debtor Morley had found to take the role of the archer who killed Mistress Harrington, those to be executed today were common folk, drawn from the main parishes in London. And it seemed that London had received the message and did not want to watch Mary's justice.

For a few moments Morley wondered if it might be possible to postpone the event. The fires were not going to light easily, Londoners had not turned out to witness the event. It was on the brink of turning into a failure. Rather than delivering a harsh message and reinforcing

Mary's will, there would be whispers through the city that the rain soaking the faggots was a show of God's displeasure with the event. That the city had shunned the spectacle as well would send a message back to the Court that they no longer cared for this royal justice.

Morley knew that he could not intervene. If he did, it would be he who would find the full force of Mary's displeasure aimed at him. None would see the sense in what he had done. It was, sadly, a better and safer route to let it run its sorry course and deal with the results later. It was unfortunate that Cecil had decided to shun the occasion. Morley wondered if this was a politic move rather than just a desire to remain both warm and dry.

As the year drew to a close, it seemed that England's tolerance for her Spanish-styled Queen was also waning. Philip had persuaded Mary in March of this year to join her forces to his and England had declared war against France. It was a move the Privy Council knew England could ill afford, and towards the end of the year the effects were now being felt by the population as well. The lack of support for the burnings at Smithfield was also a measure of public sentiment toward the war with France.

☦

Christopher Morley sat patiently waiting for Catherine de Bernay. He was in no rush, his mind applied to the latest of Cecil's problems that had been delivered to him to solve. The failure of Green's execution had been quickly forgotten. , Mary's attention was drawn to a new problem, and Cecil was helping to ensure that it remained the centre of focus. The war with France and Philip's absence had placed another issue before Mary that she could not now avoid. The question of the succession. Whilst she had been able to claim that she was with child, they could not press her on the issue, but Philip had been away fighting with the Spanish and English forces against France, and any hope Mary had for a child was now lost. The Privy Council, with Philip absent, were uncharacteristically united with a single-minded purpose, and that was to resolve the issue of the succession.

	Philip had pressed his wife to join his war against France. What would happen if he lost? Would he sacrifice England? There was a real fear that by involving the country in the fight with France, England's oldest enemy, that they were at serious risk of losing their sovereignty to Henry of France. There needed to be an answer to the question of the succession, there needed to be an assurance that if the worst happened, England would not become a part of France.

The options were limited. The final name that they had, the only real answer, was Elizabeth. It was known that she favoured the Protestant cause, disliked Philip, had shunned a foreign match and was eminently a better prospect to provide the country with an heir than her older half sister, Mary. If the succession was vested in Elizabeth, there were a number of names that could be suggested as marriage prospects. It was an issue of control, and the Privy Council were in agreement that they could control Elizabeth. The key issues now were how to secure this situation, how to persuade Mary to vest the succession in Elizabeth. They would soon raise the question with Elizabeth. Cecil was keen to ensure that the Tudor temper was kept in check and knew that a forewarned Elizabeth would be a subdued Elizabeth. Given time to consider the facts, he was sure she would see this as a vital opportunity to secure her safety and immediately improve her situation.

Catherine saw Morley sat in the arbour where the statue of Apate stood, and her mouth formed a hard line.

Morley's face split into a wide smile at the sight of her. "Why so serious? We are, my dear, on the same side."

"Are we?" Catherine replied. Realising she had no choice, she took a seat on the bench, as far away from Morley as possible.

"Of course we are, your help was really appreciated." Morley held out his hand and in his palm were two coins.

Catherine's eyes flicked from the coins to his face and back again. This time she voiced no refusal and held her own hand out next to his. Morley, smiling, tipped his hand and let the two coins slide into Catherine's keeping. Her small hand closed around them and in a moment they were out of sight.

"What have you for me to do now?" Catherine asked.

"Straight to business," Morley grinned. "This is why we get on so well."

"We don't get on." Catherine shot him a dark look. "I have no choice, you have made that very clear."

"Profit where you can, when you can," Morley said. "It is not a bad motto to live by."

"I don't want to profit, I just want what is mine," Catherine replied, sourly.

Morley sighed. "And that might happen, but at the moment I need you to pass a message to Elizabeth."

"A message? Like last time when poor Libby was arrested," Catherine shot back.

"And Libby is safe and well, remember. That as yet has come to nothing," Morley reminded her, adding, "and it kept Kate Ashley safe as well, so your actions have helped your mistress."

"Hardly!" Catherine spat back. "Remember how Kate ended up in the Fleet prison in the first place, or have you forgotten?"

Morley grimaced. "Oh Catherine, times change."

"So you keep telling me," Catherine said, grimly.

"My message for your mistress cannot be written down, and I trust you to deliver it well. There's no action required of you other than that." Morley waited for Catherine to nod in acceptance of his words before he continued. "The Privy Council are to press Mary to vest the succession in Elizabeth. She will shortly be summoned to discuss this, and my master simply wishes your mistress to consider this opportunity before it occurs."

"Is that it?" Catherine replied, confusion wrinkling her brow.

"Yes, that is all. Now, repeat the message to me, please," Morley requested.

It was an hour later, when Catherine had given Morley's message to Elizabeth where she sat alone in the garden. She listened silently. Then, her eyes fastened on Catherine's face, she quizzed her in detail about how the message had been delivered and by whom. Catherine kept her answers basic and consistent.

Elizabeth waited, and waited.

Christmas at Court came and went.

In January, Mary promised 150,000 ducats for the war Philip was waging with Spain, along with troops. The price of her support for his war was for him to visit England, which Philip dutifully did. Mary immediately imagined herself to be pregnant again. She would tolerate no advances from her Council imploring her to settle the succession upon Anne Boleyn's bastard.

Catherine was also forced to wait. She put the coins from Morley with those she already had, along with a gold chain that had belong to Kate Ashley, who was still not present to report it missing. It was over a year now since Richard had deposited her with Elizabeth, and she had accepted that the Fitzwarren brothers had truly forgotten about her.

Chapter 20

The Final Proof

Ten members of the Order, including its Grand Master, Edward Fitzwarren and Brother Rodrigo were all gathered on the Mdina bastion. A canopy had been erected to protect the powder from the heat, and pointing out over the wall was a carriage-mounted culverin. In attendance at the demonstration were Richard, Jack and a trembling Master Scranton.

"It has been, Master Scranton, over a half a year since we began this endeavour. Now is your moment of reckoning," Richard said, his grey eyes locked with those of the small man.

That Scranton was nervous was evident from his demeanour. Over his shirt he wore a linen apron, blackened with dust. His hands, creased and lined with age, rolled and squeezed the cloth through his damp hands.

It was Jack who stepped between them. "Master Scranton needs a little time. These are not things that can be rushed."

"When did you become a diplomat?" Richard said, acidly.

"I'd rather not be blown to Hell," Jack said, pointedly, and then to Scranton, "Let me assist, Master Scranton."

Scranton looked thankfully at Jack and nodded.

"Ignore everyone watching. You set the charges, and do not worry about anything else. First we are to use standard powder? Am I right?" Jack asked, holding the little man's attention, hoping that in doing so he would distract him from the intimidating onlookers.

"Standard powder, yes," Scranton said, and then stopped.

"You need to weigh it out first," Jack prompted, pointing at the balance scales set close to the ordnance.

"Weigh it." Scranton licked his lips and using a wooden scoop poured the powder into the scales.

Rodrigo stood on the other side, notebook in hand, ready to confirm the measurement before Scranton took the powder to prepare the charge with. Scranton's hands shook and a liberal quantity of powder missed the brass weighing pan, dusting the limestone flags with a thin coating of black.

Jack swore under his breath.

"Master Scranton, allow me." Jack retrieved the scoop from his hand and took a firm hold on the powder sack. Then quietly for Scranton's ears only he said, "Tell me what to do. Quickly."

"The projectile is eight pounds," Scranton's squeaky voice managed, "and we need a charge of one quarter of its weight, so two pounds of powder."

Jack nodded quickly and measured out the two pound charge, repeating Scranton's words as he did so. "A two pound charge for an eight pound shot. Agreed?" He caught Rodrigo's eyes who nodded in agreement.

Together, Jack and Scranton loaded the charge and left the remainder of the process to the Order's gunners. They added hay wadding on top of the charge ramming it home before adding the missile to the barrel.

Scranton's nerves were such that he yelped and clapped his hands over his ears when the cannon fired. After the cloud of smoke cleared, all eyes turned to the terraces stretching out below the citadel. The men below knew the range of the gun fired and the impact point of the shot was quickly marked with a white flag.

Jack had already begun to weigh out two pounds of the pellets that he had helped to make. Rodrigo confirmed the amount.

"A second two pound charge, of the new powder," Jack announced to those watching.

The charge was handed to the gunners and Jack stood back to watch the piece loaded for a second time. Jack inclined his head sideways, saying quietly in Scranton's ear, "If you pray, do it now."

Scranton managed to remain silent when the gun fired for a second time. Jack had stopped breathing.

Please God, let the distance be further.

The second flag was red. Jack let out a long shuddering breath, clapping Scranton so hard on the back that the little man staggered forward with the force of the blow. The second marker was a significant distance further on. The stone shot had cleared another two of the terraces before embedding itself in the soil.

The bastion was soon cleared of the Order's elite, Richard leaving with them. It seemed unlikely that Jack was ever going to get to speak with him. Rodrigo, Scranton and Jack along with the Order's gunners remained.

"Master Scranton, a feat indeed," Rodrigo said, coming forward to congratulate the powder manufacturer.

Scranton's arrogance of manner had returned the moment the red flag had been erected. His chest puffed out, he smiled accepting Rodrigo's praise. "I was confident that you would be impressed with this process."

Jack looked skywards and rolled his eyes.

"Does this powder process work on all shot sizes, or are there optimum sizes?" Rodrigo continued his notebook still poised.

"I've had little chance to test it on a full range of cannon. The indications from my experiments so far are that it is ideal for the mid-ranged pieces. There might be a risk involved when the charge exceeds five pounds."

"We have available here all sizes. We can perform a range of tests, even on the larger pieces. It would be interesting to see how much their range could be extended." Rodrigo mused, tapping his pen against the side of his cheek.

"Or we can achieve the same range as standard powder but with less powder," Scranton pronounced, and then added, "How many battles have there been where the ordnance remained silent for lack of powder?"

Jack left Scranton to bask in the glory of his success. Walking to lean against the bastion walls, he stared across the parched land towards the sea.

"What are you looking for?" It was Emilio's voice. The Knight had come to stand next to him.

"Nothing that I can see out there," Jack replied, wearily.

"Ah, Jack. You should celebrate your success." Emilio, his hands folded together, leant with his elbows on the top of the wall. His gaze though, was not on the far distance.

Jack let out a long breath. "I no longer know how to measure success."

"I've not seen you since we fought on the hillside," Emilio replied.

Jack glanced sideways at the Knight. "I thought I was going to get blown to Hell that day."

"Hell? Jack, you're not destined for that pit!" Emilio laughed.

"Where am I destined for?" Jack let his head fall forwards.

"I've heard you are Richard's half-brother," Emilio said. "That is a shame. The Order could have offered you much."

"Does that fact bother you?" Jack asked through his hands.

"It would have, but you are a man who has fought at my side and for that I cannot offer you anything less than respect," Emilio said, seriously.

"And if I had not fought with you?" Jack questioned.

"Then it would have been my shame, for I would not have shunned your company," Emilio answered truthfully.

"Are you so sure?" Jack said, darkly.

"Yes I am. The Apostle Peter reminds us that anyone, no matter how they came into the world, if they fear God and do what is right, will be accepted. Was not King Solomon also tainted the same, and did not your Henry I of England populate his church with his illegitimate children? And Sir Galahad whose quest for the…"

"You've made your point. Please stop before you compare me to Galahad or I will throw myself off the bastion!" Jack replied, a slight smile appearing on his face.

Emilio beamed back happily. "Today is not a day for maudlin thoughts. Your brother has laid his case before the Grand Master with some success. We should celebrate this." Then leaning closer he said, "Chaste I may be, but I'm not always sober."

Jack grinned at him. "And for that I would be extremely thankful."

†

"Andrew Kineer is no longer on Malta," de la Sengle announced as he walked into the room.

"Where is he?" Richard's eyes narrowed.

The Grand Master smiled, pulled out a chair and seated himself at the table before speaking. "Halfway to Sicily, I would imagine by now."

Richard dropped his head into his hands. "You just let him go? You have no guarantee that he will bring those arms back to the Order."

"He's a man driven by greed, and you are a man driven by loyalty," de la Sengle said, slowly.

"My loyalty is not a tradable commodity," Richard returned.

"Oh, I think it is," de la Sengle replied. "I accept, that once out of here, Kineer's self interest will guide him. It is doubtful his promises to bring the weapons to Malta will be fulfilled. He will, I have no doubt, plan to sell them to whoever has the most coin he can take quickly for the deal. His time here has taught him, if nothing else, that dealing with the Order was a mistake he is lucky to have survived."

Richard raised his head from his hands and looked at de la Sengle levelly across the table. "So why did you let him go? If you accept that he will not bring the arms back to the Order and to Malta?"

De la Sengle smiled. "To teach the man a lesson."

Richard rocked back in his seat. "What lesson is he going to learn from this?"

There was a jug of water on the table and de la Sengle, ignoring Richard, fastened his eyes on it and slowly filled one of the earthenware cups. At length he spoke. "He will indeed learn nothing from it. Already he probably feels he will profit from your endeavours." De la Sengle raised the cup to his lips and sipped the cool water. "You, however, have plenty to learn."

Richard's face hardened, but he said nothing.

De la Sengle smiled. "You are going to pay for your sin of arrogance. Granted, Kineer has a head start, but I can put you on a boat in three days that will take you to

Venice. If you are the man I think you are, and you are a man who has everything to lose, you will make it back to England first."

Richard's mind was racing and he sat rigid in his seat.

"You set your wits against the Order," de la Sengle said, slowly, "and against me. Now whilst I admire that in a fashion, it cannot be perceived to have happened. So, your men will stay here as surety. Master Scranton we have a need for. And you will go to England and ensure the Order receives the shipments you have promised it."

"And you trust me to come back?" Richard's voice was cold and level. The eyes that held those of the Grand Master were stormy grey.

De la Sengle smiled and set the simple cup down carefully in front of him. "Kineer told me before he left that I indeed held a lever over you."

"And what lever would that be?" Richard's mind began to quickly work through the possibilities, ending quickly with one word – Jack.

He was wrong.

"We have your sister," de la Sengle stated simply. "And you have some love for her, it appears."

Richard wisely remained silent.

"So we will keep her as surety, and," de la Sengle could not help a smile, "her child. Your nephew or niece."

The look on Richard's face was enough.

"You knew? I had wondered." De la Sengle picked up the cup and drained it, setting it back quietly on the table before meeting Richard's eyes again. "She is unmarried, and, I am led to believe, illegitimate herself."

Richard regarded his hands which, despite his efforts to still them, visibly shook.

"I wish you to come back. We will release them upon your return."

"I just need to bring you the flintlocks and you will free them?" Richard said. It sounded too simple.

"Not quite. I did say I wished to punish you for your sin. Are you a man of honour?"

Richard, his mind now as unsteady as his hands, sought to grapple with too much at once, but he replied with conviction, "Yes, yes I am."

"Your sister is with the Benedictines. They will raise the child and it would be right that she remain with the Order. An unmarried woman with a child."

"No… She can't stop here!" Richard blurted, his eyes wide as he stared across the table at de la Sengle.

De la Sengle continued as if Richard had never spoken. "Good men like you are the foundation of this Order. You have skills I can use. Your cousin, Edward, he wants to build a rifle corps of highly trained men. He recognises the value in what you have shown him."

There was open confusion on Richard's face. "I've given you everything I have. I will bring the arms from England into the keeping of the Order. You have Master Scranton's process for the powder manufacture. Please do not punish me by keeping her here."

"Are you so sure?" de la Sengle enquired slowly. "Loyalty, it seems, is a tradable commodity after all. I demand yours in exchange for your sister's liberty. Bring me the arms and yourself, willingly, to the Order of St John and I will release your sister."

Richard felt as if he had taken a blow to the chest.

"That is the condition for her release and my charity," de la Sengle repeated.

"You leave me little choice." Richard's voice was hoarse.

"Willingly, I said. Remember that is my condition," de la Sengle said sternly.

"Willingly it shall be." Richard delivered the words quietly.

There was a loud tap on the door, and from the smile on de la Sengle's face it was one he had been expecting. A moment later it opened and his brother, bound at the wrists, was pushed through the door. Jack's expression was murderous, there was a cut above his left eye and blood ran down his cheek.

"I would have sent you alone," said de la Sengle, "however your brother has made a good case on your behalf and wishes to go with you. I'm sure he too has a vested interest in your success as we hold some papers I have no doubt he would like back." The Grand Master rose smoothly from his seat at the table. "I'm sure we will see each other again, soon. One of our ships will take you from Malta in three days."

De la Sengle departed and the two armed men who had pushed Jack through the door left with him. Richard quickly pressed his knife to the rope holding Jack's wrists. His grey eyes met those of his brother.

"I'm sorry."

"What for this time?" Jack said, his voice angry.

"They've let Andrew go ahead of us to bring the guns back to Malta," Richard said simply.

Jack's hands went to his face, the blood from above his eye smearing across his cheek. "God's bones! Then what are we doing?"

Richard stepped back and dropped into the chair de la Sengle had recently vacated. "We have the same deal, we just need to overtake Andrew."

"You are not making any sense." Jack took hold of his brother's shoulders and regarded him with cold blue eyes. Richard didn't however get a chance to reply as the door opened a moment later and they were both taken and deposited for safe keeping in a cellar.

✝

Richard relayed the facts, or at least as many of them as he wanted to share, to Jack. That de la Sengle wanted to teach him a lesson he admitted. He also told Jack that the men and Lizbet would have to remain on Malta as surety until they delivered the flintlocks to the Order. That Lizbet was bearing a child and that to secure her freedom he had to pledge his own, he kept to himself.

He also told Jack that Andrew Kineer was no longer on Malta. That de la Sengle was giving him a head start of three days before releasing them to pursue him and make their way back to England. The brothers were in agreement on at least one fact. They would be damned if they were giving Andrew a three day lead.

☦

"Jesus Christ! Will you stay still?" Jack held a ladder, and, at the top of it, balanced on the rungs, was his brother. There was no support for the wooden frame other than the dirt floor it rested on and Jack's arms, which were already beginning to feel the strain of holding it upright.

"Just keep it upright," Richard reprimanded, not seeming at all alarmed by the precarious perch he occupied or by the warning edge in his brother's voice.

"I'm bloody trying. It would be a damn sight easier if you would stop wriggling about." Jack, feeling the ladder pull from his hands again, closed his eyes tight and fought to bring it back to the vertical, adding though clenched teeth, "Stay still, I said! Do you never listen to me?"

Above them was a trap door, a hoped-for means of escape. The door they had been propelled through earlier was steel and barred and there was no hope of escape in that direction. A grilled window admitted some light, but was far too small to offer an exit route. They were evidently in a cellar and Richard had spied the dark square outline of the trap door in the ceiling.

"Hold it steady, and I'll try and lift it," Richard advised.

"As if I wasn't already trying to do that!" Jack complained. His shoulders were burning now with the effort of holding the ladder as still as he could manage.

"Well, try harder," Richard called down.

Jack, his head tilted back, watched his brother at the top of the ladder. Richard, palms pressed flat against the underside of the hatch, feet as balanced as well as he could get them on the top rung, pushed as hard as he could. Jack felt the added strain on the ladder and fought hard to keep it vertical.

The hinged panel above Richard moved.

"It's open!" His brother sounded triumphant as the trap door lifted above him. The act of forcing the door up and over increased the weight on the ladder even more. Jack gasped and cursed. A moment later there was an almighty bang as the trap door opened fully and fell back against the floor above them. There was a sudden final push against the ladder that tested Jack's footing, then the weight he was fighting against was gone.

Light spilled down from the opening and as Jack watched, his brother disappeared over the edge of the hatch only to reappear a moment later. "Lift the ladder up so I can reach it. Quickly, come on!"

Cursing, Jack forced his tortured muscles to perform one more feat, raising the ladder high enough, so Richard could reach the top rungs from where he hung though the opening in the ceiling.

"You're wobbling it! Hold it straight or I can't reach it."

"It's bloody heavy, although not as bad as it was with your backside on the top of it. Get a hold of it. I can't get it any higher." Jack was holding it as high up as he could. A second later he felt it pulled from his grasp as Richard lifted it through the hatch.

"Just wait, I'll not be long," Richard's voice called down. Then the ladder and his brother disappeared from view.

"Don't you worry. I'll stop right here!" Jack replied, sarcastically.

In the room above he heard noises and wished dearly that he could see what was going on. But the hatch was small and the view it afforded was only of a white plastered wall in the room above. Suddenly the ladder reappeared and began to descend back towards him. The bottom rung dangled above his head.

Richard's head appeared over the edge. "I've tied it to a meat hook in the ceiling, that's as far as I can get it to you. The rope's not long enough."

Jack could just reach the bottom rung.

"Will it hold?" Jack asked, shaking his shoulders out.

"Who knows?" came the honest reply. "I've tested it with my weight but you're quite a bit heavier."

"What are you trying to say?" Jack fumed as he prepared to jump for the ladder.

"Get on with it. It'll hold or it won't," Richard replied. "Anyway it's not the hook I'd worry about but the rat-chewed rope I've had to use. If I was you, I'd make haste getting up that ladder."

Jack jumped. He hung by his arms from the bottom rung. The ladder swung and twisted on the rope making the climb a difficult one. Hauling himself up the first three rungs, he was able to press a toe to the bottom rung, and with his weight now thankfully on his feet, he was up the rest of the ladder in a moment.

"It did hold!" Richard, annoyingly, sounded both genuinely surprised and delighted. "But can you squeeze through the trap? It would make a comic scene, wouldn't it, if you got stuck there during your escape. Come on, hurry up. Someone somewhere must have heard the noise that door made when it opened."

"Will you shut up? You're enjoying this!" Jack growled as he began to fit his shoulders through the opening.

"Undoubtedly."

Jack, hands on the floor, levered himself over the edge of the hatchway, and knelt, breathing heavily, next to his brother.

"Lounging on Malta has made you quite unfit!" Richard remarked. Neatly, he untied the rope, lowering the ladder back into the cellar.

Jack, glaring at him murderously, closed the trap door a lot more quietly than when it had been opened.

"Do you have any idea how to get out of here?" Jack hissed in Richard's ear as they emerged from the room into a corridor beyond. "There will be a guard on the main door."

"I'll think of something. Will you just keep your voice down? This way," Richard replied, his voice sounding annoyed as they set off down the narrow dim corridor.

As they got to the end, Richard laid his hand on the door, but before he could press it open, they both heard a voice they recognised behind them.

"Fortunately for you, we need your services." It was Edward Fitzwarren.

Richard stopped. His hand dropped to his side and he turned back to face his cousin. "We wished only to set on a course to bring you Monsinetto's cargo as soon as we can."

"You were told to wait three days," Edward growled. There were three other men standing behind him. "Those were our terms. What made you believe you could vary them?"

"If we delay, you might not get the cargo you want," Richard pointed out. "To leave sooner is to lessen the risk."

Edward ignored Richard and pointed to Jack. "Bring him to my room and put the other back in the cellar. And make sure they cannot get out this time."

Jack shook off the hand of the man who took a hold on his arm to lead him down the corridor. Richard, pinioned between the other two, was dragged back towards the cellar they had recently escaped.

Edward stood with his arms folded. Jack was pushed hard in the small of the back and stumbled into the room. The door closed noisily behind him.

Edward waited until Jack recovered and stood straight before he spoke. "I know who you are."

Jack nodded, and replied, "And I you."

"I've seen the papers that were taken from you. I've no reason to doubt them," Edward stated, eyeing him coldly. "I don't care overly for my family anymore."

Jack squared his shoulders and matched Edward's stare. "I'm not enamoured of them either. I have been shown little kindness."

Edward regarded him silently for a moment. "You seem to be a man of honour. You fought well against the infidel, even though your case was hopeless."

Jack was past being intimidated. "I was curious!"

"Curious?" repeated Edward.

"I wished to see if the Order was as good as the tales Brother Emilio tells," Jack supplied.

Edward's eyebrows raised at that. "And were you disappointed?"

Jack shook his head. "No."

"You have an inheritance you could gift to the Order. Its significance could offset your circumstances," Edward replied, bluntly.

Jack smiled. So this was what he wanted. He swallowed the rebuke he was going to make and said instead, "A kind offer, and one worth considering."

"You would do well to consider it. No matter what you think, a man raised as you have been could never have a place in society." Edward then added, "And the company you keep does not help your cause."

That was too much for Jack. "I choose my company well."

"I think time will prove you wrong." Edward's voice bore a hard warning edge.

Jack, wisely, backed down. "Life is a lesson. I have much to learn."

"And the Order has much it could teach," Edward pronounced.

The interview was soon over and Jack was escorted back to the cellar. And into the company of his brother.

"I will be happier when we are no longer on this island," Jack said as the door closed behind him.

"What did Cousin Edward want?" Richard said, from where he was sat on the floor, his knees drawn up.

Jack crossed the room and dropped down onto the floor next to him. "Not a lot. He smelled a profit for the Order, that's all." When he saw the questioning look on his brother's face, he added, "They have the papers proving my inheritance and they'd like a share."

"I'm sorry, Jack. It's my fault that they have a hold over you," Richard said, quietly.

"They have a hold over me while I am on Malta, but when we're off this island they won't," Jack replied, "and if they think I'll come back here willingly after this is over, they're fools. I'd rather die a poor man in England than spend the rest of my life shackled to this burning rock and subject to the whim of the likes of Edward Fitzwarren."

Richard didn't reply. The cellar was dark and Jack couldn't see the look on his brother's face.

After two and half days, they were finally allowed to leave Malta. During the late evening, after curfew in the Citadel, accompanied by Emilio and three of his men, they made their way quickly through the silent blackened narrow streets of Mdina to the gate on the western side. At a quiet word from Emilio the gate opened, and a moment later they emerged into the warm night air of Malta. A short distance away, two of Emilio's men waited, and beside them five saddled horses ready to take them to Birgu, where a carrack was readying to take to the sea and set her prow towards Sicily, and then to the Italian coast.

The Italian Knight carried with him written orders from the Grand Master that would lay at their disposal the resources of the Knights throughout Europe to transport them north, and back to England a lot faster than they had made the journey south. De la Sengle wanted the contents of Monsinetto's cargo in his armoury as quickly as possible. Releasing Kineer would, he knew, add a sense of urgency to their journey that otherwise it might have lacked. He had no doubt at all that the group escorted by Emilio would arrive first.

✝

Robert had resigned himself to having to wait until William's demise before he could sell any of his property. Although he was now legally in charge, not as much money seemed to flow in his direction as he had hoped. There might be rents and dues, but there were also high expenses for maintenance, upkeep and wages for William's staff. There was not as much left as Robert had wanted, and worse, what money did arrive trickled in.

His father had given him a manor near Chichester when he reached his majority. It had been his father's before him and as the Fitzwarren heir it had passed to him. Robert never used it. The accommodation was poor and the hunting even worse. However the Chichester estate was an answer to a more immediate problem. Robert had debts, and selling this estate would clear them and leave him with a full purse.

The adjacent landowner was Henry Merton and he had already offered to buy the manor twice, but William had turned him down. The property had always vested in the Fitzwarren heir and his father had no intention of selling it, or of allowing his son to sell. Now though, things were different. Robert's father was out of the way, locked behind doors in his London House. The manor belonged to Robert, the title documents were vested in his name, so he could legally sell it.

Henry Merton had agreed a price and Robert had set Clement the task of transferring the title to the property and managing the transaction. Robert might not like his lawyer, but he needed to ensure that Merton did not cheat him on the transaction. The deeds to the Chichester property were with his father's lawyer, Luttrell. Clement had prepared the Deed of Feoffavi, for the bargain and sale of the manor, sending this to Luttrell for him to action. It should have been a simple process from there. Clement's addendum would have been attached to the deed roll for the property, and all of it would have been passed to Merton's lawyer in exchange for the agreed sum.

However it was not going as Robert had planned. Clement's bargain and sale deed, headed in Latin "dedi concessi feoffavi et vendidi," had been returned to Robert. Attached to it was another sheet of parchment, and the words at the top had made Robert's stomach twist.

"Title indigentiarum."

His hands shook as he read the words Luttrell had added to Clement's addendum before he returned it.

"Title indigentiarum."

No title.

William's lawyer, Luttrell, was refusing to execute Clement's deed because Robert lacked the legal capacity to sell the manor. Robert had balled the parchment, and, howling, sent the creased sheets towards the wall before storming through the house towards his father's rooms.

†

William sat back and looked at the portrait of his long dead wife. Tonight, the severe gaze she laid upon him seemed to have softened. He was sure he could detect a smile in her eyes. William found himself smiling back at the painting.

"Eleanor, lass, you always did get your way. No matter how long it took." William spoke quietly, his eyes gazing adoringly at the face of his wife. William had always harboured a secret worry that she had known what he had done all those years ago. On reflection, he could see there had been little he had gained from it. She had resented his mistress, a woman whose name he could not even remember, never mind recall what she had looked like. She had been one of Eleanor's servants, who had provided for his needs for a few nights while Eleanor had been pregnant. He'd had no feelings for the woman, he'd have given her bastard little thought either, if it had not been for Eleanor. Eleanor, who wanted them both gone. Eleanor, who pitted her will against his. William could not let her win. The fault of it was hers. She'd been furious that he wanted to keep his bastard son as well as their child and her temper had risen. Lord, what a temper she had. William smiled. It was so easy to make her mad.

William could now see that his victory had been a feeble one. To spite his wife, he'd swapped the children, sent away her son, their son. He'd meant to tell her what he had done, reinstate her child and teach his wife a lesson. But that had never happened. He'd gone to Court, Eleanor was pregnant again, and when he came back there was a new child in her crib. Eleanor had nearly died, he remembered her surrounded by her ladies and a priest. They'd told him she'd not live to see the morning. They'd been wrong and Eleanor had recovered, but that had not been the time to tell her what he had done with her first child. William had resolved to deal with the situation later.

His wife took such pride in their first born, Robert. Eleanor doted upon Robert, marvelled as he learnt to walk, to run, to ride a horse. He was the heir, and William had realised that there was little he could do about it. He had pushed the issue to the back of his mind and forgotten about it.

Or at least he had tried to.

He wasn't often at his brother's house, but he could remember seeing Eleanor's son there when he had visited once. Even though it was shoulder length, filthy and matted, he'd recognised the blond hair as belonging to Eleanor's son. It had the quality of white gold, and his face, beneath the grime, was hers. He'd heard the child calling the other boys, heard his rough peasant's voice, his ripped breeches showing his backside, and he'd known then that it was too late to take this child back into his house.

Now he'd met the man that boy had become.

The first time he'd taken him to be a thief, poorly dressed, nervous, and Jack had fled from his house. The second time however, he had stood before William with an air of confidence, the eyes that had met William's full of reserve. William remembered the meeting well. He'd seen the man's temper flare easily – just like his mother's.

In the lonely hours, William, more and more, began to fashion this man he had briefly met into the son he did not have in Robert. Into an ally, a man of honour, possessing the best traits from his beautiful wife and from himself. Robert's character was tainted, ruined by the curse of his bastardy and there was nothing, William told himself, that he could have ever done to have remedied that.

He was drawn from his reverie by the sound of the door being pulled open. There was no knock, no announcement. Looking up, he saw Robert standing on the threshold glaring at him.

"It didn't take you long to find out, did it?" William said, with clear satisfaction in his voice.

"What have you done?" Robert growled the question for the second time.

"What I should have done a long time ago. Clipped your wings," William spat back.

"You've breathed your last, old man." Robert advanced towards William and snatched the counterpane from the bed. It was plain on his face that he meant to suffocate his father with it..

"Do that and you'll inherit nothing," William snarled. "Nothing. Do you hear me?"

Robert stayed his advance.

"Kill me and everything I own vests in your brother," William said, slowly and clearly. "And there is nothing you can do about it."

"But he is a traitor," Robert spat back. "He can't inherit."

"I didn't vest it in Richard, you fool," William replied, his voice cold.

Realisation struck Robert with the force of a physical blow. His hand opened and the counterpane slipped from his grasp to the floor. "You left it to him, to that bastard?"

William's smile was answer enough.

Robert's hand's covered his face and he let out an anguished howl.

"Kill me and you'll end on your arse on the street," William growled.

"I let you live so you can toy with me like this?" Robert shouted, through his fingers before dropping his hands from his face and staring deep into William's eyes.

"You have no choice," William stated, and Robert knew he didn't.

☦

Lizbet had cried. It was just the once, and they were tears of frustration. Imprisoned within the precincts of the Benedictine Order in Mdina, she had no news at all of what had happened to Jack and Richard. She'd asked and asked, then after weeks of receiving the same answer, she finally gave up asking. Lizbet was trapped, and in more ways than one.

Physically she was trapped inside the walled confines with the nuns, unable to see or hear beyond the walls, forced to live within the narrow limits of their world. She was also trapped by her body as it began to betray her. That she carried a child was now unmistakable. Lizbet was also held captive by her own thoughts. They lurked at the back of her mind. The truth of the child she carried was a truth she did not want to face, one she did not want to dwell upon. The abhorrent reality was that she carried the child of a man whom she hated, a man who had tried to kill Richard, who had driven him to the edge of his reason.

Had she been in London it would have been a simple matter, coins would have been exchanged and weeks ago she'd have taken a mixture of henbane and milkwort that would have purged the child from her before it had even become one. Now it was too late. It had a form within her. It was beginning to possess her.

The steps down to the garden were white marble, their edges rounded and smooth. In total there were fourteen. Lizbet stood looking down at them for a long time before she finally moved, taking three careful slow steps back away from them. Reaching out a hand, she steadied herself against the wall.

"Oh God, I'm sorry." Lizbet's words, spoken aloud to herself, sounded around the garden, her alien English accent seeming incongruous amongst the lemon trees, white tiles and vine clad walls. Lizbet knew she did not belong here.

She ran forwards on light feet. The first two steps landed on the marble slabbed balcony. The third connected with nothing as she flung herself from the top of the stairs and into the void.

Lizbet's fall was only broken when she hit the ninth step down, the noise of it rattling around inside her head. For a moment she was reminded of another time, beneath the water when her head, with a seeming finality, had struck a rock. Strong hands had pulled her free. Now there were no hands, no help, only helplessness.

EPILOGUE

Both brothers agreed, in the few moments when they found themselves alone on that journey north, that the Knights had impressive resources at their disposal. The days they had waited in Malta had allowed time for the logistics of their onward journey to be put into place. Their stops were planned, provision had been made for changes of horse, their accommodation was excellent and their safety guaranteed. They left each stop after what was considered sufficient time for food and sleep, with an escort that would take them further north through Europe and hand them on to the next escort. None of the men they met were interested in who or what they were. The men strictly and efficiently obeyed their orders: "Move them north – quickly."

Jack felt he had little time to catch his breath, so brief were the stops. All responsibility for the journey had been taken from them.

When he complained to Emilio, he was told curtly that when he had the skills to get them where they were going at an equal speed then Emilio would defer to him. Jack had stalked off, cursing loudly. He had found his exit blocked immediately by one of Emilio's men and was forced to turn on his heel and rejoin the group.

"Shall we go in?" Emilio said, gesturing to an opened door behind him. "There is food ready for us.

We are not scheduled to stop here for long. And we both know, Jack, what a high regard you have for your stomach."

Jack's blue eyes locked with the Italian's for a moment, before he pushed past him and entered the hall behind him.

Jack seated himself at the table, where there was indeed an annoyingly good meal laid out. Jack gave it his full attention, ignoring Emilio and Richard who had joined him at the table.

"Jack always travels better when fed," Richard remarked, as Jack finished his meal.

"My point was that we could have made this journey equally well on our own," Jack said, his words directed at Emilio. "I resent being treated like a letter. One that the Knights wish to impress the Lord with their speed in delivering."

Emilio, seated opposite Jack, had finished his meal. Unlike Jack, he'd drunk sparingly, the glass in his hand still half full. Dropping his gaze from Jack, he addressed Richard, who sat on Jack's left. "Does he adopt such an attitude just to annoy me, or is it a permanent condition?"

Richard looked up and met the Italian's gaze. "Don't feel you are being singled out."

"Surely he cannot resent the fact that you will make your destination as quickly as possible," Emilio said, directing his reply to Richard.

"I believe that Jack holds his freedom in higher regard than your efficiency," Richard replied, dryly.

"I'm sat here!" Jack said loudly, putting his empty glass down with bang.

Emilio laughed. "How many times have I told you that you are easy prey?"

Jack shot the Knight a murderous look before returning his attention to refilling his empty glass.

A moment later a letter was brought to the table for Emilio. He had received similar dispatches on their journey. Emilio did not share their contents, but the brothers guessed that they contained details of the provision made for the next leg of the journey. The letter was sealed and then further tied with a light blue ribbon threaded through the paper and secured under the wax seal, a security device against tampering. The Knight broke the seal roughly with his thumb and pulled the ribbon free of the paper, discarding it on the table. Unfolding the sheet, he read the brief contents over the rim of his glass. A moment later he secured the folded sheet inside his jacket.

"Gentlemen, we have only a few hours, so I suggest you get some sleep." Emilio rose from the chair and left them alone.

"What I wouldn't give for a good night's sleep," Jack said, his head in his hands. "I'm starting to lose track of whether it's night or day."

Richard didn't reply. Reaching out, he picked up the blue ribbon that Emilio had discarded. Folding it neatly, he tucked it into his doublet. Lizbet's favourite colour was blue.

Printed in Great Britain
by Amazon